Nantucket Nights

Elin Hilderbrand

St. Martin's Paperbacks

This is a work of fiction. All of the characters, organizations, and events portrayed in this novel are either products of the author's imagination or are used fictitiously.

NANTUCKET NIGHTS

Copyright © 2002 by Elin Hilderbrand.
Excerpt from *Summer People* copyright © 2003 by Elin Hilderbrand.

All rights reserved.

For information address St. Martin's Press, 175 Fifth Avenue, New York, NY 10010.

Library of Congress Catalog Card Number: 2001058860

ISBN: 978-0-312-98976-7

Printed in the United States of America

St. Martin's Press hardcover edition / July 2002
St. Martin's Paperbacks edition / July 2003

St. Martin's Paperbacks are published by St. Martin's Press, 175 Fifth Avenue, New York, NY 10010.

10 9 8 7 6 5 4 3

Critical Acclaim for
Nantucket Nights

"What a perfect summer pleasure Elin Hilderbrand provides in *Nantucket Nights*, mixing the complexities of family life and friendship with suspense, romance, and moonlit Nantucket nights."

—Nancy Thayer, author of *Custody*

"Dips deep into *Peyton Place* country."

—*Kirkus Reviews*

"Ms. Hilderbrand paints a picture of idyllic Nantucket life that slowly starts to unravel as the ugly underbelly is revealed. Hidden secrets, a mysterious disappearance, and the pain of betrayal form the basis for this haunting read."

—*Romantic Times*

"The novel is fast-paced and suspenseful enough to keep readers interested. A likely candidate for summer-vacation reading."

—*Booklist*

St. Martin's Paperbacks Titles
by Elin Hilderbrand

The Beach Club

Nantucket Nights

Summer People

The Blue Bistro

For my friends
Richard and Amanda Congdon,
who taught me what I know
of patience, devotion, and
the strength of the human spirit

Kayla

It is December on Nantucket Island—a month of white skies and the first truly cold winds of the winter, a month made bearable by Christmas cheer. When Kayla stands next to the big Douglas fir in front of Pacific National Bank, she gazes down Main Street at the rows of trees with their fat colored lights, the snow flurries dusting the cobblestones, and the people she has lived amongst for twenty years, who are hurrying into the warm shops.

Kayla has shopping to do as well. At The Complete Kitchen, she buys an ice cream scoop for Luke's teacher, and the woman behind the register offers her an hors d'oeuvre from a silver platter: smoked salmon on rye bread topped with caviar that looks like black pearls. At Nantucket Sleigh Ride, they're handing out hot cider in paper cups. Kayla buys ornaments and a strand of scallop-shell lights. At Johnston's of Elgin cashmere shop, Kayla splurges on a cherry red pashmina for a party she and Raoul have been invited to on the fifteenth. The salesgirl wraps the pashmina in cream-colored tissue paper, ties it up with red ribbon, and then slips it into a fancy shopping bag with silk cord handles.

Walking back to her car, Kayla marvels at how, on the outside, everything in her life appears to be back to normal. And on a day like today, better than normal.

Antoinette has been missing for three months.

As Kayla walks into her house, the phone rings. She still can't bring herself to answer the phone because she's afraid.

"Afraid of what?" Raoul asked her once.

Afraid of this very thing: She waits for the machine to pick up, and then she hears a voice.

"Kayla," the voice says. "This is Paul Henry. I have news. Please call me."

Kayla deletes the message and begins pacing the house, still clutching her shopping bags. She is grateful that she's the only one home. No one else heard the message.

I have news.

Afraid of what?

Afraid that everything is *not* back to normal. Antoinette, the woman whom Kayla once called her best friend, was swept off the coast of Great Point while swimming in the middle of the night on Labor Day weekend.

Was Antoinette dead? Alive? There was no way to know.

Until now.

Kayla

At two o'clock on the Friday of Labor Day weekend, the phone rang. Kayla was eating lunch: half a tomato sandwich and eight Lay's potato chips. As she ate, she paged through the Dutch Gardens catalog, looking for spring bulbs.

Kayla plucked the phone off the kitchen wall. It was her friend Valerie Gluckstern's secretary.

"Hold for Val," the secretary said.

Twenty seconds later, it was Val herself. Kayla heard her shut the door to her office. Val always took her personal calls behind closed doors.

"Kayla?"

"Yes, Counselor," Kayla said, licking salt off her fingers.

"Have you talked to Antoinette?"

"Not yet."

"But we're on for tonight? Eleven-thirty, and not a minute later? You're driving?"

"As promised."

"God, I'm so happy, I could just burst. I have, like, sixteen closings this month, and I don't care. John said something last night about running for selectman again in the spring, and even that didn't bother me."

"And tonight you're going to tell us who's making you so happy?" Kayla said. "The mystery man?"

"As promised," Val said. "I'm bringing a bottle of champagne I picked up when I was in France. You bought cheese?"

"I'm going to the store this afternoon. When I talked to Antoinette last week I asked her to bring the lobsters, but I'll call and remind her."

"It's a full moon tonight," Val said. "Can you even believe the romance in that? Has there ever been a full moon for Night Swimmers before?"

"I don't remember one."

"So this is the first time in twenty years," Val said. "Twenty years, can you believe it? God, we're old." She sucked in her breath and let out a long stream of air. It sounded like Val was smoking a cigarette, but Kayla knew better.

"Are you lifting your weights?" Kayla asked.

"Twenty reps, bicep curl," Val said. "You can fight age, you know."

"*You* can fight age," Kayla said. "It's too late for me. I have to ration potato chips. Count them out, seal the bag, and hide it away."

"I know what you mean," Val said.

"You don't know," Kayla said. "Ms. Size Two."

"Size four."

"I envy anyone over forty in the single digits," Kayla said.

"You know this book I'm reading?" Val said. "By the Swiss therapist? She has a lot to say about Americans suffering from poor self-image, and she actually recommends having an affair. So for once in my life, I'm doing something right. Something European." Kayla heard the weights clunk to the floor, and then Val said, "Whew! I don't like to hear you getting sensitive about your weight."

"I can't help it," Kayla said.

"Do you want to borrow the book?"

"When you have a book that deals with the potato chip syndrome, let me know," Kayla said. She heard the other phone in Val's office ring—no doubt, important business, money to be made. Kayla let her go. "I'll see you tonight."

Kayla clicked off the phone and returned to her lunch and the seventy varieties of daffodils, but her mind stayed on her conversation with Val. Val had spent the shimmering summer months having an affair. With someone they all knew, Val said, but she wouldn't tell who. Kayla had been guessing all summer—Charlie, who owned the fish market; Thebaud, the chef at 21 Federal; Alan, the mail carrier. Nope, nope, nope, Val said. Kayla's other best friend, Antoinette, refused to play guessing games.

"I have better things to do with my time than speculate about Valerie's illicit sex life," Antoinette said. "For example, I could be conducting an illicit sex life of my own."

Kayla poured herself a glass of lemonade and drank it slowly. The house was quiet, and for just a minute she felt lonely, like the last housewife left in America. Her husband was building the biggest house in the history of Nantucket Island, her four children were out enjoying the final days of freedom before they had to go back to school, and her two best friends were conducting lives that brimmed with sexual energy—strangers' hands running up the insides of their thighs, the electric sensation of a first kiss. These feelings were lost to Kayla, buried in her past. As far away as Europe.

Dutifully, she put her plate and glass in the dishwasher.

Although she occasionally felt sorry for herself, Kayla's life wasn't dull. True, Nantucket was small and stranded thirty miles off the coast of America, but it had endless stretches of beach, hundreds of acres of moors dotted with freshwater ponds, and a charming town of cobblestone streets, spired churches, and historic homes built with whaling fortunes in the nineteenth century. It was popular to believe that things only happened on Nantucket during the summer. Summer was a slice of heaven, but the same was true for the rest of the year on the island, and Kayla felt sorry for anyone who missed the days of October that were as red and crisp as an apple, or the snow silently blanketing Main Street on Christmas Eve, or the seals that lounged on the rocks of the jetty and flapped their fins at the people who rode the ferry into the icy harbor in winter. It was true, though, that most of the excitement on Nantucket arrived in summer, and such was definitely the case this year, even for a housewife like Kayla.

Back in June, Kayla's husband, Raoul Montero, owner of Montero Construction, landed the biggest job ever on Nantucket—the Ting house out in Monomoy. Val had represented Pierre and Elisabeth Ting when they bought the vacant lot for six million dollars, and the house they wanted to build would cost another ten million. The day Raoul had found out the job was his, he came home on his lunch hour, something he rarely did. Kayla had been weeding the garden, wearing a bikini top and jeans shorts, her bare knees stained with dirt. Just before Raoul pulled into the driveway, she'd had a sense of glorious freedom. Her kids were all elsewhere: her oldest, Theo, worked part-time as a ramp attendant for Island Airlines; her girls, Jennifer and Cassidy B., had babysitting jobs; and her eight-year-old, Luke, was at camp every day until four. After nineteen years of marriage and eighteen years of child-rearing, she woke up to discover that it was summer and she had a day all to herself; she dug in the garden, inhaling the scent of rosemary and basil, listening to Cat Stevens sing "Oh Very Young" on the kitchen radio. Then Kayla saw Raoul's red pickup pull into the driveway. She'd panicked at first—construction could be a dangerous business, people fell off roofs and high ladders—but when she saw Raoul's face, she knew he had good news.

"I got Ting," he said. He strode through the backyard to the garden and reached her before she could even stand up.

"Lucky, lucky man," she said. "How did you get so lucky?"

"It's not luck, baby; it's skill," he said. He took Kayla's sweaty body in his arms. Raoul was not only lucky, but blessed, as well. He was tall and strong with Spanish coloring—dark hair, golden brown eyes, rosy lips. Their kids worshiped him. They ate the same things that Raoul ate—for breakfast, two banana muffins and a bowl of fruit; for lunch, egg salad on a sub roll. They all loved Chevy trucks, skiing, The Rolling Stones singing "Street Fighting Man," Tom Brokaw, scary movies, coconut cream Easter eggs. It baffled Kayla at times—they'd had four children who were carbon copies of Raoul. Sometimes it was like she'd had nothing to do with their creation. Sometimes it was like she was just a visitor to their planet.

Raoul scooped Kayla up in his arms. She wasn't a petite woman by anyone's standards, but that day when Raoul carried her into the house, she felt as light as a size two. "Anybody else home?" Raoul asked.

"Nope."

He'd carried her upstairs to the bedroom, untying the string of her bikini top with his teeth. He laid her across the bed and slid her shorts and her underwear over her dirty knees. Nantucket was a small place, and there had been rumors during the nineteen years of their marriage that Raoul had had affairs with two women. But Kayla tried not to believe it.

Raoul whistled. "You're beautiful, Kayla."

"I'm glad you got the job," she said. "I know how much you wanted it."

"We wanted it," Raoul said. "Didn't we?"

"We did," she said. "We all did. When the kids find out, they're going to flip."

Raoul unbuttoned his jeans and reached for her. He had a flat, brown stomach that rippled with muscles. He was a gorgeous, lucky man who had landed the job of a lifetime. What a way to start the summer—enough money was headed for their bank account to let them to grow old without a care in the world.

Maybe it was remembering that sweet afternoon hour of making love with her husband, or maybe it was all the talk of illicit affairs, but Kayla decided, after she got off the phone with Val, to drive out to Raoul's job site. She did this occasionally, because after Raoul started the Ting job, he was rarely at home. He left the house at six in the morning with his metal lunch box (muffins, fruit, egg salad), and then he ordered pizzas for his crew for dinner, or he treated them to Faregrounds or A. K. Diamond's. He had yet to make it home before their youngest, Luke, went to bed, and now that this had been going on for a couple of months, the kids were starting to show signs of frustration. Their hero, the parental sun they revolved around, was missing.

"Do you love the Tings more than us?" Cassidy B. asked him one Sunday morning.

"What kind of question is that?" Raoul roared, picking up Cassidy B. in a giant bear hug. He looked over Cassidy's shoulder at Kayla—she was scrambling eggs at the stove. "The Tings are paying for your college education. Not to mention the braces you might need in a few years, not to mention a ten-speed bicycle, not to mention it looks like your doll-house could use a new roof. Do you have any idea how much it costs to reshingle these days?"

Cassidy B. put her hands over Raoul's mouth. "Daddy!" she protested.

"You can hardly blame the kids," Kayla said. "They never see you anymore. They miss you."

"Well," Raoul said, a dangerous edge to his voice, "we all decided that this was what we wanted."

What they wanted, yes—but lately Kayla had been listing all the things that a million dollars couldn't buy. It couldn't buy happy, well-adjusted children; it couldn't buy a happy marriage.

Monomoy was a breathtaking part of the island, a fitting place for a ten-million-dollar home. The Ting property had five hundred feet of waterfront with its own beach, its own dock, and sweeping views across Nantucket Harbor toward town; you could see the north and south church spires, the wharves, and the red beacon of Brant Point lighthouse. Buying a va-cant lot for six million dollars set a Nantucket real estate record, but it was just a drop in the bucket for Pierre Ting, who was the scaffolding baron of Hong Kong. Most year-round islanders were unhappy about the best pieces of Nantucket being snapped up by ultra-wealthy people who didn't appreciate Nan-tucket and would only spend a few weeks a year on-island. Raoul had caught a lot of flak from his fellow builders and the antidevelopment people for agreeing to build the Ting house, or "the cathedral," as everyone called it. Raoul didn't back down. "They're jealous," he said. "They'd do it themselves in a heartbeat."

Kayla pulled into the quarter acre of dirt that had been cleared for a driveway, next to five pickup trucks, although Raoul's truck wasn't among them. Her spirits sagged until she remembered that Raoul sometimes let his crew borrow his truck to run to Marine Home Center, or to Henry Jr.'s for sandwiches. So she got out of the car. There was a huge yellow Dumpster, and boards, tool belts, and empty soda cans lying around. A boom box blasted her son Theo's favorite band, The Beastie Boys. Kayla weaved her way toward the house. She was proud of Raoul's design, although a small, secret part of her agreed with the islanders who found it ostentatious. Raoul had taken her on a tour after the framing was done. The entryway of the house had a wonderfully airy, spacious feel, with enough height to plant a tree, which was what the Tings intended to do—plant a Japanese cherry tree that would weep its fuchsia blossoms all over the marble floor. One moved into the formal living room, the formal dining room with built-in china cabinets, the gourmet kitchen featuring three islands to be topped in pink granite, the walk-in pantry, the den shelved for TV, DVD, and five hundred–CD changer, the atrium where the indoor pool would go. Up a huge, curved staircase were the five guest rooms, the children's playroom, the master bedroom suite including his and her bathrooms, a study, a sitting room, and four walk-in closets (one just for Elisabeth Ting's summer shoes). Outside, the house had eleven decks and nine hundred square feet of patio that led to the outdoor pool, the hot tub, and the beach.

It was Raoul's most challenging design; already, *Architectural Digest* had called, wanting to feature the house the minute it was complete. But today it was still just plasterboard walls and plywood floors covered with shavings. It smelled wonderful, like fresh lumber, newly planed boards. It was Raoul's smell, and Kayla loved it better than anything. Looking out the living room window at Nantucket Sound, she breathed in the fragrant wood and decided that maybe the house wasn't so preposterous after all. Before they knew it, there would be another house on the island dwarfing this one.

Someone touched Kayla's back.

She whipped around. It was Jacob Anderson, one of Raoul's workers. Jacob had curly dark hair and green eyes, and he looked absurdly handsome in jeans and work boots. When Kayla saw him, she thought, *Illicit affair*, and her face burned.

"Jacob," she said. "You startled me."

"Did I?" he said. Jacob had the alarming quality of speaking to every woman, including her—the boss's wife—like she was a *woman*.

Kayla cleared her throat. "Is, uh . . . is Raoul here?"

Jacob shook his curly head. He was wearing a baseball hat backwards, and the curls at his forehead, underneath the plastic strap, were damp with sweat.

"He went into town to see about something."

"Into town?"

"Yeah, that's what he said. He said he wasn't sure how long he'd be gone."

"Oh," Kayla said. Her forehead wrinkled, and she knew it wasn't attractive, so she raised her eyebrows trying to smooth it. There was no reason to be concerned; Raoul probably had twenty reasons to go into town—building department, the post office, the bank. "So he went into town and you don't know when he'll be back."

"That's right." Jacob smiled at her—a charming, boyish smile. "Can I show you around the house?"

"Thanks, but I've seen it already," Kayla said. "Raoul gave me the tour a few weeks ago."

"I've been trimming out one of the bedrooms," Jacob said. "Okay, listen to this—each guest room is plumbed for its own washer and dryer. Rumor has it Mrs. Ting doesn't want the *linens* to get mixed up." He shook his head. "It blows my mind what people will spend their money on. A washer and dryer in each room, fancy sheets for each bed, and a dancing troupe of cleaning girls to do the work. I'm lucky if I have time to change my sheets at home once a summer."

"I know what you mean," Kayla said. A picture of Jacob's rumpled bed presented itself in her mind. "Listen, I should go."

"Let me show you upstairs," Jacob said. "It's come a long way since you were here before."

"Another time," Kayla said.

"Oh, Kayla, you're breaking my heart," Jacob

said. Then he did an unbelievable thing. He reached out and touched Kayla's lip. She thought, *He's going to kiss me*. And she wondered where the rest of the crew was—it was a big house, the closest person could be a hundred feet away—but then Jacob lifted his finger from her lip and held it up for her to see. "Potato chip," he said, and sure enough, there was a fleck of Lay's potato chip on his fingertip.

Kayla exhaled. There was moisture under her arms. "Guilty as charged," she said, and she carefully moved herself around Jacob. "Well, when you see Raoul, tell him I stopped by." She was almost to the entryway of the house when she remembered something else. "Oh, and Jacob?"

Jacob was still studying his fingertip. "Yeah?"

"Can you remind him that I have Night Swimmers tonight?"

"Night Swimmers?"

"That's right. Night Swimmers. He'll know what it means."

"But I don't know what it means. Is it some kind of secret society? Is it something that involves you taking your clothes off?" He licked the potato chip off his finger in an incredibly suggestive way, and Kayla was out of there with a wave because he was right on both accounts, although she surely couldn't let him know that.

Kayla pulled out of the site, thinking about the fleck of potato chip and Jacob's impossibly light touch and Raoul gone into town, saying he didn't know when he'd be back. Panic rose in her as she recalled the rumors of years ago: Raoul with Pamela

Ely—a leggy woman with long brown hair and an upturned nose—and then the luscious nineteen-year-old Missy Tsoulakis. The rumors were unsubstantiated, but also hard to disregard when the whole town was talking about it, and when Pamela Ely positively *would not* make eye contact when Kayla saw her at the Stop & Shop. For Raoul, having an affair would be as easy as telling his crew, *"I'm going into town. Don't know when I'll be back."* Kayla's thighs ached.

You're being stupid and predictable, she told herself. The combination of that damn potato chip and Jacob in those paint-splattered jeans (which looked as good on him as jeans could look on a man) and Valerie cheating on her husband, John, and Antoinette, who was cheating on no one because she belonged to no one, but who hinted she'd been having crazy sex herself lately, led Kayla down this path of suspicion. There had been times in the last five years when she'd watched Raoul sleep, when she'd reached over and touched his penis, hot and erect, and she'd wondered, *Is he dreaming about me?* How could she ever be sure? Raoul always assured Kayla that he thought she was beautiful, but she had gained weight after four children, and she waged a constant war with herself to stay in shape. She looked okay for forty-two, but not great—certainly there were women on the island who were ten times as attractive, thanks to gyms and plastic surgery and plain, old-fashioned good genes. Kayla closed her eyes for a split second. Maybe she was too sensitive; maybe she did need one of Val's goofy books—*You're*

Okay But I'm Better; *Ten Steps to Your Own Uniqueness*; *Stop Biting Your Nails, Start Building Your Future*. When Kayla opened her eyes she relaxed, because she saw Raoul's red truck coming down Monomoy Road toward her.

They stopped in the middle of the road, Kayla in the Trooper, Raoul in his big red truck, and he turned down the radio and smiled and said, "Hi, baby."

Kayla unfastened her seat belt and slid her body out her open window far enough to kiss him. He tasted like himself.

"Where'd you go?" she asked.

"Town Building. I had to check on some easements. I bumped into Valerie, and she reminded me about your séance tonight."

Kayla slithered back into her car. "It's not a séance, Raoul."

He checked his side mirror, but no one was coming. Even in summer, two people could sit in the middle of the road and have a conversation without interruption. "I'd just love to know what you ladies do out there in the middle of the night."

"I'm sure you would," Kayla said. "But it's none of your business."

"I know, I know. It's a woman thing. Estrogen required for inclusion," Raoul said. "Now tell me, how did Theo seem this morning?"

"The same. I asked him if he was excited about school next week, and he didn't answer. I asked him to pick Luke up from camp at four o'clock, and he sort of grunted."

Raoul tapped his head against the headrest. "Tell you what. This weekend I won't work Sunday or Monday. I'll take Theo fishing and have a heart-to-heart with him."

"Let's hope that works," she said.

"What time are you leaving tonight?" Raoul asked.

"Eleven-fifteen," she said. "I'll be back in the morning before you go to work."

"Good," he said. He kissed his fingers by way of good-bye and drove off.

It was half past three, which gave Kayla enough time to dash into the Stop & Shop for two pints of raspberries; then it was down to Fahey & Fromagerie on Pleasant Street, where she bought a hunk of pale, creamy Saint André cheese and two slender baguettes dusted with flour. There was a selection of olives and red peppers, marinated mushrooms and salami—the kind of special, wonderful things her kids wouldn't eat. They also had chicken salad without too many unidentifiable chunks, and a cucumber–dill–sour cream thing and she got two pounds of each for dinner. By the time Kayla left the cheese shop, it was two minutes to four, and she had to head over to the school to spy on her sons.

Kayla wished she didn't have to do this, but Theo's odd behavior of the last month or so left her no choice. She meandered through the back streets so that she cruised by the school at ten past four, and sure enough, there was Luke in his green Nan-

tucket Day Camp T-shirt, holding two cupcakes on
a paper plate and a purple balloon, squinting against
the sun. Her fifty-year-old son trapped in an eight-
year-old body. Luke had been an old man since he
was born. He liked order, he liked adhering to rules,
he liked promptness. Kayla had him on a schedule
when he was only three weeks old, and later, he
refused to eat unless he was wearing a bib. Kayla
had read somewhere that the youngest child in the
family was the most likely to be footloose and fancy-
free, but not this one. Kayla and Raoul had dubbed
Luke the child most likely to develop an ulcer. The
inefficiency of the world around him was always letting him down.

Kayla pulled up next to the curb, and Luke
opened the door. The plate of cupcakes covered
neatly with plastic wrap went on the seat between
them, and then he tucked the balloon into the car.

"Theo never showed," he said, and in his voice
was the unmistakable tone: *Kids today. You just
can't trust them.*

"It's only ten after," Kayla said, pulling into a
vacant parking spot. "Let's give him the benefit of
the doubt. We'll wait here five minutes and see if
he shows up."

Luke sighed deeply and fastened his seat belt.
There was a faint pink juice stain above his upper
lip. He tapped one of his little black soccer shoes
against the floor mat.

"So how was the last day of camp? You had a
party, I take it."

Luke nodded, crossed his arms over the front of his T-shirt.

"I'll bet you're glad you don't have to wear that shirt anymore," Kayla said. "We can use it for a rag."

Luke plucked the shirt away from his body and sniffed it. "Be sure to wash it first," he said.

They watched the cars pass on Surfside Road. People were leaving the beach, the tops of their Jeeps down, damp towels wrapped around the roll-bars. Contractors who kept normal hours headed home in their pickups. A few cars honked their horns joyfully; it was, after all, the start of a holiday weekend. The last weekend of summer.

"Mom," Luke said, staring resolutely out the window. "Theo isn't coming."

Kayla turned the key in the ignition. "Okay," she said. "Let's go."

Predictably, at home, Theo's Jeep was in the driveway. Luke refrained from saying anything, and Kayla followed suit. They headed inside. Theo sat at the breakfast bar in just his swim trunks, inspecting his toenails. He did not look up when they came in.

"Hello," Kayla said. She put the groceries in the fridge. Theo stood up and intercepted the cucumber salad; he got a fork and started eating right from the plastic container. Luke glared at him as if to say: *Barbarian.* Luke wrote his name in block letters on a piece of masking tape and put the tape over the plastic covering his cupcakes.

"These are mine," Luke said.

"Fuck off," Theo said.

Luke looked at Kayla as if to say: *Are you going to tolerate this?*

"Theo," Kayla said, as nonconfrontationally as possible, "that salad is for all of us."

"You're contaminating it," Luke said. "With your fork."

Theo stopped, stared at his little brother. "I said, fuck off."

Kayla ushered Luke out of the kitchen, and he whispered to her, "You forgot to yell at him for not coming to get me."

"I didn't forget," she said. "I'm just picking my moment."

"I'm telling Dad," Luke said.

"Me, too," she said, and this seemed to satisfy him.

The girls were in the living room. Jennifer was watching *Oprah,* and Cassidy B. was reading the latest Harry Potter book, finishing the bag of Lay's potato chips.

"I can't believe you're eating those," Jennifer said to her. "You might as well be ingesting poison."

Cassidy B. shrugged.

"Hi, girls," Kayla said.

"Theo forgot to pick me up," Luke announced.

"So?" Jennifer said.

Cassidy B. didn't look up from her book. Kayla's girls were like before and after pictures of adolescence. At fourteen, Jennifer was showing all the signs of womanhood: She had breasts, and long, shiny dark hair, her voice was throaty. She worried about her weight and her complexion; she read the nutrition information labels of everything she ate. Cassidy B. was eleven and still a child. She had baby fat and a clear, untroubled look in her eyes. When she had friends over, they read or played with Cassidy's dollhouse.

Kayla loved her children so much that she kissed the three of them. First she kissed Luke's juice-stained lips; then she kissed the side of Cassidy B.'s face while she read, and even Jennifer let Kayla kiss her, a quick, dry kiss on top of her sweet-smelling hair.

Theo came into the living room, still eating the cucumber-dill salad. "What the fuck is going on in here?" he said.

Now Kayla had three kids looking at her as if to say: *Are you going to tolerate this?*

And then the phone rang.

"Kayla?"

It was Antoinette. The woman had the sexiest voice on the planet. It was dark and exotic, like sandalwood, like expensive chocolate.

"Hi."

"What's going on?"

"You're supposed to bring the lobster tails," Kayla said. She checked the kitchen clock; it was half past four. "Can you swing it? If not, I'll send

Theo to East Coast Fish. He owes me." Kayla turned around, and there was Theo, staring at her. He was such a handsome kid—brown hair bleached a shade lighter by the sun, golden brown eyes, and an incredible tan—he was his father all over again. Yet the way he looked at her was disturbing. Always, now, these disturbing looks, like he knew something about her that she didn't know herself.

"I can swing it," Antoinette said. "I have time."

"Of course you do," Kayla said. Antoinette was the freest person Kayla knew, and as if to illustrate the concept, Luke stepped through the sliding glass doors onto the deck, holding his purple balloon, and he let it go. It floated away.

Kayla put her hand over the receiver. "Luke, honey, why did you do that?"

Luke came back inside, glared at Theo, and marched off, stomping his soccer shoes.

"Do you want to borrow a couple of kids?" Kayla asked Antoinette.

"Looks like I might be seeing my own this weekend," Antoinette said.

"Your own what?"

"My own kid."

Kayla was silent. Back in the reaches of Antoinette's past was a daughter whom she'd given up for adoption and never seen again.

"You mean . . ."

"She called a few days ago. Her name is Lindsey. *Lindsey*. A white name if ever I heard one."

"Is . . . is she white?" Theo was still glaring at

Kayla, and she covered the receiver again with her hand. "Do you mind?" she asked.

"No," he said coldly, his eyes not leaving her face. "I don't mind."

Kayla stepped out onto the deck and scanned the horizon for Luke's balloon, but it was gone already.

"She wasn't white when I knew her," Antoinette said. "She wasn't black or white. She was . . . well, I remember thinking she was the color of a wine cork. Obviously I'm a woman who drinks too much. This whole thing has hit me sideways. This whole thing is fucking me up."

"Yeah, I believe it," Kayla said. "So she's coming this weekend?"

"Tomorrow. I tried to explain to her that I live in the woods on an island thirty miles out to sea. I tried to explain to her that I wasn't much of a people person. Didn't seem to faze her."

Kayla felt vaguely uncomfortable, and when she turned around, there was Theo standing in the sliding glass door, staring at her.

"Let's talk about it tonight, okay?" Kayla said. "I have to go."

"Lobster tails?" Antoinette said.

"Yeah."

"You'll pick me up at quarter to twelve?"

"Not a minute later."

Kayla clicked off the phone, and Theo immediately lost interest in her. He put the top back on the cucumber salad, delivered it safely to the fridge, and deposited his fork in the dishwasher. Model child. He disappeared while Kayla stood there thinking about Antoinette's long-lost daughter *showing up*, tracking Antoinette down like something off *Geraldo* or *Oprah*. Tracking down a birth parent—it was cliché by now, wasn't it? And yet Kayla, at least, was interested. What had it felt like to give up a child? And what would a child of Antoinette's look like? Antoinette never told Kayla if her husband was black or white, and Kayla had been too afraid to ask. The color of a wine cork? What did that mean? More white than black? More black than white?

Before she determined why this question intrigued her or if it even mattered, Theo was back—he'd put on a T-shirt and a pair of flip-flops, and he was rattling his car keys.

"You're going out?" she said.

He, naturally, did not respond. Pointless to ask where he was going or if he'd be back for dinner. He climbed into his Jeep and drove away. Kayla stood in the door and watched him go.

"Do you think they'll all act this way?" Kayla asked Raoul later that night. She told Raoul about Theo forgetting Luke, about the foul language, the staring, the aggressive silence. It was more of the same.

Raoul leaned back in the dining chair and it creaked. It was almost ten o'clock. Luke and Cassidy B. were in bed, Jennifer was sleeping at a friend's house, Theo hadn't returned. Kayla and Raoul finished up the cold salads by candlelight.

"I don't know, Kayla."

"Do you think we should take away the car?"

"Then you'd have to shuttle him around," Raoul said. "No. Grounding him is grounding ourselves."

Kayla sighed. "You're going to have to talk to him," she said. "Maybe all he needs is one-on-one with you. Maybe the fishing will do it."

"Maybe," Raoul said. He rubbed his eyes. "This will pass, Kayla."

Easy for you to say, she thought. *You're never home*. And so, all of Theo's defiance seemed aimed at her. The summer had started out fine. Theo worked at the airport, and he drove around in his Jeep. Did Kayla need errands done? Theo was there to help—to run to the Stop & Shop, Bartlett's farm, East Coast Fish. Nights, he squired his friends and an endless stream of girls to parties and bonfires at the beach. Theo was already close to being the most popular kid at Nantucket High School, and when he got the car, the phone never stopped ringing. Kayla could have easily filled her day being Theo Montero's personal secretary.

And then, at the end of July, something happened. Theo turned, like sour milk. He stopped answering phone calls from his friends; he vanished for long periods of time without explanation. He swore. He locked himself in his bedroom and masturbated—Kayla heard him more than once, the heavy breathing, the moaning—and she sneaked away from his room hot-faced, embarrassed. It was natural, she knew, but it was as if he wanted her to hear him being openly and defiantly sexual in the house.

Kayla scanned her mind over the last few weeks. Nothing unusual jumped out. By that time, the summer had a rhythm: the sun, the garden, burgers on the grill, baby-sitting, camp, the phone ringing. One night while Theo was out, she and Raoul searched his room. Kayla felt evil and intrusive, doing this thing she swore she'd never do—opening his drawers, checking between his mattress and box spring. They were looking for Baggies of weed or warm beers, but they didn't find so much as a *Playboy*. Theo's room was messy with baseball mitts and boxer shorts and a copy of *The Scarlet Letter*. Raoul picked up the book.

"Somehow I don't think Hawthorne is behind all this," he said.

It was a phase, Kayla kept telling herself. Theo was eighteen, a year older than the rest of his class-mates because he'd contracted mono in the third grade and they'd decided to hold him back. Theo was suffering from growing pains, maybe. Many of his friends were a year ahead of him, and they were graduating, leaving the island for Amherst, Burling-ton, Charlottesville.

Back when the behavior started, Kayla stumbled upon Theo in the kitchen in the middle of the night. He was standing before the open refrigerator drink-ing milk from the plastic container. She watched him a minute before she spoke, the light from the fridge cast a bluish glow on his half-naked body—her beautiful, angry son.

"Theo," she said. "Is something bothering you?"

He paused his guzzling. "Yeah," he said. "You."

"Did you have a fight with your friends? Did something happen at work?"

Theo didn't answer.

"Theo," she said, "just tell me what you're thinking."

Theo put the milk back into the fridge and returned to his room, slamming the door.

Two weeks ago at her yearly checkup, Kayla told Dr. Donahue that Theo's behavior was keeping her up at night. Dr. Donahue was sixty-nine years old, working through retirement, and he was infamous for healing what ailed you, or what didn't ail you. He prescribed Ativan, a sedative, for her nerves. "How old is that boy?" he asked. "Eighteen? He'll be out of the house before you know it."

In another hour, Raoul was fast asleep and Kayla got ready for Night Swimmers. She changed into sweatpants, a red MONTERO CONSTRUCTION T-shirt, tennis shoes. When she stepped out onto the deck, the yard was bathed with moonlight. The first full moon in the history of Night Swimmers. Maybe it was a sign.

Here was how Night Swimmers began:

When Kayla was twenty-two years old and new to Nantucket and didn't know a soul, she rented a room in a cottage on Hooper Farm Road for the summer. The cottage was small and poorly constructed, but she had just finished living in a dorm at UMass, so to her, the cottage was a castle. Also renting rooms in that cottage were Valerie McIntyre and Antoinette Riley. Like Kayla, Valerie was just out of college, and headed to law school at NYU. Val wanted to take law school by storm—impress the professors, date the smartest guy in her section, and land a job with Skadden, Arps in New York City. She wanted Law Review and a year clerking for Judge Sechrist on the Fifth Circuit Court of Appeals. All this so she could one day get married, have children, and open her own practice on Nantucket. Kayla admired Valerie's ambition; she admired her plans. Kayla had no plans other than to buy a bicycle and find a job and maybe a boyfriend and go where the summer took her.

Antoinette was three years older than Kayla and Val; she was dark-skinned like an Egyptian priestess. That was one of two things Antoinette told them about herself on the day she moved in. "Three quarters African American, one quarter French Huguenot. My maternal grandmother was the Huguenot. Now you know, so you can quit gawking."

Kayla never imagined having a black roommate. But she was thrilled. Valerie, who was into her self-help books even then, said to Kayla, "There is one big difference between us and Antoinette, and it has nothing to do with skin color. You and I are fusers. We like other people. But Antoinette, she's an isolator. She prefers to be by herself."

It seemed true: Kayla and Valerie were fast friends. They each got jobs in town. Kayla worked at Murray's Toggery peddling Lilly Pulitzer skirts and Top-Siders, and Valerie sold tiny gold lightship baskets at a jewelry store. They spent their free days on Nobadeer Beach, and their free nights doing the bump at the Chicken Box. Kayla reveled in the new friendship, but she felt uncomfortable excluding Antoinette. It *did* feel like a racial issue—the two white girls leaving the black girl at home. And so, Kayla invited Antoinette everywhere—to the movies, to the bars, to the beach. Antoinette always declined in the same taut, definitive way. "No." And then, as an afterthought, "Thanks."

Antoinette didn't have a job that summer; she was spending her time "recovering." That was the other thing she told them when she first moved in: She had come to Nantucket to recover. Recover from what? It was an endless source of speculation between Kayla and Valerie. Antoinette wasn't a recovering alcoholic—she purchased cold chablis at the liquor store, poured it into one of the Waterford goblets she had brought to Nantucket, and drank alone in her room. She wasn't a recovering drug addict—when Kayla and Valerie lit up a joint before they went out to the Chicken Box, Antoinette would poke her head out of her bedroom and ask if she could have a toke. They pushed the dope on her eagerly, hoping it would make her talk, but it shut her up even more. After smoking, Antoinette's eyelids drooped, her mouth clamped shut, and she retreated back to her room, arms crossed over her chest.

Antoinette was a dancer. She wore black leotards and dirty pink ballet slippers, and every once in a while, Kayla found her in the backyard spinning and leaping and moving her arms in a way that reminded Kayla of an elephant's trunk. Antoinette danced until her leotard was soaked with sweat, and when she finished, she downed a jug of water, wiped her face off with a towel, and looked around the backyard as if she'd just stepped off a bus in a strange town.

One time Antoinette noticed Kayla peeking at her from the open kitchen window, and Kayla felt like she'd been caught watching Antoinette undress or something. "Part of your recovery?" Kayla asked meekly.

Antoinette did not respond.

Kayla remembered that first summer on Nantucket vividly. As soon as she stepped off the ferry she knew she'd found her spiritual home. The island was peaceful, simple, the historic home of Quakers and Native Americans. Kayla loved the colors of Nantucket: the gray of cedar shingles, the blue of the sky reflected across the harbor, the green of the dune grass, the red of ripe tomatoes in the back of the Bartlett's farm truck. But what made Nantucket special was the people. In mid-July, Kayla met Raoul at the Chicken Box, but their relationship didn't grow serious until the fall. That first summer, Kayla immersed herself in life with her two roommates, the one who liked her and the one who didn't. Kayla tried everything in her power to draw out Antoinette—she made a fancy dinner and set the table with three places. Candles, Chablis, marinated swordfish; she even went so far as to slide an invitation under Antoinette's bedroom door. *Dinner party here! Tonight!* the invitation said. *Please come as you are! Seven o'clock!* At quarter to seven, Antoinette slid the invitation back out. *No!* it said. *Thanks!* Kayla and Val ate the swordfish and drank two bottles of Chablis by themselves.

"I don't know why you try so hard," Val said. "She's obviously a mental case."

Right before Labor Day that first summer, a heat wave hit. Walter Cronkite announced on the evening news that Nantucket Island was the most comfortable location on the eastern seaboard, and immediately people from Boston, New York, and D.C. flocked to the island. But even Nantucket was hot and sticky, and when Kayla stood in the close, un-air-conditioned showroom of Murray's folding and refolding the Shetland sweaters they'd ordered for autumn, she felt like crying. It was hard to ride her bike, it was hard to lift her hands above her head, and it was impossible to sleep.

One night during the worst of it, she rose from bed and went into the kitchen, dug into a half gallon of Rocky Road, and lit up a joint. She heard footsteps, and she expected Valerie to appear, but instead, Antoinette walked into the kitchen, completely nude. Kayla tried to hide her surprise. One of the things she and Valerie had agreed on was that no matter how strange the things Antoinette did were, they would not act shocked.

"Kayla," she said.

Kayla handed Antoinette the joint, trying not to stare at her dark pubic hair, her purplish nipples. "It's hot," Kayla said.

Antoinette inhaled the smoke and after a moment let it go. "You got that right."

"I couldn't sleep."

Antoinette looked at Kayla then, and Kayla got the feeling it was the first time Antoinette had ever really seen her. "Let's swim," Antoinette said.

They woke Val, and the three of them climbed into Antoinette's CJ7, a great old Jeep that Kayla and Valerie had both admired but never ridden in. Kayla thought they would go to Steps Beach, where the water was calm, or possibly to Surfside or Nobadeer, which were close to the house, but Antoinette was driving—still nude—and when she took unfamiliar roads, Kayla said nothing. They headed out Polpis Road, where Kayla sometimes rode her bike, and took a left toward Wauwinet. They continued down a road with a lot of trees—Kayla could remember thinking that nowhere else on Nantucket had she seen so many trees—and then Antoinette pulled onto the shoulder, turned off the Jeep, and got out of the car. They were sitting in complete darkness amid the chattering of crickets. Valerie pressed her fingertips into Kayla's shoulder blade, and Kayla knew what she was thinking: *Now we've done it. Antoinette's deserting us here. Or worse, she's going to march us back into those woods and shoot us.* Then Kayla heard a hissing sound and she leaned over the driver side and peered out the window. She saw, through the darkness, the even darker form of Antoinette, crouched down, letting air out of the tires.

That was Kayla's first time up the beach to Great Point, the tip of Nantucket, the beginning and end of the island. It was the first time she'd driven over sand at all—the Jeep bounced and jiggled over bumps and in and out of ruts, and Antoinette's breasts jiggled, too. Kayla watched as Antoinette gripped the steering wheel, eyes straight ahead. They said nothing.

Antoinette stopped out past Great Point lighthouse. There was no moon that year, but there were billions of stars, and the kind of distinct Milky Way you could see only when you were a hundred miles away from the nearest city. When they stepped out of the Jeep, they were surrounded by water on three sides, with the lighthouse behind them like a stately guard. A division was visible in the water: a current pushing toward the sound, a current pushing toward the ocean. The foam on the waves was iridescent. For a moment, Kayla forgot it was hot.

She and Valerie stripped, and the three of them waded into the water and fell backwards. Chill. That's the best way to describe the sensation: sweet and chill. Kayla's life at that moment was all about the temperature of that water, the relief, the beauty of it. She could have stayed there forever.

Maybe Antoinette was feeling the same way, because as she floated on her back, she began to tell them things.

"I got married three years ago," she said. "A year ago I became pregnant, and while I was pregnant, I found my husband cheating on me. I had a baby girl, but I gave her away."

Kayla kept treading water, and Valerie, somewhere near her, did the same. Because it was dark, they didn't have to worry about the expressions on their faces: shock, horror, and perverse interest.

"You were *married*?" Kayla asked. That explained the Waterford goblet, at least. "You had a *baby*?"

"Was. Had." Antoinette spoke to the sky. "All past."

"So that's what you're recovering from, then?" Kayla said.

"Recovering, yeah. That's the bullshit I told myself when I got here. But if this summer's taught me anything, it's that I'm never going to recover. I have these dreams, you know, nightmares, where I hear my baby crying and I'm searching through a big house, but behind each door instead of finding my baby I find my husband having sex with different women."

"Why did you give away your baby?" Val asked.

"After she was born I tried to kill myself," Antoinette said. "I took pills. My neighbor found me and I was hospitalized and social services took the baby. But in the end, I decided to put her up for adoption."

"Because?"

"Because," Antoinette said, like it was obvious. "Because I can barely live with my own pain. Taking care of someone else, being that *responsible*, you know, for another person's welfare, I'm just not healthy enough. I want to be able to kill myself if that's what I decide."

"Please don't decide that," Val said. "Don't kill yourself over a man. They're not worth it."

Antoinette kicked her feet. "He wasn't just some *man*. He was my husband. Not that I expect either of you to understand."

"I understand," Kayla said, though of course she didn't. But she sensed in herself the power to understand someday, and she realized the magnitude of Antoinette's confidence. "Thank you for telling us. We thought you didn't like us."

"I don't want friends," Antoinette said. "Nothing against you personally. I just don't have the energy. Besides, in a couple of weeks you're leaving. You'll go back to your lives; you'll forget I even exist."

"I'm not going anywhere," Kayla said. She didn't realize the words were true until she spoke them. "I'm staying here on Nantucket."

"I'm leaving for law school," Val said. "But I'll be back. Next summer I'll be back. We can come up here again. We can tell more secrets."

"I might be dead next summer," Antoinette said.

"No," Kayla said. "Don't say that."

"You have no idea how I feel," Antoinette said. "You have no idea how much effort it takes to survive each day."

"Telling us the truth is a really crucial step," Val said. "That's why you brought us up here in the first place. You wanted us to know what happened. You wanted to share."

Antoinette almost smiled, but instead she dipped her head back and came up spouting water from her mouth. "You white women," she said. "*Share* is your middle name. You two can't even go to the bathroom by yourselves."

"Friends are important for personal growth," Val said.

"I lost the only two people who meant anything to me," Antoinette said. "It's not like I can replace them."

Kayla swam over to Antoinette and took her hand. Val joined them, and the three formed a circle in the water.

"We can't replace them," Kayla said. "But I agree with Val. I think we should come back here every summer."

"I don't know if I'll make it to next summer," Antoinette said.

"You'll make it," Val said.

"We'll see to it," Kayla said.

"I don't want you future Junior Leaguers on my charity case," Antoinette said. "You hear me? Don't knock on my door in the middle of the night to check if I'm still alive."

"Of course not," Kayla said.

"And like I said, I don't want friends."

"We'll be better than friends," Kayla said. She was sucked into the idea immediately: Great Point at midnight, the stars, the chill water, three women sharing the secrets of their souls. "We'll be the Night Swimmers."

Kayla picked up Valerie first because she lived closer, on Pleasant Street, near Fahey & Fromagerie.

Her house was smaller than Kayla's, but more attractive—gambrel-style, like a barn, with neat hunter green shutters, pink geraniums in the window boxes, and a healthy violet-blue hydrangea bush on either side of the front door. Two cars in the driveway: Val's slick, sexy BMW convertible and her husband's quieter black Jaguar. Race cars, the cars of professionals who could afford landscapers and a cleaning lady, the cars of people without children. After that first summer on Nantucket, Val had accomplished most of what she set out to do: Law Review, clerking for Judge Sechrist, a job as an associate at Skadden, Arps in New York, where she met and married John Gluckstern, a Wall Street superstar. Within five years they had enough money to leave Manhattan behind and move to Nantucket year-round. Val set up her own law practice in an office overlooking the Easy Street Boat Basin. She was tremendously successful, handling all the biggest real estate deals on the island.

John worked as an investment adviser at Nantucket Bank, a job he took so he could meet other islanders with money to invest. Kayla and Raoul had been to see John twice—once when they set up Raoul's business and then again in June, when Raoul landed the Ting job. John wore a three-piece suit to work, and at first that made one think that John was no different professionally from how he was socially: a self-important, puffed-up jackass. John had run for local office four times and had never been elected. He was unlikable. He was a one-upper, and he didn't listen. But what Kayla found after going to see him at work was that in his job, he was different. He was eager and excited and friendly, and although he knew everything in the world there was to know about money and investing, he wasn't pushy. He explained options to Raoul and Kayla carefully, he asked pertinent questions about the kids' college educations, and he let them make their own choices—choices that made them feel confident, smart, successful.

After their second visit with John at the bank, Kayla wanted to gently suggest to Val that if John treated his friends and neighbors the way he treated his clients, he'd be better liked. But by that point, Val had lost interest in making John seem less reprehensible. Back in April, John ran for selectman for the fourth time and garnered only sixty-seven votes. Val called Kayla from the high school cafeteria in tears, and Kayla went to pick her up. It was a rainy night, and the two of them drove out to the deserted parking lot of Surfside Beach. The rain was so heavy that Kayla couldn't even see the ocean through the windshield. Val sopped up her tears and slugged coffee and Kahlúa from a thermos that Kayla had brought. Val talked about how humiliating it was to have received only 67 votes when the winner got over 1,300.

"John doesn't even see what that means," Val said. "He doesn't understand that nobody likes us."

"Everybody likes *you*," Kayla insisted, though she knew this wasn't true. Some people *didn't* like Val— they thought she was too uptight for Nantucket, too tough for a woman. She was wealthy, she was powerful, she intimidated people. But Kayla defended Val against the people who muttered *bitch* or *dyke* when Val's name came up in conversation. Val was Kayla's first friend on the island; she'd known her longer than she'd known Raoul. Still, Kayla was well aware that Val didn't help John at all in the polls.

"I feel this deadly combination of disgust and pity for John," Val said. "Actual pity for him because running for office is his passion. How do I ask my husband to stop pursuing his dream? Do I just say, 'Honey, please give up your aspirations, you're embarrassing me'? Is that what I say? Maybe it is. Because I can't handle another loss like tonight."

Six weeks later, when Kayla and Val met for coffee at Espresso Café, Val told Kayla she was having an affair. Her passions, she said, lay elsewhere.

Valerie came out of her house holding the largest bottle of champagne Kayla had ever seen. It was almost as big as Luke; the cork was level with Valerie's head, and the bottom of the bottle was at her waist. Kayla flung open the car door.

"What have you got there?" she asked.

"It's a Methuselah of Laurent-Perrier," Val said. She set the bottle down on the seat between them. "I brought it back from France for this very occasion. They had an absolute fit in customs, but they made an exception when I told them it was for Night Swimmers."

"You don't suppose we'll drink all that?" Kayla said.

Val shrugged. "We have a lot to celebrate after twenty years. I'm finally happy, you're finally rich—"

"I'm not rich," Kayla said.

"You will be soon enough," Val said. She closed her door, and Kayla backed out of the driveway. "It's okay to have money, Kayla, though I know you don't believe it."

"I think it's okay," Kayla said defensively. "In fact, I think it's fine."

Val shook her short hair. She wore a pressed white linen shirt that was so crisp it looked like parchment, and baggy linen pants the color of wheat bread. Beige suede Fratelli Rossetti sandals. She was deeply tanned (from sunbathing nude every weekend at Miacomet Beach), and she wore three gold chains around her neck that were as thin as strands of web. Those chains were her signature jewelry, she said. They defined who she was. Kayla cringed when Val said things like "signature jewelry" in public because it just gave people another reason to dislike her. Who on earth had signature jewelry? Princess Diana? Zsa Zsa Gabor?

As if reading Kayla's mind, Val fingered her chains. "Did you talk to Antoinette?" she asked.

"I did."

"How did she sound?"

"She sounded fine." Kayla threw the car into reverse and backed out of the driveway. "Why do you ask?"

"Oh, I don't know," Val said. "We had lunch last week, and she seemed a little reflective."

"You had lunch?" Kayla said. "You didn't tell me that."

Val shrugged. "It was no big deal. It was just lunch."

"Yeah, but you could have . . ." Kayla almost said *"invited me along,"* but she caught herself. "You could have mentioned it."

"I also had lunch with Merrill and Kelly. I also had lunch with Nina Monroe."

"Yeah, but those are your friends."

"Antoinette is my friend. Please, Kayla, don't get sensitive about this. It was only lunch."

"You're right," Kayla said. She couldn't help but feel jealous in the most adolescent way—there was no reason why Val and Antoinette shouldn't have lunch alone. No reason why they shouldn't pursue a friendship independent of her. But, in fact, Kayla had always believed that she was the glue that held Val and Antoinette together; she was closer to both of them than they were to each other. "So she sounded reflective?"

"Yes," Val said. "Has she told you anything?"

Kayla considered mentioning Antoinette's daughter, if only to prove that she had some inside information first, but she shook her head. The announcement about the daughter could wait until midnight, when Night Swimmers officially began.

The Night Swimmers had evolved over the past twenty years into an evening of rules and rituals. It was a rule to eat decadent food—lobsters, cheese, berries. It was a rule to drink champagne. And it was a time to share secrets, like the one Antoinette had shared with them twenty years earlier.

As Kayla drove through the moonlit night toward Antoinette's house, she thought about the secrets she'd shared over the past years. She'd told Val and Antoinette all the secrets from her past—about sneaking out in the middle of the night to meet a high school boyfriend at a disco, cheating on a chemistry test in college, stealing a pair of duck shoes from Murray's when she worked there her first summer. She told them one year that she was pregnant with Cassidy B.—before Raoul even knew. Val and Antoinette's secrets were always more interesting than her own. Val told about sleeping with a professor to get on Law Review, she told about a bank account abroad that she kept a secret from John, she told them she overcharged one of her best clients on a regular basis. Antoinette told about being cut from the Joffrey Ballet School when she lived in New York before she was married, she told about how her mother ran out on her when Antoinette was at boarding school in New Hampshire.

This year Antoinette would tell about her daughter coming to visit, and Val would disclose the name of her lover. Kayla—well, Kayla would talk about Theo. The three women would accept each other's secrets like valuable gifts to be kept safe from the rest of the world.

Antoinette lived off Polpis Road down a long, bumpy dirt path bordered on both sides by scrub pines. Antoinette bought the land with a portion of her enormous divorce settlement, and she hired Raoul to build her four-room cottage. She invested her settlement with John Gluckstern in the early eighties, and he bought her a load of Microsoft at two dollars a share. Val had let it slip that Antoinette now had close to thirty million dollars. She was worth more than Kayla and Raoul and Val and John put together, but her lifestyle required very little. She danced, she went for walks in the woods, she drank chardonnay, she read novels. It sounded enviable at first—Antoinette had enough money to do whatever she pleased, and what she pleased was to go for days, even weeks, without talking to another soul. She had claimed twenty years earlier that she didn't want friends, but over time she had given in to Kayla and Val in small ways. She joined them for an occasional meal, she sometimes remembered their birthdays, she called just to talk every once in a while. Her desire to kill herself subsided, although she experienced dark periods when she didn't eat, didn't dance, didn't leave the house. The dark periods lasted a few days, maybe a week, and then they ended and Antoinette went back to what she did best, cultivating her loneliness. "I'm lonely all the time, every day," she told Kayla. "But there are far worse things than being lonely. Like being betrayed."

Once a year Antoinette opened herself fully to Kayla and Val, she played their game, she returned their love. Every year Kayla worried that Antoinette would withdraw from Night Swimmers, deem it silly and worthless, but she never did. Deep down, Antoinette respected the bond they'd nurtured for twenty years.

Antoinette emerged from her cottage dressed entirely in black: black leotard, black leggings, and her vintage black Chuck Taylor basketball shoes. She was a woman in permanent mourning.

"I come bearing crustaceans," she said, sliding a plastic tub of lobsters covered with aluminum foil into the backseat. She touched both Kayla and Val on the shoulders. "Hello, white women."

"Hello, you beautiful black woman, you," Val said. "When are you going to brighten your wardrobe? I'm reading this book about positive self-image, and it said other people respond to the colors you wear. They tie it right in with your personality."

"I think Antoinette looks lovely in black," Kayla said.

"Thank you," Antoinette said. "It's been a long time since I've been called lovely. Beautiful, sexy, reclusive, yes. Lovely, no. *Lovely* seems better suited to describing a summer day, or a bride. *Lovely* is a poem by Robert Frost. I view myself as a Gwendolyn Brooks poem. Something grittier, more complicated. Do you want to reconsider your choice of adjective, Kayla?"

"No," Kayla said. "I don't. I find you lovely."

"I should read more poetry," Val said. "I don't even know who Gwendolyn Brooks is."

"I smell Coco Chanel," Antoinette said. "Is that you, Kayla?"

"What can I say? Women are the only ones who appreciate perfume. I don't know why I bother to waste the stuff on Raoul."

"What's this?" Antoinette asked, inspecting the champagne.

"It's for our twentieth anniversary," Val said. "I wanted to do something special."

"Val brought it back from France," Kayla said. "She was thinking of Night Swimmers as she toured the Champagne region."

"Well, thank you, madam," Antoinette said. "I'm sure tonight will be a night we'll remember for the rest of our lives." She pointed to the blue numbers of the car's digital clock. "It's eleven-forty-seven, ladies. We'd better get a move on."

Kayla drove down the Wauwinet Road, past the gatehouse, and onto the crooked finger of land that stuck out into Nantucket Sound. Great Point. It was so secluded, so remote, it was Nantucket's only real destination, the place year-round islanders went when they wanted to get away, when they wanted to feel like they'd *been* somewhere.

Kayla cruised along the shoreline a good ten feet above the water line. The tide was going out, the water silvery in the moonlight, and Kayla had a feeling that this silence would be the best part of the evening. This peaceful coexistence.

She parked in the usual spot, beyond Great Point lighthouse. "Here we are."

They sprang into action. Val grabbed the bottle of champagne by the neck as though it were an unruly child and dragged it onto the sand. Kayla turned around to greet Antoinette. Antoinette's frizzy dark hair was pulled back in a rubber band, and she had something green on her lip. Kayla reached out to wipe it off, exactly the way Jacob had reached for the potato chip that afternoon on the job site, but Antoinette recoiled from Kayla like a serpent, a wild look in her eye.

Kayla retracted her hand. "You have something on your lip."

Antoinette wiped at her mouth defensively.

"Sorry," Kayla said. "I didn't mean to frighten you."

"You didn't frighten me, Kayla," Antoinette said, and she smiled. "I'm just feeling a little guarded about my personal space."

Because of her daughter coming, Kayla thought. The daughter whose existence had explained so much twenty years earlier.

"It's eleven-fifty-eight, people," Val said. "Let's hurry."

Kayla pulled a blanket out of the back of the Trooper and spread it in the sand. Val wrangled the wrapper and cage off the champagne. Kayla set out the cooler that held the cheese, the berries, and three champagne glasses. Antoinette plopped the tub of lobsters down, and Kayla handed Antoinette a chilled glass. Valerie let the cork fly out of the Methuselah with a deep, resounding *thwop!* The cork sailed toward the water.

Val poured the champagne. The three women raised their glasses. In the moonlight, bubbles rose to the surface of the flutes.

Val checked her watch. "Okay, ladies, it's . . . midnight! Say it, Kayla."

Kayla addressed the ocean. "To the night, to the water that surrounds us, to the island of Nantucket, and to our friendship. These things are eternal."

"Eternal," Val said.

"Eternal," Antoinette said.

"Your secrets," Kayla said, "are safe with me."

"And safe with me," Val said.

"And safe with me," Antoinette said.

They drank the first glass of champagne all the way down—and the golden rush that went to Kayla's head encouraged her. This part of the ritual always made her feel wild and daring—a nearly overweight, nearly middle-aged mother of four buzzed on champagne at Great Point at midnight. It made her feel exciting things were possible. They set their glasses carefully in the sand and joined hands. Val's hand was warm and moist, like the hand of a preschooler, and Antoinette's hand was dry and bony, like a bunch of sticks. They walked in a circle. *"Our friendship . . . no beginning . . . no end,"* Kayla said under her breath. Then they dropped their asses onto the blanket, and Val poured more champagne. Night Swimmers had begun.

It took only one more glass of champagne to make Val antsy about her secret. She cleared her throat, sucked in a deep, dramatic breath, and said, "I can't wait another second. You know I've been seeing someone, a man, not my husband—I've been sleeping with someone. And I'm ready to tell you who it is. Now I don't want you to freak out, okay? Especially not you, Kayla. You won't freak out on me, will you?"

The muscles around Kayla's heart steeled themselves for a blow. Why did Val think she would freak out? Was Val going to say *Raoul's* name? Kayla dug her feet into the cool sand as she remembered the year when her secret had been this: *I think Raoul is having an affair.* This was back when Luke was a toddler and Kayla was still fighting to lose the weight she'd gained while carrying him. Her first suspicion was about Missy Tsoulakis. A picture of Missy popped into Kayla's mind: her nineteen-year-old blondness, her tennis skirt with matching bloomers that peeked out when she bent over to pick up a ball. Missy had taught Jennifer tennis at the 'Sconset Casino, and Raoul had always been the one to drop Jennifer off and pick her up. He'd insisted on it. Once when Kayla happened to show up, he was engrossed in the tennis lesson, his fingers wound through the wire fence like claws as he watched them. Missy's strong tan arms were wrapped around Jennifer, showing her how to execute the perfect backhand. Kayla felt the air being pressed out of her lungs as she watched Raoul watch Missy. *He loves her*, she thought. *He's obsessed with her.* Kayla felt fat and dowdy—and unbearably matronly in her station wagon with Luke in the car seat in back. She drove past the courts and headed home, thinking of how the first thing she would do was cancel Jennifer's tennis lessons, and the second thing was go on a diet, and start walking like the other women in her neighborhood. Raoul and Missy Tsoulakis. That night, she asked Raoul if her suspicions were true and he said, "She's a *girl*, Kayla. Are you *crazy*?"

Antoinette nudged Kayla with her foot, and she snapped back to life.

"Speak, Val," Antoinette said. "Confess."

Valerie sipped her champagne with excruciating slowness, prolonging the dramatic moment. She wiped the lipstick smudge from her glass. "It's Jacob Anderson," she said.

"Jacob Anderson," Kayla repeated. "Jacob, who works for Raoul?"

"Yes."

Antoinette drained her champagne. "Jacob Anderson. That name rings a bell. Do I know Jacob Anderson?"

"He's on Raoul's crew," Kayla said. "You know him, Antoinette. Dark hair, green eyes, a real sweet-talker."

"Excuse me?" Val said.

Kayla thought of Jacob reaching out and touching her lip. How sure she'd been that he was going to kiss her. She had wanted him to, she realized now. She had wanted Jacob Anderson to kiss her—and so a part of her was stung by this news. A part of her did want to rebel against it. Valerie was sleeping with Jacob. He was her secret.

"He has a very sexual nature," Kayla said. "He's about thirty, he drives a blue-and-white Bronco."

"He's thirty-two," Valerie said. "Antoinette doesn't know him."

"I know him," Antoinette said. "He helped Raoul build my house." She looked at Val. "Congratulations."

"Thank you," Val said. She poured herself another glass of champagne. "We're in love."

"You're in *love*?" Kayla said.

"What?" Val said. "I'm not *allowed* to be in love with Jacob Anderson?"

"Of course you're allowed," Kayla said. "It's just . . . Oh, I don't know."

"You do know," Val said. "You think it's silly. You think he's too young."

"There's no such thing as too young when you're a woman over forty," Antoinette said. She kicked off her Chuck Taylors, peeled off her leggings and leotard until she was nude before them in the moonlight. "Now I don't know what you ladies came here for, but I came to swim. I'm going in."

"Me, too," Kayla said. She slid out of her sweats and her T-shirt. She examined her own naked body, but she knew how different she looked from Antoinette and Val. Antoinette had a ballerina's body: tall, slender, and lithe. Statuesque. Val was more muscular—lifting free weights in her office was no joke—her arms were perfectly toned and she had a teeny-tiny little butt that probably fit into one of Jacob Anderson's hands. Kayla, in comparison, was thick—full, droopy breasts, rounded belly, dimpled thighs. She tried not to get discouraged by this.

Valerie pried off her sandals. "You guys aren't happy for me," she said.

"I'm happy for you," Kayla said. "I'm glad it's Jacob. I like Jacob."

Val unbuttoned her crisp white shirt. "You're not angry?"

"Why would I be angry?" Kayla asked.

"I don't know," Val said. "I'm just so happy, and I want you to be happy, too."

"I'm happy!" Kayla said. It was difficult not to feel like everyone's mother when the people around her acted like children. "You have my blessing. Really."

They heard a splash and turned to see Antoinette plunge into the water. Kayla and Val hurried in behind her.

The water was the perfect foil for Val's news. Soft waves rolled over Kayla's shoulders. Her anger and confusion subsided. She didn't wonder about the trajectory her thoughts had taken in the last ten minutes—why she felt Val was going to say Raoul's name, why she felt a pinch of jealousy when Val said Jacob's name instead. She didn't consider these things. Or rather, she considered them and then let them go, like Luke letting go of the string of his purple balloon that afternoon. Kayla concentrated on the simple perfection of the water, the moonlight, the lighthouse, the Methuselah of champagne. Swimming with her two dear friends.

Antoinette dived and surfaced like a dolphin, her dark hair sleek against her head. "My daughter arrives tomorrow," she said.

She obviously said this for Val's benefit, since Kayla already knew. But Val was quiet. Antoinette went under again.

"Did you hear Antoinette's secret?" Kayla asked Val. "Her daughter arrives tomorrow. The daughter she gave up for adoption."

Val was bobbing in the waves; Antoinette was the only one of the three of them who actually swam. Val shrugged. She didn't seem surprised at all.

Antoinette surfaced.

"Start at the beginning," Kayla said. "When did she call you?"

"Wednesday night," Antoinette said.

"And what did she say? Did she . . . did she introduce herself?"

"Obviously."

"Well, I mean, did she say, 'Hi, I'm Lindsey, your daughter'?"

"Something like that."

"Lindsey wasn't what you named her, though, was it?"

"I didn't give her a name at all," Antoinette said. She dived under and stayed below water a long time. Kayla got the message: Antoinette didn't want to talk about it. Kayla tried to imagine what it would be like to be in Antoinette's place. A daughter she'd given away. What if the daughter looked just like the husband? It was too bittersweet, too powerful. You'd want to see the girl more than anything else, your own *child*, but it would be scary, too. All the emotion Antoinette had escaped twenty years ago would come walking across the tarmac tomorrow.

"What are you going to do with your daughter?" Kayla asked. "Do you have plans?"

"No plans," Antoinette said.

"What are you going to say to her?" Kayla asked. "What are you going to tell her?"

"I'll answer her questions," Antoinette said. "I explained the basic story to her over the phone."

"Will we get to meet her?" Kayla asked.

"I'm busy this weekend," Val said. "With Jacob."

"I want to meet her," Kayla said.

"Maybe you can pick her up at the airport and take her to your house," Antoinette said. "Maybe you could pretend you're her mother, Kayla. I'm sure she'd be happier with you."

"Come on, Antoinette."

"No, I'm serious," Antoinette said. "Why don't you take her?"

"You *are* the consummate parent, Kayla," Val said, playing with the chains at her neck. In the moonlight they looked like strands of golden thread. "The perfect mother of four perfect children. We agreed on that at lunch the other day."

Kayla pictured Val and Antoinette sitting together at lunch—at 21 Federal or the Galley—someplace expensive and elegant. She was more than just jealous, more than just hurt at not being asked along. She was angry that they had talked about her. "Shut up," Kayla said. "Just shut up."

She swam to shore with some difficulty, because

the tide was going out and waves kept washing her
backwards. She struggled back to the beach, where
she buried her face in one of the towels she'd
brought—it was scratchy and dry and smelled like
Bounce. She toweled her body and hair and stepped
into her clothes. Her heart was beating wildly. Why
was she so angry? She wondered if this was how
Theo felt—consumed with unreasonable anger, with
rage that seemed to come from nowhere. Or maybe
she was so angry because of Theo. Because her
friends were telling her that she was the perfect
mother, and she knew they were being sincere. Antoinette gave her child up, and Val had no children—
they had left the mothering to Kayla. Kayla had
spent her adult life doing the best job that she possibly could, and yet when she thought about Theo,
she knew she had failed. Her oldest child was a bril-
liant, blazing example of how she had failed.

Kayla unwedged her purse from underneath the
front seat of the car. She rummaged through it until
she found the bottle of Ativan Dr. Donahue had prescribed, and she put a pill under her tongue. Then
she poured herself another glass of champagne and
swallowed the pill, thinking that she would go to the
airport tomorrow and spy on Antoinette and her
daughter. She would witness the awkwardness between them, the inevitable disappointment when
they saw each other's faces—and maybe that would
give her some small, mean satisfaction, watching
Antoinette fail, too.

Val and Antoinette emerged from the water, dried
off, and wrapped themselves in their towels. Kayla

poured them each another glass of champagne, and without conversation, the three of them started in on their feast: Kayla pulled lobster meat free of the scarlet shell and dipped it indiscriminately into the melted butter, she smeared hunks of baguette with the Saint André, and she popped raspberries into her mouth like bonbons. The food was so delicious that Kayla started to cry. It was the Ativan kicking in. Soon, she was sniffling and sobbing, and Val and Antoinette stared at her. She poured herself another glass of champagne, then one for Val and Antoinette.

"Did I say something that upset you, Kayla?" Val said.

"It's not you," Kayla said, reaching for another hunk of baguette. She was feeling light-headed and drunk. "I guess it's time for me to tell my secret. It's about Theo."

There was a spectacular silence. She was coherent enough to notice that—a silence that was different from quiet, different from lack of conversation. She raised her head and watched Val and Antoinette exchange a look.

"What about Theo?" Val asked.

"Something's happened to him," Kayla said. "He's changed. He hates me, he hates his brother and sisters, he even hates Raoul. He's turned vile and disgusting and scary." Then she remembered something she had been trying to erase from her mind since the moment she discovered it, a week before. "He drove his Jeep through my garden." The words sounded pale and insufficient for what had happened. Kayla woke up one morning and found her garden ruined. Every single vegetable, herb, and flower had been buried in a crosshatch of deep ruts. Theo had run the Jeep back and forth until every plant was torn to bits, every vegetable smashed. And he made no move to hide it: the tires of his Jeep were muddy. He'd had the gall to park the Jeep in the driveway with muddy tires. It was then she knew that her child hated her, because that garden was her project, it was her avocation, it was hers and hers alone. Raoul didn't even notice anything wrong. "It took me three days to dig everything up, to get it cleaned out. The whole thing is gone. He stole it from me."

After a second, Val turned to Antoinette. "Well, what do you think of that?"

Antoinette said, "He's a teenager, Kayla. He'll get over it."

They drank more champagne. They finished the lobsters and the cheese and the berries. Kayla leaned back in the sand and closed her eyes. The Ativan was working its magic. Val and Antoinette spoke words that made no sense, a code. Or maybe the words made sense but just not to her because she was asleep; maybe the words got jumbled up with a dream she was having. Kayla dreamt that the string of Luke's purple balloon was wound around the legs of a baby seagull, and tangled, so that the bird couldn't fly. The gull tried to fly and Kayla chased after it, wanting to cut the string. But she couldn't get close enough.

Kayla heard herself snore, and she jolted awake. She reached instinctively for her glass of cham-

pagne, drank what was left, and filled it again, lifting
the Methuselah with ease now. The huge bottle was
half empty.

"What were you guys talking about while I was
asleep?" Kayla asked. "Were you discussing what a
bad mother I am?"

"You're not a bad mother at all, Kayla," Val said.
"I'm sure whatever Theo's problem is, it has nothing
to do with you. You're being too sensitive again."

"What is it, then?"

Val patted her knee. "It's school or something.
Friends. A girlfriend."

Kayla shook her head. "No, if it were that kind
of thing he would have told Raoul. He tells Raoul
everything."

Antoinette interrupted them. "I have something to
say. I have my secret to tell."

"You already told your secret," Kayla said.
"About your daughter, remember? Only one secret
per customer."

"Maybe you should stop drinking, Kayla," Val
said. "It's really bringing your emotions to the surface."

"So what? I thought that's what tonight was
about. Letting it all hang loose."

"I have a confession to make," Antoinette said.

Kayla turned to her friend. Antoinette was looking
at her in a meaningful way, and Kayla got an awful
vibe. "Oh, God," she said in a voice she didn't recognize as her own. "Don't tell me. Are *you* having
an affair with Raoul? Are you screwing my husband?"

Antoinette sat perfectly still for a moment, staring at Kayla. Kayla stared back at first with accusatory fire, then with defensiveness, and finally with shame. She was ruining everything. But before Kayla could find the words to apologize, Antoinette rose and her towel fell away, exposing her beautiful dark body. Kayla thought she was going to drive off in the Trooper, leaving them there. Kayla wouldn't have blamed her. But Antoinette didn't get into the car. Instead, she put her arms out like she was holding an imaginary beach ball, and she pirouetted into the water. Kayla watched in a stupor; she *was* drunk. Antoinette swam straight out.

Kayla turned to Val. "I shouldn't have said that."

Val blinked. "Kayla, what is *wrong* with you?"

"I don't know," Kayla said.

Kayla waited for Antoinette's dark head to surface so that she could call out an apology. She had no idea why those words escaped her lips—*Are you screwing my husband?* It was the Ativan talking, and the champagne, combined with the awful memory of Missy Tsoulakis. Even after nineteen years of marriage, Kayla was insecure—and especially when she saw forty-four-year-old women with incredible bodies like Antoinette's and Val's. But still, how dumb of her. Insensitive. And inappropriate for Night Swimmers. It was their twentieth anniversary, and she'd ruined it.

Kayla missed Antoinette surfacing; she was looking in the wrong place. Her mental clock ticked:

How long was too long? The water was dappled by moonlight; it was all bright surfaces and dark troughs. After a minute, she stood up.

"Do you see her?"

Now Val was the one lying down with her eyes closed, probably off in dreamland with Jacob Anderson. "Do I see who?"

"Antoinette." Kayla's insides felt like they were filling up with something dark and syrupy. Foreboding. Fear. "I don't see Antoinette," she said. Her voice sounded calm; the Ativan reined her in.

"She's swimming," Val said.

"I don't see her," Kayla said. She walked closer to the water, which reflected the moonlight like a mirror. Was Antoinette out there floating on her back? "Antoinette, I'm sorry! Hey, I'm sorry! I'm stupid drunk. Please come out! Antoinette!"

Kayla looked around Great Point to the harbor side. The rip current was raised in the water like a scar.

"I don't see her," Kayla said.

Val sat up on the blanket. "What do you *mean* you don't see her?"

"Do you see her?" Kayla asked. Panic grabbed Kayla—a child running out in the road, a piece of hard candy lodged in a throat—imminent danger.

Val joined her at the water's edge. "Holy shit," she said. "Antoinette!"

"Antoinette!" Kayla called. "Antoinette, please!"

No answer.

Kayla tore off her clothes and dived in. Val followed. Kayla wasn't a strong swimmer, but she went underwater and opened her eyes. The water was greenish black, too dark to see a thing, and immediately she was terrified of this dark, silent world. Her eyes stung. She flailed her arms through the water hoping to hit something warm and familiar, a body, Antoinette's body.

She surfaced but saw no sign of Val. "Val!" she screamed.

Val raised her head. "I'm over here!"

"Antoinette!" Kayla called. She went under again and batted her arms and legs in all directions. She could see nothing but water—so much dark water. Her children were home safe in their beds, dry, warm, her husband, too, and she was submerged in the Atlantic Ocean searching for Antoinette. Kayla broke the surface and tried to put her feet down, but the water was too deep. A wave crested over her; she came up coughing. The current pushed her out; water had gotten up her nose, and her whole face stung. A voice whispered in Kayla's ears—a *shushing* that washed over her with each wave. The Ativan and the champagne wanted to slow her down, rock her to sleep. She could just close her eyes and let the waves carry her away. But she lifted her arms and started swimming back to shore, and as she did, she saw a figure crouched on the beach, and she allowed herself a moment of sweet relief until she saw that the figure was Val, hugging her knees, crying.

Kayla let the waves wash her up next to Val.

"Oh, Jesus God. Oh, sweet Jesus," Val said. She looked at Kayla. "We have to get some help."

This sounded right—*get help*—but Kayla couldn't make her mind work properly. How would they get help?

"I'll stay here," Val said. "You go. Call the police from the Wauwinet gatehouse. Go right now."

"I'm too drunk to drive," Kayla said. Another Night Swimmers rule was that no one left the beach until sunrise, when they'd had enough time to sleep off the champagne. "And I took a sedative. I can't go."

"You have to go!" Val said. "I'm just as messed up as you, and it's your car. You have to go, Kayla, right this second!"

Kayla moved heavily, like she was still underwater. She pulled on her clothes and floated over to her car. It smelled like lobster. She eased the car over the ruts in the sand and headed back toward the Wauwinet. She started convulsing with the cold; water ran down her back. Oh, God, she thought, please, please, please God. *Why* had Kayla said what she said? Her head swelled until it felt like it was the size of a watermelon. The dunes to her right grew larger. How would she make it to the phone? Kayla yanked on the steering wheel to get the Trooper to stay in the tracks. What if she got stuck? Everything blurred; the car bounced as Kayla tackled the dunes. *Antoinette is going to be fine*, Kayla thought. *This is just a joke. She's angry at me for saying something so stupid.*

When Kayla reached the Wauwinet gatehouse, she grabbed a handful of change from the console of her car and ran to the pay phone. She stared at the receiver of the phone, and the buttons. Did 911 require money? Certainly not. But Kayla slid a quarter and a dime into the slot anyway and dialed her house. She needed to talk to Raoul.

After two rings, Theo answered the phone. "Hello."

"Put Daddy on," Kayla said. Her voice sounded calm, maybe tinged with low-grade anxiety, as if to say, *I have a flat tire*, or *I'm stuck in the sand*.

"Mom?" Theo said.

"Theo, put Daddy on, please. It's important."

Theo hung up the phone.

Kayla thought, *Call 911!* But she put more change into the slot and dialed her house again. The phone rang until the answering machine picked up. Kayla called back a third time. After three rings, she heard the hoarse croak of Raoul and she burst into tears. Time was of the essence—she knew that—but it took Kayla several seconds to regain her voice enough to tell him that Antoinette went swimming and didn't come back to shore.

"Where are you?" he asked.

"The Wauwinet."

"Where's Val?"

"Back at the Point."

"You've called the police?" he asked.

"Not yet."

"Well, call the fucking police, Kayla. Call 911, right now. I'll call the fire department. Jesus, Kayla."

"I want you to come out here," Kayla wailed. "Leave the kids. They'll sleep."

"Call 911," he said. "Do that one thing and then

drive back out and wait with Val. Don't go in the water, Kayla, do you hear me?"

He hung up and Kayla called 911. The dispatcher was a reedy-voiced woman—Charlotte, her name was. She had a daughter in Luke's grade. Kayla told her there was a woman missing in the water off Great Point.

"This is Kayla Montero. I'm calling from the pay phone at the Wauwinet. This woman is a friend of mine. Can you send someone out right away?"

"We'll send the Open Water Rescue Squad," Charlotte said.

"And they'll be able to find her? Even in the dark?"

"They'll do their best," Charlotte said.

Driving back out to Great Point, Kayla remembered Antoinette's daughter, Lindsey. What if she showed up in the morning to find Antoinette missing? *I'm sorry, but Antoinette's missing. She danced into the water last night, and now she's . . . gone.* Lindsey would blame herself. Because maybe Antoinette had disappeared on purpose to avoid this child of hers. Motherhood was firmly ensconced in Kayla, anchored like her soul in her body, but she could imagine what a terrific fear it might be for Antoinette to be faced with motherhood when she had rejected it so long ago. And Antoinette was just about to confess something. Maybe the confession was that she was planning to disappear for a few days, to ditch the daughter. This sounded cruel, not to mention unlikely, but Kayla liked it better than the thought that Kayla's accusation had made Antoinette retreat to the water and that, once swimming, Antoinette was swept out to sea. Because then it would be Kayla's fault.

By the time Kayla got back to the lighthouse, the approaching lights of a boat were visible. Val paced the beach wearing her white shirt and a beach towel tied around her waist. She had Antoinette's Chuck Taylors on each of her hands and she banged the soles together like a child playing with blocks.

"She's gone," Val said. Her eyes were round and empty. "She just danced away."

The remains of their picnic lay about. Kayla picked up the Methuselah and ran with it to the water's edge, where she heaved it into the ocean.

"What are you doing?" Val said.

Kayla picked up the three champagne glasses and tossed them into the water as well; they shattered against the wet sand.

"It's called destroying the evidence," Kayla said. "You're a lawyer, Val, you should know that."

"We have nothing to hide," Val said. "It's not like we committed a crime here, Kayla."

"We're drunk!" Kayla screamed. "Antoinette was drunk!"

Kayla tossed the food and trash into the middle of the blanket and shoved it in the back of the Trooper. She loaded in the empty cooler. The lights of the boat got closer; she could hear the motor. She saw two more pairs of headlights driving up the beach. *Please let that be Raoul*, she thought.

"You're crazy," Val said. She ran to the water's edge. "If they find that bottle, they're going to think we're guilty of something."

Guilty of something. Kayla watched Val wade into the water and retrieve the Methuselah. Kayla hadn't thrown it very far, and unlike Antoinette, the bottle had washed back to shore, whole and unharmed.

Soon, Great Point was swarming with men. How incongruous, Kayla thought, that their women-only ritual was being invaded by these foreign creatures. A true sign that something was wrong. And what did it say about her that she was relieved, happy even, to see all these men—the men in the coast guard who piloted the search boat, two men on WaveRunners, the men of the police and fire departments who arrived in their Suburbans with their lights flashing, and finally Raoul, who trundled up the beach in his red Chevy? He ran to her like a hero from the movies. Raoul was the luckiest man Kayla had ever met. Just his presence would help.

Paul Henry, a policeman Kayla had known for years, climbed out of one of the Suburbans. Paul was short and wiry, quietly intense. He dressed like a math teacher, or like Mr. Rogers, in cardigan sweaters and canvas sneakers, and he had a crew cut. Kayla asked him once if he'd ever been in the military. Navy, he said—but the crew cut he'd had since he was six years old, and he'd never seen any reason to change it.

"Kayla, Valerie," Paul said. "Tell me what happened."

"We were swimming," Kayla said. "I mean, Val and I were sitting here on the beach and Antoinette danced into the water."

"She what?"

"She danced into the water. She put her arms out like she was holding a ball, and then she pirouetted into the water. Look, here are her footprints." Kayla showed him the deep gouges that Antoinette's toes had left in the sand. "Once she started swimming, we lost track of her."

Paul Henry pinched his lips together like he'd just eaten a bad clam. "Never, never swim up here without a spotter. At night, no less. It's irresponsible. Because this is what can happen. This is the danger. Do you see that rip, Kayla?" Paul Henry pointed. "You know better than this. You've lived here, what, twenty years? You wouldn't let your kids do it, and you shouldn't be doing it yourself."

"Paul," Val piped up. "Scolding us now isn't helping Antoinette."

Kayla and Val walked with Paul Henry to the water line. The waves lapped over Kayla's feet, and over the tops of Paul Henry's canvas sneakers.

Val pointed to an imaginary spot in the dark sea. "I saw her out there."

"And she swam straight out?" Paul asked. "You're sure?"

"Yes," Val said.

"I'm not sure," Kayla said. "Now I can't remember where I saw her."

"It was here," Val said.

"What was she wearing?" Paul Henry asked. "Did she have anything on—a sweatshirt or anything—that might weigh her down?"

"She was nude," Val said.

"Why in the world were you ladies out here in the middle of the night swimming nude?" Paul Henry said. "What was going on out here?"

"We come every year," Kayla said. "For Night Swimmers."

"Night Swimmers?"

"It's a tradition," Kayla said. "We're always careful."

"Well, not careful enough," Paul Henry said. "Not tonight." He radioed the coast guard boat. The boat had a roaming searchlight, there was more talk of the rip current, and they were all silent when someone on the coast guard boat cut through the radio static and said, "With a rip tide like this, a person could be washed out to sea in a matter of minutes."

Jack Montalbano, the fire chief, approached them. He was a big, hearty Portuguese with a crushing handshake. His wife had died of ovarian cancer the year before, and Kayla hadn't spoken to him since she'd dropped a roasted chicken off at his house after the funeral.

"Hi, Jack," she said.

"We'll find her," he said, putting his arm around Kayla. "Don't you worry. The boys will pull her out on the WaveRunners. They always do."

"Thank you, Jack," Kayla said. "We know you're doing the best you can."

Jack shook hands with Raoul. "Heard you're working on the Ting house," Jack said. "Heard that job is so big you have your own phone number for the site."

Raoul shrugged. "Lots of job sites have their own phone numbers. You know how it is."

Jack rubbed his hand over his black hair. He was in street clothes: a denim shirt, khaki pants. Jack's wife, Janey, had been a secretary at the elementary school. She knew every kid's name by heart, and she had always called when one of Kayla's kids was sick or in trouble. "No, I don't. I'm sure as hell not making any money off the wash-ashores the way some folks are. And these Tings, they're Chinese, right?" Both Jack and Janey had been born and raised on the island; they were warm and kind people, although Jack was known to be close-minded about anyone who wasn't a native Nantucketer. *Round-the-pointers, wash-ashores*—this was what he called the summer people and even folks like Kayla and Raoul, who'd lived here for twenty years.

"Does their ethnicity matter?" Raoul said.

"Jack, I want you to find my friend," Kayla said.

"Rumor on the scanner has it that you ladies were out here fooling around."

Rumors were everywhere on Nantucket, Kayla thought. Even the police scanner. "Depends what you mean by fooling around."

"I mean drinking," Jack said. "Drinking and swimming in waters that would be a challenge for a good swimmer, sober. It's two o'clock in the morning, Kayla."

"We've been coming out here for twenty years," Kayla said. "We're not a bunch of drunk teenagers you can just *chastise*, Jack." But her voice sounded whiny and overly defensive, like that of a drunk teenager.

He let a "Chrissake" out under his breath and then stuffed his hands deep in the pockets of his khakis. "It might be best if you all stepped out of the way," he said. "Maybe you could wait in your car?"

Kayla and Val sat on the front bumper of the Trooper with Raoul between them. Kayla watched Paul Henry pick the empty Methuselah out of the sand. He read the label as he walked over to them.

"You ladies drank all this?"

Kayla huffed. "We're over twenty-one, Paul."

"I asked you a question," Paul said. "I'm your friend, Kayla, but I'm also a policeman and I'm trying to help. Was your friend drinking champagne?"

Kayla threw her hands up. "The rumors are confirmed. We were drinking! Blatantly breaking the open container law!"

Paul scowled at her, unamused. "So you estimate that the woman we're looking for drank a third of this bottle?"

Kayla looked at Val. Val was asleep with her eyes open. "Not a third. Just a couple of glasses."

"Two glasses?" he asked.

"Two or three," Kayla said.

"And how much did you have?" he asked. "This is a huge bottle."

"Does it matter, Paul?" Raoul asked. "They come out here every year to have some champagne and go for a swim. Celebrate the end of summer. That's all this was."

"I'm not insinuating anything else," Paul said. "But I like to know what I'm dealing with. There's a big difference between a swimming woman and an intoxicated swimming woman. A big difference."

A young policeman whom Kayla didn't recognize approached Paul with a handful of glass shards he'd gathered from the shoreline. The remnants of the champagne glasses.

"Don't get excited," Kayla said. "Those are our glasses. I threw them in the water."

Paul picked up a piece of glass and turned it in the moonlight. "Was this before or after Ms. Riley disappeared?"

"After," Kayla said.

"So it wasn't as if you had a fight with Ms. Riley before she decided to go swimming?"

Kayla disliked the way Paul said the words "go swimming." He said them like they were a euphemism for something else. "No," she said.

Paul gave the piece of glass back to the young policeman, who was wearing surgical gloves. The coast guard boat moved farther out, and the WaveRunners zipped back and forth closer to shore. Jack Montalbano watched them, smoking a cigarette.

"Why aren't they diving?" Kayla asked. "Jack, why aren't they diving?"

"They're looking above the surface right now," Jack said. "They'll dive only if they have to."

Paul's walkie-talkie rasped, and Kayla heard the sound of a helicopter.

"Coast guard sent a copter," Paul Henry said. He sounded impressed.

The coast guard helicopter had a searchlight that swept over the water like the eyes of God. Paul Henry squinted at it, the tendons of his neck stretched tight.

"That baby has a sensor that detects body heat above the water," he said. "The helicopter will locate her, Kayla. You can bet on it."

They waited while the helicopter circled the area. At one point it was so far away that Kayla lost track of it, and her stomach turned at the thought of Antoinette all the way *out there*. Everything keeled to one side like a capsizing boat. Kayla vomited in the sand—the champagne, the lobsters, one stinky, lumpy mess. How had this *happened?* She wanted to hit reverse, rewind, she wanted to rewrite the way the evening had gone. One moment all of them were safe, the next moment not. Raoul patted her back and gave her a towel to wipe her mouth. Paul Henry handed her a thermos of cold water, which was so unexpectedly beautiful and welcome, tears came to her eyes. She drank nearly the whole thing, letting it drip down her chin. Raoul smoothed her hair.

"Ssshhh, it's okay."

But, of course, it wasn't okay. The helicopter was out of sight, the rescue boat a mere blip on the horizon, and then the WaveRunners pulled onto shore and the riders climbed off, shaking their heads.

"She's not out there anywhere, boss," one of the riders told Jack Montalbano. "Do you want us to dive?"

Jack answered them facing the water, so Kayla didn't hear his response. He pointed thirty or forty yards out and the riders climbed back on the WaveRunners taking masks and snorkels with them. *Out looking for Bob*—that was what the fire department called it when they were searching for a body. Kayla couldn't bring herself to tell Raoul the worst part—that, seconds before Antoinette danced away, Kayla had accused Antoinette of sleeping with him. Kayla added to her list of things that money couldn't buy. It couldn't buy words back once they were spoken; it couldn't buy her best friend back from the dark ocean.

Kayla woke when she heard the helicopter hammering toward them. She was still sitting on the bumper of the Trooper, crushed up against Raoul, who stared at the helicopter as it approached. The Suburbans were parked nearby, but now the men who had formerly been all action sat in the sand or stood with their hands dangling at their sides. Waiting. Then Paul Henry got static over his walkie-talkie, and he moved away as he listened to the report. He looked their way once, and Kayla's heart fluttered with optimism. But his slumping shoulders suggested defeat. He spoke into his walkie-talkie and slowly headed back to them.

"They're not picking her up with the heat sensor," Paul told them. "They want to start a recovery mission."

"What does that mean?" Kayla asked.

Paul tucked his hands into his armpits so that his arms made an X across his chest. "It's been almost four hours already, Kayla. The general consensus is that if she entered the water at the time and place you said she did, they would have found her by now. Since the coast guard hasn't located her yet, it means something very unusual has happened."

"She's dead," Val said, emerging from the car, her face eerily blank and zombielike. "What they're telling us, Kayla, is that they think she's dead and they're not going to spend any more time and money trying to rescue her. She's a woman, and a black woman at that. Now, if it were a white male out there, if it were a *policeman* or a *fireman* out there, you can bet things would be different." She pointed her finger at Paul, and in doing so, she teetered like a drunk. "You, buddy, are looking at a lawsuit."

"What if it were your wife?" Kayla asked Paul. "Would you call off the rescue? What if it were your daughter?"

"Calm down, ladies. The pilot just asked me if it's possible this woman's not out there at all. It's highly unlikely that if she entered the water at the time you said she did, that our men wouldn't have picked her up on the radar. The coast guard uses mathematics, Kayla. They know where to look. They also know how long a person can survive in waters like these. I promise you, if they thought Ms. Riley were alive out there, it would still be a rescue mission."

"She's dead," Val said.

"Is there any chance your friend swam down the

beach instead of out?" Paul asked. "You said she lives in Polpis. Is there any chance she headed home?"

"Why would she do *that*?" Val asked. "That's the stupidest thing I've ever heard."

"You ladies have had a lot to drink," Paul said. "And this thing about her *dancing*, well, it sounds odd to me, like she was kidding around or something. Maybe she swam down shore and climbed out, and you never even saw her."

"Ridiculous," Val said.

"Where does she live?" Paul asked. "We'll check her house."

Kayla told him the address; then she said, "Can we come with you?"

"This is turning into police business," Paul said.

"Paul," Kayla said. "Please. She's our best friend. We've known her for twenty years."

"Okay," he said.

Kayla climbed into the Trooper, but Val stood in the sand with a strange look on her face.

"I'm going to ride with Raoul," Val said. "I want to talk to him about something. Is that okay with you, Raoul?"

Raoul tossed his keys in the air and caught them. "Sure thing. Hop in. We'll see you at the house, sweetie," he said to Kayla. "Think positive."

"I'll try," Kayla said. A pesky jealousy gnawed at her heart. Why should Val ride with Raoul? Kayla thought about the warm cab of Raoul's truck, Raoul fresh from bed, and Val sitting next to him with just a towel wrapped around her waist. Val's linen pants were in the back of the Trooper, along with her ridiculously expensive Italian sandals. She was riding next to Kayla's husband half naked. Val wasn't afraid to cheat on her husband; she was fucking Jacob Anderson. Anger, jealousy, and fear surged through Kayla, and she almost slammed into Raoul's back bumper.

Why did Val want to talk to him? Was she going to tell him what Kayla said before Antoinette entered the water? Here were other things that money couldn't buy: loyalty from your best friend or your husband or your wife.

Their caravan pulled down Antoinette's long dirt driveway: Raoul and Val in the truck, Kayla in the Trooper, Paul and his partner in a police Suburban. When Kayla saw the cottage, her heart soared. Every light in the place was on, the front door was wide open. Antoinette was home! Kayla jumped out of the Trooper and ran to Raoul, reclaimed him.

"Oh, thank God," she said. She tugged on Raoul's arm like one of the kids: *Love me, love me best. Forget what Val has told you and love me. I'm not a murderer after all.* "Thank God."

"Let Paul go in first," Raoul said quietly.

Val pulled Kayla toward the open front door. "I can't believe this," she said. "She left us on Great Point thinking she was dead. Now I *am* going to kill her. Antoinette!"

Paul Henry and his partner brushed by them; the partner had his hand on his gun. Kayla didn't even know Nantucket policemen carried guns, but this guy carried surgical gloves and a gun.

"Stand back, ladies," he said. He peered inside the open door. "Oh, baby."

Paul Henry looked in over his shoulder. "Uh-oh. Whoa." He knocked on the door frame. "Ms. Riley? Ms. Riley, it's Paul Henry with the Nantucket Police Department. Are you in there?"

"What's going on?" Val said. Her bottom half was still swathed in just a beach towel, and Kayla had an urge to tell her to put on her pants.

Raoul stayed in the driveway, studying the outside of the house. At first Kayla thought he was admiring his handiwork in the moonlight. The house had only four rooms, but it was one of his favorite designs. Huge living area, huge kitchen, huge bathroom, huge bedroom. High ceilings, big windows, lots of custom touches. He once told her he could stare at his houses for hours, the same way she had watched enthralled as the children slept when they were babies.

"She's not in there," he said.

"Raoul?"

He shook his head. "She's not in there, Kayla. What does Paul say?"

Paul and his partner had just taken their first steps through the front door into the living room. Val was close behind them, and Kayla was a few steps behind Val. When Val poked her head in the door, she screamed.

Antoinette, hanging from the exposed beams?
Antoinette, lying in a pool of blood?
"What is it?" Kayla asked, afraid to move.
"Ms. Riley?" Paul Henry called out.
Kayla looked through the front door.

The place had been torn apart. Antoinette's things were everywhere. The floppy beige cushions of her sofa were strewn about, her books had been swept off her built-in shelves, the hand-dipped candles that she ordered from Woodstock, New York, had been snapped in half. Her Norfolk pine lay on its side. Bottles of Stag's Leap chardonnay were scattered across the floor like bowling pins.

"Oh, dear God." Kayla took a step inside, but Paul Henry raised his hand.

"Don't move," he said. "This really is police business now, Kayla. Is it safe to assume this place didn't look this way when Ms. Riley left this evening?"

"We didn't come inside," Kayla said. She turned to Val, who was back to wearing her wide-eyed, doped-up expression. "Did we, Val?"

Val shook her head.

"So it *could* have looked like this," Paul Henry's partner said. He put his surgical gloves on before he started picking things up. "For all we know, Ms. Riley could have made this mess *herself*. Meaning she was in a certain frame of mind when she headed to the beach." Every light in the house was on—the in-ceiling track lighting, the Tiffany lamps, the lights in the kitchen and the bathroom. Antoinette hated lightbulbs. She preferred sunlight, candlelight.

"These lights weren't on when we picked Antoinette up," Kayla said. "Someone else has been here."

"Is anything missing?" Val said. "Was she robbed? You might as well let us look around because we're the only ones who will be able to tell you."

"The TV is missing," Paul Henry said. He nodded at the big square blank spot in Antoinette's built-in shelves.

"Antoinette doesn't own a TV," Kayla said. "Val's right. You should let us in."

The partner glowered at them. *"Don't touch anything,"* he said. "And you," he nodded at Val. "Put on shoes."

"They're in the back of my car," Kayla said. "Along with your pants."

Val disappeared to dress. Raoul remained in the driveway, but now he was drawing patterns in the dirt with his feet. He kicked up clouds of dust.

"Antoinette is still missing," Kayla said.

"Yes," he said.

Kayla and Val moved through the house behind Paul Henry and his partner, whose name Kayla learned was Detective Dean Simpson—an actual detective here on Nantucket!—ogling the mess. They found Antoinette's checkbook and wallet hidden deep in a pile of clothing that had been dumped out of the drawers onto her bed. The checks were all accounted for on the register and there was cash, $227, in the wallet. Detective Simpson dusted the handles of the dresser drawer for fingerprints. They were all of a sudden in the middle of a *crime scene*. Kayla tried to remember what Antoinette had been like at the beach. She had been in a good mood, Kayla thought, although maybe a little nervous about her daughter. But then there was the confession she was going to make. What was the confession?

They entered the bathroom. Everything from the medicine cabinet had been thrown onto the floor or into the toilet. "This could have been a person looking for drugs," the detective declared. He picked up the prescription bottles.

Kayla yanked Val into the kitchen. "All right. Tell me what you think. Did Antoinette come back here and make this mess herself?"

"Why would she do that?" Val asked.

"Maybe she *wanted* to disappear," Kayla said. "Maybe she wanted to ditch the daughter."

"Speaking of the daughter," Val said. She pointed to a note on the fridge—a cocktail napkin smeared with blue ink: *L., Cape Air, noon Sat.* "That's in a matter of hours. We're going to have a lot of explaining to do."

"She was going to confess something, Val," Kayla said. "Maybe she was telling us she was going to disappear."

Val looked doubtful. "I don't think so."

"Why? Do you know what she was going to say?"

"No."

"What were you two talking about while I was asleep?"

Val fiddled with the refrigerator magnet—from

the Islander liquor store—and furrowed her brow. "I can't remember. I was probably doing most of the talking. I usually do."

"So she didn't tell you her secret?"

Val put her hands on Kayla's shoulders. "No, friend, she didn't."

"Well, do you think she—? I mean, we know she tried to kill herself before."

"That's true."

"You think she's dead, don't you?"

They heard a voice-clearing from the bathroom and then Paul Henry, "Ladies, would you come in here, please?"

Val raised her eyebrows and mouthed the word *ladies*. Kayla looked out the front window at Raoul, still in the driveway, systematically smoothing the dirt with the edge of his work boot.

They entered the huge, brightly lit bathroom.

The floor alone, jade green tiles, was worth *several* thousand dollars, according to Raoul. Paul and the detective had their paws all over Antoinette's collection of little brown bottles—they were popping the child-proof caps off and shaking a few pills out onto the countertop between the double sinks. The detective wrote the names of the drugs into a little notebook.

Out the window Kayla saw the sky brightening; it was almost half past five. If things had gone as planned, they would be waking up on the beach ready to hit the Downyflake for some chocolate doughnuts before heading home. Raoul would be putting on his boots, sliding his lunch box from the

top shelf of the fridge and driving out to the Tings',
who, Jack Montalbano had so pointedly reminded
them, were *Chinese*. But no. No.

"Do either of you know why Ms. Riley had so
many prescription drugs?" the detective asked. He
pronounced *either* "eye-ther," which Kayla found
annoying.

"Menstrual cramps," Val said. "Bad ones."

Kayla looked away. *Migraines*, she thought, *de-
pression*. Was Antoinette's committing suicide such
a far-fetched idea? Kayla remembered back to the
first Night Swimmers: *I want to be able to kill myself
if that's what I decide.*

On the back of the toilet Kayla saw a perfect
whelk shell that she and Antoinette had found on
Tuckernuck, back when Theo was a little boy. Kayla
remembered the afternoon well—they'd borrowed a
seventeen-foot Mako from one of Raoul's workers,
and Antoinette had motored them through Madaket
Harbor and out past Smith's Point until they reached
the next island over, Tuckernuck, which was still
mostly wilderness. Kayla had Theo bundled in an
orange life jacket, and she made him sit on the floor
of the boat with both arms wrapped around her legs.
And then Antoinette lifted him onto the deserted
beach and they had a picnic and swam and collected
a bucket of perfect shells like this one.

Kayla lifted the whelk shell, disobeying the detective's orders to not *touch anything*, but he was
engrossed with Antoinette's Fiorinal and his notebook, and didn't notice. Underneath the whelk shell
Kayla saw a white plastic stick that made her catch

her breath. She practically slammed the whelk shell back down.

Val had moved around her to look at the pills with the police. "These are the ones for the cramps," she was saying. "These blue ones, I'm pretty sure."

Seven green tiles separated Kayla from Val and the policemen. Val was shielding Kayla from view. Kayla picked up the whelk shell again and slid the plastic stick into the pocket of her sweatpants, completely unobserved.

Detective, ha!

They probably wouldn't even have known what the stick was, but Kayla, the mother of four children, knew only too well.

A pregnancy test, with two purple stripes showing. Positive.

When they emerged from the house, Raoul was still smoothing the dirt in the driveway. The detective flipped out.

"What are you doing?" he shouted. His voice was sucked into the dark woods surrounding the house. "Have you given any thought to footprints? Tire tracks? You just destroyed evidence!" He threw his hands up in the air and with them, his dinky notebook, which fluttered to the ground like an injured bird.

Raoul looked stunned. And exhausted. "Sorry, man. It was just a nervous thing. You know, something to do while you snooped around."

"Well, shit," the detective said. He couldn't have

been older than thirty. He wore wire-framed glasses and had dark hair turning gray around the ears. Funny, Kayla hadn't really looked at him until then.

Paul Henry retrieved a coil of yellow police tape from the Suburban, and he and the detective wound it around Antoinette's house, sealing off the doors. They were going to head back to the station to file a report and send the fingerprints and some other samples to a forensics lab on the Cape. The coast guard would do a sweep of the outlying areas in the chopper at seven, and the divers would start their recovery mission. But now it was clear that neither Paul nor the detective thought Antoinette was in the water. They thought something else was going on.

"We'll have our men check the airport and the Steamship right away, see if they find her leaving the island," Paul said to Kayla before she left. "Can you get us a photograph of Ms. Riley? I didn't see any pictures in the house."

"Antoinette isn't fond of the camera," Kayla said. "But I'll look at home. I think I have one."

"Thanks," Paul Henry said. "We'll call as soon as we get any news."

Kayla drove home as the sun was coming up. The sky was a band of deep rose along the horizon, then yellow, then dark blue. A *V* of Canadian geese passed overhead. Val snored softly in the passenger seat. Kayla had insisted that Val ride with her. Besides, Raoul said he wanted to stop by the Hen House, where his crew gathered for breakfast every morning, to let them know he wouldn't be working today.

"Tell Jacob I'll call him," Val said, and Raoul had simply nodded. So he knew about Jacob. Kayla wondered if *that* was what he and Val were discussing in the truck: Val's secret was a secret no longer.

Well, now Kayla had a secret, too. Antoinette was more than just a missing woman. She was a missing woman with a long-lost daughter showing up; she was a missing woman with a house that had been ransacked; she was a missing woman who, at the age of forty-four, was pregnant. By whom? It wasn't as if Antoinette had been celibate since she divorced—she had flings every once in a while, the most notable with a man who stumbled across her house by accident when he was on his bike looking for Jewel Pond. But these were week-long summer flings, or one-night stands, no one sticking around, and certainly no one leaving behind anything as lasting as a baby. Kayla was at a loss. Who had fathered the baby? That part of the secret Antoinette had taken with her, wherever she went.

Kayla woke Val up when they reached her house. Kayla didn't know what to say. "Get some sleep? We'll talk later?" The pregnancy test was practically glowing in her pocket, but she wasn't ready to tell Val about it. Not yet, anyway.

Val nodded. "I want to leave John."

Kayla groaned. "Oh, Val."

"What?"

"Not today, Val, okay? Don't leave him today."

"I'm miserable with him. I'd like to be less miserable. I'd like to do something drastic, something dangerous."

Kayla looked at the perfect façade of the house; it was hard to believe so much unhappiness lived inside. "Do you think Antoinette disappeared on purpose?" she asked. "Do you think she did this to be *drastic?*"

"Of course not," Val said.

"So you think she's dead?"

"They didn't find her alive, Kayla."

"They didn't find her dead, either. They didn't find her at all. It's like she vanished into thin air."

Val smiled sadly, and with obvious fatigue. "You're right. Call me later." Val shut the car door and limped across her manicured lawn to her house. Kayla sat in the driveway until Val disappeared inside, and then she headed for home.

Kayla's house looked the same, which seemed odd, given all that had happened. It was almost as though she expected it to be burned down or torn apart, but it stood solid and steady. She had beaten Raoul home, and from the looks of it, Theo had already left for work. Island Air flights started at six, and since this was when Raoul usually began his day, Theo didn't mind getting up early. He and Raoul rose together and drank coffee quietly in the kitchen before going to their respective jobs, although since his outbursts started, Theo had taken to getting up half an hour earlier and drinking his coffee at Hutch's at the airport. Or so he told Kayla the one time she was brave enough to ask.

Kayla extracted herself wearily from the car, looked in the back at all the picnic stuff—the towels, the tub of lobster shells that would start to stink as soon as the sun came up, the empty Methuselah— but she didn't have the energy to deal with it. The lobster shells, though. She opened the back of the Trooper and managed to lower the tub to the drive-way, where she could just leave it for now. And then she saw Antoinette's black Chuck Taylors and she welled up with tears and hurried into the house. She needed sleep.

As soon as Kayla entered the kitchen, she remem-bered that Jennifer was sleeping at a friend's house, which meant Luke and Cassidy B. were here alone. An eight-year-old and an eleven-year-old—she was one hell of a mother. True, Theo had probably only left twenty minutes before, but still. She was lucky the house *hadn't* burned down. Before she went up-stairs, she checked the answering machine. There was one new message. Kayla imagined hearing Paul Henry's voice pumped with the adrenaline of vic-tory, *We found her!* Or better still, Antoinette's voice. But it was dead air, a hang up: Kayla calling from the Wauwinet.

She checked on Luke and Cassidy B. All four of her children had Raoul's thick, dark eyelashes, which curled against their cheeks when they slept. God, she loved them. She stumbled into bed herself, too tired to even take off her clothes. The sun was up now, peeking through the rosewood blinds. She put Raoul's feather pillow over her head and let the waves of sleep wash over her.

Twice Kayla tried to float to the surface of her sleep and break into consciousness—once when Raoul joined her in bed, and once when Luke padded in wearing his blue pin-striped pajamas, like a little business suit—and both times she failed. Her eyelids fluttered, and she was sucked back down.

She finally awoke with Raoul shaking her. "Kayla. Kay-la."

Kayla focused her eyes. The blinds were up, the room filled with sunlight. It was hot, and she felt sticky and hazy and uncomfortable. She had a pounding headache; the inside of her mouth was powdery and tasted like egg yolk, her hair was stiff with salt. Then it all flooded back: too much champagne, Antoinette gone.

She blinked. "Are the kids okay?"

Raoul touched her cheek. He was showered, dressed, his dark hair damp. "Of course they're okay. Jennifer came home and left again to sit for the Ogilvys. She ate a banana, but that was all I could interest her in. Cass and Luke are downstairs watching TV. I told them it was okay until you got up. They want to see you. They're worried about you."

"What did you tell them?" Kayla asked. "Do they know Antoinette is gone?"

"*Gone* is a strong word. I said you had a rough

night. I said Antoinette got lost and we're having trouble finding her."

"Fair enough," she said. "Can you get me some water? What time is it?"

Raoul went into the bathroom and brought her water in the green plastic cup that held their toothbrushes. Not a cup she wanted to drink from, but she kept quiet. "It's twenty past eleven," he said.

Kayla drank the water, handed Raoul the cup, and swung her legs so that they rested on the floor. It felt wildly luxurious to have him at home waiting on her like this, and she wanted to stay and enjoy it, but she couldn't. With effort, she stood up.

"I have to go," she said.

"Kayla."

"I have to go to the airport to meet Lindsey," she said.

"Lindsey who?"

"Antoinette's daughter," Kayla said. "A daughter that she gave up for adoption a long time ago and who is coming to visit today. I can't explain it all to you right now, but I have to go meet her."

"Whoa," he said. He stuffed his hands in the back pockets of his jeans. He was wearing a crisp white polo shirt instead of his usual MONTERO CONSTRUCTION T-shirt. He looked so beautiful: clean, tan, barefoot in his jeans and white shirt. What a handsome, lucky man. Kayla felt sure right then that she would never get enough of him, even if they both lived to be a hundred, and especially not if he continued to work the way he did. "What are you going to tell her?"

"I don't know," Kayla said. "But if she wants to stay here tonight, I'm going to let her."

"She'll stay where—on the pullout?"

"We'll put her in Luke's room," she said. "Luke can sleep in here with us." Luke would pretend not to like that—he would say he was too old to sleep with his parents, but secretly he'd enjoy it. Kayla's mind traveled a predictable path: changing the sheets on Luke's bed, vacuuming, clearing space in the closet. God, she was such a *housewife*.

"She might not show up," Kayla said. This was, of course, her hope—that this girl the color of a wine cork would get cold feet about seeking out her birth mother and find an excuse to miss her plane. Nantucket was tricky to get to, she reasoned, especially on a holiday weekend.

"It's possible," Raoul said, but Kayla heard doubt in his voice. He was lucky; she was not.

Kayla showered quickly and put on a pink sundress with thin straps. It looked summery and nonthreatening, and it flowed nicely over her stomach and thighs. She took three Advils, spritzed on a little Coco, which she hoped would mask the smell of hangover, and went downstairs.

If Luke and Cassidy B. were worried about her, she couldn't tell. They were engrossed in a wildlife program about the Komodo dragon.

"Here it is almost noon on a beautiful day and you're inside," Kayla said. "Are you being punished?"

Cassidy B. jumped up from her position on the floor—probably half out of excitement to see her and half out of fear that Kayla would scold her. Sitting too close to the TV was a no-no. Kayla couldn't even remember why anymore.

"Mommy, you're home!" she said. She hugged Kayla in an exaggerated little-girl way. "Daddy said Auntie A. got lost."

Kayla pressed her close and glanced over her head at Luke, who was wearing his green Nantucket Day Camp shirt even though today was Saturday, even though camp was now over.

"Good morning, Luke," she said.

"Good morning," he said seriously. "Did Auntie A. drown?"

"No. Who said that?"

He shrugged. "Nobody."

Raoul must have let more slip than he intended, although it was impossible to keep the truth from an eight-year-old. Eight-year-olds were perceptive and suspicious by nature.

"I have some exciting news," Kayla said. "We may have a sleepover guest tonight."

"Who?" Cassidy B. said. "Is Sabrina coming?"

Sabrina, Raoul's mother, who never visited without her head scarves and séance candles, was another one of the kids' favorites.

"Not Sabrina," Kayla said. "It's someone you've never met before. It's a woman named Lindsey . . ." Lindsey what? Not Riley. "She's Auntie A.'s daughter."

"Auntie A. doesn't have any children," Luke pronounced. He glared at her as if to say: *Can you please get the facts straight?*

"Yes, she does. Antoinette hasn't seen her in a long time, and that's why you've never met her. But I'm going to pick her up right now, and she may stay the night. We're going to let her sleep in Luke's room and Luke can sleep with Daddy and me."

Before Luke could protest, Cassidy B. said, "Lucky." That did the trick; Luke smiled smugly.

Kayla snapped off the TV and checked the clock. She had to go. "You two play outside. See if you can get Daddy to throw the Frisbee. I'll be back in a little while."

Before she left, Kayla put the pregnancy test in a plastic sandwich bag and dropped the bag into her purse. Then she checked three photo albums for a picture of Antoinette. She thought there was one picture from long ago of Antoinette at their house for dinner, holding one of the children in her arms. Kayla flipped back and forth through the laminated pages, past baby shots and birthday parties, Jennifer riding a horse, Theo in his baseball uniform, but she couldn't find a single photo of Antoinette. The picture Kayla remembered was missing.

Kayla reached the airport with five minutes to spare, and so she called the police station to see if they had any news. Paul Henry wasn't in; Detective Simpson wasn't in. The woman who answered the phone said there had been no news about the missing woman; they hadn't found her at the Steamship or the airport.

If Kayla wanted a report on the recovery mission, she should call the fire department.

Kayla called the fire department, keeping her eyes on the Cape Air gate. Jack Montalbano came to the phone.

"We haven't found her yet, Kayla," he said. "But, hey, the good news is that she might not even *be* in the water. I heard you found some mischief up at her house."

"*Mischief* is toilet paper in the trees," Kayla said. "This was a lot more than just mischief." She wondered if Jack had been up all night; with his wife gone, he probably avoided his empty house as much as he could. "Are you still . . . out looking for Bob?"

He cleared his throat. "The diver is out there now, yes."

Kayla felt nauseated. She hadn't eaten anything since the night before—the lobsters, the cheese. "Keep me posted," she said, and she hung up.

The Cape Air gate still looked quiet, so Kayla made a dash to Hutch's to get a sandwich from the take-out. And a cold Diet Coke. The girl behind the counter was about seventeen, from Eastern Europe somewhere, and she had hair the color of Bing cherries. She made Kayla think of Theo. Kayla was afraid to find Theo to say hello; she was afraid he would bully her in public, or worse yet, look at her with absolute blankness as though he'd never seen her before. Kayla wolfed down half a dry turkey sandwich and took two long swills from the Diet Coke and immediately felt better. Food. Out the window, she watched the Cape Air plane land and she thought, *Okay, I can do this*. The plane taxied to its spot. Kayla still had time. She threw the rest of the sandwich away and strolled over to the Island Air counter. Just in case Theo was hanging around.

"Kayla!" Theo's boss, Marty Robbins, saw her right away and came up to the desk. "Where's your son?"

Kayla smiled as benignly as she could, but her voice was weary. "I'm not sure what you mean, Marty."

"Theo never showed," Marty said. "True, Monday is his last day, but I need him now. It's a holiday weekend."

"He didn't call?" she asked, knowing the futility of the question. She closed her eyes and tried to remember: The Jeep had definitely *not* been in the driveway, but what about the door to Theo's room? Open? Closed? It hardly mattered. If the Jeep was gone, Theo was gone. Kayla didn't have time for another missing person, and although she was ashamed to admit it, part of her was relieved that Theo wasn't at the airport. One less distraction, one less stressful encounter. The encounter she had coming would be stressful enough.

"I'll try to round him up, Marty," she said, backing away from the counter. "Right now I have to meet someone."

There was no doubt as to which of the women coming off the Cape Air flight was Antoinette's daughter. Even Antoinette would have been startled at the resemblance. Lindsey was tall and thin like her mother, with the same unruly black hair and the same dark eyes. Her skin a shade lighter, her nose pointier, her gestures more hurried than Antoinette's, but otherwise it was as though Kayla had stepped back in time to the kitchen on Hooper Farm Road as Antoinette poured Chablis into her Waterford goblet. Kayla wanted to cry at the incredible unfairness of it—this young woman so much like her mother, whom she had never seen, and because of some cruel trick of fate, would not see today. *Oh, Antoinette, how could you miss this moment? Your own child.* Kayla's heart was breaking as she approached the girl.

"Lindsey?" she said.

The girl's eyes widened just a bit, though Kayla could see she had steeled herself for anything. Well, anthing except Kayla—blond and big-boned. Lindsey was carrying a Louis Vuitton backpack, and her knuckles whitened as she clenched the strap.

"Antoinette?"

"No," Kayla said. The poor girl. Kayla sensed her relief immediately. "I'm a friend of your mom's." *Mom*—that sounded way too familiar. "I'm a good, dear friend of Antoinette's. My name is Kayla Montero."

Lindsey smiled—gorgeous teeth, the perfect shade of plum lipstick—and offered Kayla her hand. "Lindsey Allerton. Nice to meet you." Incredible poise. Here she was—what, twenty years old?—and she was as smooth as a newscaster. She wore loose-fitting white cotton pants, a sleeveless hot pink T-shirt that showed one inch of midriff, and sandals that laced up her calves. Jennifer would love her clothes. Theo probably, too.

"It's nice to meet *you*," Kayla said. "Do you have luggage?" Kayla wanted to get out of the airport before she told Lindsey anything. That would give her time to figure out what she wanted to say.

". . . brown like this one . . ." Lindsey walked over to the baggage area and reached for a matching Louis Vuitton duffel.

"Where did you come from?" Kayla said. "Where do you live?"

"Right now I'm living in Boston," Lindsey said. "I'm a junior at Emerson."

"What do you study?" Kayla asked.

"Art history," Lindsey said. "I know, I know—my parents tell me it's totally useless."

"Your parents," Kayla repeated.

"My adoptive parents," Lindsey said. "Claude and Denise Allerton. They live in New York. That's where I grew up. I told Antoinette all this already over the phone."

"Of course," Kayla said. "Well, anyway, the car's out here. Have you eaten lunch?"

"No," Lindsey said. "I wanted to eat with Antoinette."

"That was thoughtful," Kayla said. The longer she waited to tell Lindsey the news, the more Kayla felt like she was *deceiving* her. "Okay, look, my car is over here. The Trooper." Kayla walked ahead of Lindsey and opened the back so she could load her luggage in, and *wham*—the stench of old lobsters.

Even more alarming were Antoinette's black Chuck Taylors sitting there like a ghost that only Kayla could see. Kayla climbed in the driver's side and let down all the windows and turned on the air-conditioning. Lindsey got in the passenger side, backpack at her feet. Now what? Drive away? Explain things here in the smelly car, in the hot airport parking lot? Kayla sat tapping her palms against the steering wheel, letting the cool air blast the dampness between her breasts and under her arms.

Lindsey cleared her throat. "Is everything okay?" she asked. "Where's Antoinette?"

I wish I knew, Kayla thought. The car had cooled down some, so she put up the windows. "Your mom . . ." She had to stop saying that!

"Antoinette and I have been friends for twenty years, since just after you were born. It was just after you were born that your mother moved here."

Lindsey nodded. "She told me."

"I'm not sure how to put this," Kayla said. "I have some bad news."

"She doesn't want to see me."

"No, that's not it. She *does* want to see you. But something's happened. Last night, your mom and I and another friend of ours went swimming. We went swimming in the dark and Antoinette disappeared." Kayla paused. This sounded ridiculous, even to her. "We called the police and the coast guard, and they had a helicopter searching, but they haven't found her. As far as I know. I mean, there may be a message waiting for me at home. But when I left the house half an hour ago, they hadn't found her yet.

Your mom . . ." *Stop it!* Kayla told herself. "Antoinette is missing."

Lindsey made a noise like a hiccup; then she lit into Kayla. "That is such *bullshit*!" she said. "Disappeared while *swimming*? That's the best you can do?" She pulled a small package of tissues from her bag. She was crying now, her smooth façade melting. "I know this is difficult. It was the hardest thing in the world to board the plane this morning. *I* was the one who was abandoned. How do you think *that* feels? How long do you think it took me to summon the courage to even contact the agency? And then Antoinette tells me over the phone that the reason she gave me up was because my father cheated on her in this disgusting way and she developed suicidal tendencies. That wasn't exactly what I wanted to hear." Lindsey looked out the window at the car next to Kayla's—a rusty red Wrangler with the top off. "Okay, well I guess I can't *make* her want to see me. And if she doesn't want to see me, I'm sure as hell not sticking around." She reached for the door handle. "Thank you, Ms. . . . I'm sorry, I forgot your name."

"Kayla. Kayla Montero." Kayla didn't know what to do. What would be more painful: to think this was some kind of elaborate hoax, or to know the truth—that the day you were to meet your birth mother she actually did disappear? Drowned, possibly.

Kayla touched Lindsey's arm. Lindsey had goose bumps; the air-conditioner was going full-blast now, and Kayla turned it down.

"I understand what you're thinking," Kayla said. "I wish this *were* all made up, Lindsey, but it's not. I'm telling you the truth. Antoinette, we *think*, got lost in the water off Great Point. I say 'we think' because nobody's sure. The coast guard seems convinced that if she had been swimming, they would have found her. Anyway, we checked her house, because if she wasn't in the water we figured she just went home without our knowing it. But the house had been *ransacked.* Like someone broke in or whatever. To be perfectly frank, we have no idea what's going on."

Lindsey's lip curled in an unattractive way. "Ransacked," she said. Her voice could not have been more deadly.

Kayla sighed. "You don't believe me. Okay, I don't blame you. You don't know me, and here I am telling you these preposterous things. Why don't we get some lunch and we can talk a little and then I'll drive you out to Antoinette's house and you can see for yourself? Who knows, maybe by then she will have turned up. Maybe we'll have news."

Lindsey wiped the tissue under her eyes, mopping away the smeared mascara. "Fine, whatever," she sniffed. "I could do with some food."

They went to lunch at The Brotherhood because it was dark and quiet and full of tourists, so Kayla would be unlikely to see anyone she knew. Although she'd polished off half the turkey sandwich, by the time they sat down at a table for two in the corner, she was hungry again. The restaurant smelled of French fries. Their waitress was a young blonde wearing a long patchwork skirt; she bore a disturbing resemblance to Missy Tsoulakis. Missy, Kayla knew, had moved to Greece right after graduating from college. This was her younger sister, maybe, Heather. Kayla ordered without looking up from her menu: clam chowder, green salad, iced tea. Lindsey got a burger. Kayla played with the spoon sticking out of the tiny pot of ketchup. This felt a little too civilized: sitting down to lunch, when twelve hours earlier all hell had broken loose. What if there was news? Raoul was expecting her home at any minute. Just as Kayla was about to excuse herself to call Raoul, Lindsey spread her fingers out on the scarred wooden table. She had a French manicure, and her nails were as smooth and pearly as shells.

"What's she like, my mother?"

"Oh." Kayla deflated in her chair. "Antoinette is . . . well, she's one of a kind. You look remarkably like her."

"Do I?" A flicker of pleasure crossed Lindsey's face.

"It's astonishing. Antoinette is tall like you, and slender. Bronze skin. Curly hair. She's into her dancing and her meditation, and she reads."

"What does she read?"

"Novels, I think. Charles Dickens, J. D. Salinger. Toni Morrison." Kayla closed her eyes, remembering the year when Antoinette's Night Swimmers secret had been that she spent three months memorizing *The Bluest Eye*. And then to prove it, she started reciting.

"Does she have a job?"

"No," Kayla said. "She hasn't worked the whole time I've known her." Kayla stirred the ketchup. She wasn't about to bring up the divorce settlement or Antoinette's money. "She seems to have her own life work to do. The dance, the reading. She takes a lot of walks, rides her bike."

Their food arrived, and they were quiet as they ate. Kayla sipped her buttery chowder, trying to ignore the fact that it held thousands of unnecessary calories, wondering what else to say about Antoinette. She danced, she read—and she had a lover who made her pregnant. Pregnant! Kayla could really alarm the girl with that piece of news, although to Lindsey, who was Antoinette but a woman who'd once been pregnant?

"Your mother is a private person," Kayla said. She stabbed a perfect coin of cucumber lying on top of her salad. "She had her heart broken a long time ago, when your father betrayed her, when she decided to give you up. Those losses hardened her. She built herself a life of inanimate objects, you know. Her life is her books, her wine, her bicycle. Things that can be replaced."

"She loved my father," Lindsey said.

"Obviously." Kayla lifted two purple rings of onion off her salad and dumped them in her empty soup bowl. "But she's never even told me his name."

"Darren Riley," Lindsey said. "They told me that at the location agency."

"Giving you up broke her heart," Kayla said. "Now she lives in the woods by herself."

"Sounds lonely," Lindsey said.

Kayla took a swallow of iced tea, added two Sweet'N Low packets, and stirred them in with her straw. The sweetener kicked up in the bottom of the glass like dust, and it reminded her of the dirt in Antoinette's driveway as Raoul smoothed it with the edge of his work boot. In Kayla's memory, Raoul was careful about this task. The detective had accused him of destroying evidence, and in her mind Kayla could see that Raoul *was* erasing something— footprints, tire tracks. While they were in Antoinette's house, he'd cleared the whole area in front of the house. What was he clearing? *His* footprints? *His* tire tracks? Before coming out to Great Point, had he stopped at Antoinette's and torn the place apart, removing any signs that he'd been her lover? Clothing, tools he might have left behind; maybe he'd even been hunting for the pregnancy test. Kayla spit a chunk of red pepper into her napkin. She was making herself crazy.

"She was lonely," Kayla said. "Is lonely." Except that Antoinette was having an affair, an affair even more secret than Val's. Kayla wondered if that was why Antoinette danced away when Kayla accused her of sleeping with Raoul. She was caught! And pregnant by him, no less. That would have been quite a confession. Kayla pushed her plate and bowl to the side. "If you'll excuse me, I have to use the phone."

Heather Tsoulakis approached the table. "Are you ladies finished?"

Kayla brushed by her and bolted for the pay phone in the entryway, fumbling for thirty-five cents from her change purse. She wanted to take another Ativan while she was at it, but she couldn't find the bottle of pills. The ceiling in The Brotherhood was low and the floors slanted. Kayla felt the restaurant closing in on her. Her stomach churned; her mind screamed out, *You fool! You idiot! You stupid, blind woman!*

No one answered at home, and the worst came to Kayla's mind. Raoul running away to meet Antoinette, taking Luke and Cassidy B. with him. And possibly Jennifer and Theo. Whisking them away to live elsewhere with a new mother, and their new brother or sister.

Kayla didn't leave a message. When she turned around, she saw Lindsey plunk some bills down on the table and stand up. She came toward Kayla, a concerned look on her face.

"Are you all right?" Lindsey asked.

"Let's go to Antoinette's house," Kayla said. "So you can see for yourself."

On the way from the restaurant to Polpis Road, Kayla was too frantic for conversation. She turned on the radio for distraction—her semi-oldies station was playing the top three hundred songs "of all time" as a special thing for Labor Day. "Got to Get You into My Life," by The Beatles; "Show Me the

Way," by Peter Frampton. Lindsey put her window down, and a warm wind filled the car. It was a gorgeous day, and Kayla had never felt worse. Her head was throbbing, her stomach engorged from too much food too quickly, and she reeled with her new theory, puzzle pieces that she feared would fit if she found the courage to put them together.

Kayla accused Antoinette of sleeping with Raoul. Antoinette disappeared. Kayla called Raoul and *told* him Antoinette was missing. He drove out to Great Point. Kayla racked her brain: Did he have enough time to stop by Antoinette's house and tear the place apart? *Someone* had been there between the time they picked Antoinette up and the time they returned, and it wasn't a house found by people who didn't know of its existence. So, Kayla reasoned, it could have been Antoinette herself, or it could have been Raoul.

Once at Antoinette's, Raoul had stayed in the driveway and systematically wiped away all the evidence of footprints and tire tracks, except for what they'd left themselves. Pretending it was a nervous habit. But Kayla knew her husband, and she recognized his face when he was at work on something. He'd even said, *Let Paul go in first*, because he wanted Paul and the detective to be distracted by the mess so that he could clear his tracks. But what about fingerprints? What about the other "forensic samples" the detective claimed to have found? Did Raoul have work gloves in his truck in the middle of summer? And then there was the troubling detail of Val wanting so desperately to talk to Raoul in his car. Talk to him about what? Was she in on it, too? It was possible; anything was possible at this point.

They turned into Antoinette's driveway. "This is it," Kayla said. "Your mother's property."

"Do you think she'll be here?" Lindsey asked. She was gazing into a compact, reapplying her purple lipstick, like she was about to meet a blind date.

"No," Kayla said.

Kayla turned to watch Lindsey's reaction, and so she didn't notice the car headed toward them. Lindsey saw it a split second before Kayla did, and she gasped and put a hand on the dashboard to brace herself.

Kayla slammed the brakes, and the Trooper bucked to a stop, stalled out. Lindsey's compact and lipstick went flying into the windshield. Kayla had just missed hitting the front of John Gluckstern's black Jaguar. *John Gluckstern*. Ugh. He was alone in the car. Val must have told him what happened. He backed his car into a clearing on the left, and Kayla pulled alongside him.

"Hi, John," she said, as pleasantly as she could. "I guess you heard. Did Antoinette turn up?"

His voice was battery acid. "No," he said. "She did not *turn up*. I can tell you one thing, though, Kayla. You and *my wife* are in some deep shit here. I don't care if I'm the one who has to start shoveling it your way. This isn't right, and it's your doing."

"*What* is our doing?"

"Antoinette disappearing. It may look innocent to

the police, but there's no way a woman like Antoinette would let herself get swept away. That woman is tough. Physically and mentally." He tapped his graying temple to emphasize the word *mentally*. Kayla wondered about John's knowledge of Antoinette's mentality. Of course, he invested her money, so Kayla supposed he had some right to be concerned. He was wearing a shirt and tie even though it was Saturday. But Saturdays for John meant work.

Kayla wrinkled her brow. "What are you doing here?"

"Taking a look, same as you. You won't get too far. They have a summer cop guarding the house."

Kayla glanced in the direction of the house and then at Lindsey, who was busy fixing her lipstick. "John, this is . . . this is Lindsey Allerton. Antoinette's daughter. She just flew in this morning."

John poked a finger out his window at Lindsey. "Be careful of this woman, and my wife, too, if you're lucky enough to meet her. They're to blame here."

"*Blame?*" Kayla said.

But John was finished. He revved his engine and drove off down the driveway, his tires leaving behind a brown cloud.

"Asshole," Kayla said. "I'd like to know what his agenda is."

"Who is that guy?" Lindsey asked.

"John Gluckstern," Kayla said. "Husband of my friend Val, the other woman who was with us at Great Point."

"And he knows my mother?"

"He's her banker," Kayla said. "Believe me, his only interest in her is monetary." They pulled up to the front of Antoinette's house, next to the police car. A kid of about eighteen sat in the driver's seat reading *Rolling Stone*. He straightened when he saw the Trooper; then he put down the magazine and got out of the car.

"Can I help you?" he asked. He was dark-haired and had some sore-looking acne on his chin. His name tag said JONATHAN LOVE. *Officer Johnny Love.* Behind him, the house was aflutter with yellow police tape, like a badly wrapped gift.

"Has Ms. Riley returned?" Kayla asked, though anyone could see the answer was no.

"No, ma'am. The fire department is still up at Great Point on the recovery mission."

"I see," Kayla said. "Well, Officer Love, this is Ms. Riley's daughter, Lindsey. I brought her by to see the house."

Johnny Love took a long, appreciative look at Lindsey. "No one can enter the house, ma'am."

"So Mr. Gluckstern, the gentleman who was just here—he didn't go into the house?"

"No. Mr. Gluckstern wanted to look in the window, and I did allow that." Johnny Love pointed to the back deck. "If you stand on the deck, you can see into the bedroom. But no crossing the police tape. I would be in hot water if I allowed you to cross the police tape."

"We don't want to get you in trouble," Kayla said. "But I think we'll have a look. Did Mr. Gluckstern say what *he* was looking for?"

Johnny Love picked at his chin. "Something about his wife being a friend of Ms. Riley's and her telling him to come out here and see for himself if he didn't believe it. I figure there's no harm in *looking*."

"Yes, we just want to look," Kayla said.

She and Lindsey stepped onto the deck, and Kayla ushered her toward the bedroom window. "Go ahead," she said.

Lindsey cupped her beautiful hand around her eyes and peered in. "Ransacked," she said. "As reported." She straightened up and looked at Kayla. "Okay, so now what do we do?"

"What would you like to do?"

Lindsey turned toward the woods and took a deep breath. Her shoulder blades protruded through her pink T-shirt. "I'd like to know what's going on here. I prepped myself for a lot of shit, you know, but not this."

"I understand," Kayla said.

"No," Lindsey said, "I don't think you do. I have a space, you see, right here—" she tapped her breastbone "—and that space needs to be filled. I need to see my mother. Only now I'm beginning to think this dream isn't going to come true for me. Not today, maybe not ever." She pronounced *ever* "evah," and this small bit of street accent caught Kayla's interest. She studied the girl. Lindsey was trying hard to keep it together—makeup, hair, clothes. Until now, she'd been acting like seeing Antoinette was simply a choice she'd made, rather than a burning desire. A way to fill a weekend, rather than a life-defining moment. But Kayla recognized her desire—

no, her *need*—to see Antoinette. Just to meet her for a moment, to stand face-to-face, say hello, and touch—God, *touch*—the person who had given birth to her.

"You're right," Kayla said. "I don't understand. I'm sorry."

"Can we go to Great Point?" Lindsey said.

"That's what you'd like to do?"

Lindsey pulled a clump of hair into her fist and held it so that it strained the skin of her forehead. "Yes," she said. "Take me to the place where she disappeared."

And so, fourteen hours later, Kayla made the same trip she'd made the night before: first to Antoinette's, then to Great Point. It wasn't a bad idea—the police might have missed something in the dark that would be clear now that it was two in the afternoon.

Because it was Labor Day weekend, the parking lot by the Wauwinet was crowded with happy beachgoers: rental Jeeps and trucks crammed with children. Someone else was playing her radio station loudly; Eric Clapton's "Wonderful Tonight." Kayla wanted to separate herself from their frivolity, but she had to let the tires down. She jumped out of the Trooper with the gauge. She saw the tires were plenty low—they hadn't been refilled from the night before. One good thing. But then the gatehouse attendant motioned for her to stop.

"I have a sticker," Kayla said. "And my tires are already low."

Another teenager, with a brown ponytail and bangs, serious looking in her dun-colored uniform with her clipboard. "I need to advise you that the fire department is conducting a recovery mission off the end of the Point," she said. "We lost someone last night."

Lost someone.

"We know," Kayla said. "Thank you."

Even under the circumstances, it was impossible to find the ride out to Great Point anything but beautiful. The white sandy beach, the *Rosa rugosa* in its final bright pink bloom, the harbor on one side dotted with sailboats, and the ocean on the other, the seagulls, and the distant figure of the lighthouse. Kayla wasn't surprised when Lindsey caught her breath and said, "Wow."

"There's a map in the glove compartment," Kayla said. "I'll show you where we're going."

Lindsey pulled out the map, and Kayla pointed to the spit of land sticking out into the sea. It was daunting to see how isolated Great Point was—*surrounded* by water.

"Why did you go swimming out *here*?" Lindsey asked. "It seems kind of reckless."

"It was your mother's idea," Kayla said defensively. "A long time ago. Twenty years ago. We drove out here in the middle of the night, and it's been a tradition ever since. It's not reckless because we're careful. We're good swimmers and we understand the water. And Antoinette is the best swimmer of the three of us. How she got swept away, *if* she got swept away, is a mystery to me."

"What was she like before she went into the water? Was she okay? Was she upset about seeing me? Did she want to see me?" Lindsey's neck splotched. "I can't shake the feeling that it's my fault. That Antoinette, you know, chickened out."

Kayla touched Lindsey's arm. "It wasn't you, Lindsey. It was me. *I* said something that upset her. And after I said it, I thought she was going to take the car and drive away. But instead she held her arms in a circle, like she was holding a ball, and she danced into the water." In fact, something about the dancing bugged Kayla. It had seemed so, well . . . so staged. Like she'd been planning it.

"*You* said something to upset her?" Lindsey asked.

"She was upset because I . . ." *This* felt reckless—confiding the truth in someone she barely knew. It was like stripping off all her clothes and letting Lindsey see her naked. But the poor girl deserved as much of the truth as Kayla could give her. "I accused her of sleeping with my husband."

Lindsey fingered the hollow at her throat. "Oh, God," she said. "So you're telling me that you upset my mother, and then she went swimming in this dangerous water." She let her window all the way down, and they both watched the waves sweep up onto the beach. The water didn't look dangerous at all—it was blue-green, crystal clear.

"The fact is, Lindsey, your mother was hiding something."

"Oh, really?"

They passed other cars that had made camp—beer, sandwiches from Henry's, boom boxes playing Kayla's station (Lynyrd Skynyrd, "Free Bird"), umbrellas, shrieking children. Before Ting, Kayla and Raoul had enjoyed days at the beach just like this with their kids.

"Yes." The news of Antoinette's pregnancy coated Kayla's mouth. The test was in her purse.

"What do you think she was hiding? Do you really think she was having an affair with your husband? Is that something she would do?"

"She was having a relationship with *someone*," Kayla said. "That much I know."

"Because she told you?"

"No," Kayla said. "She was about to tell me. Before she went in the water. But she never got the chance."

"So you're assuming she was having a relationship, then," Lindsey said. "I mean, if Antoinette didn't tell you."

"I have evidence," Kayla said.

"Oh, please," Lindsey said. "*Please*. You're being very melodramatic, Kayla, you know that? I appreciate that you're my mother's friend and everything, but *really*. You come off as a bit of a drama queen."

Kayla hit the brakes and reached for her purse, dug through it like a smoker hunting down her last cigarette. Then she found it—the sandwich bag containing the pregnancy test. She held it up before Lindsey's face.

"This," Kayla said, "is a positive pregnancy test. I found it at your mother's house last night. Believe me, there is *no way* it belongs to someone else. This is Antoinette's. There is no way someone else's positive pregnancy test was going to be lying around your mother's house."

Lindsey stared at the bag like it was a severed head. Okay, fine. Melodrama. Kayla hit the gas, and panic washed over her. They were getting closer to the spot where they'd been swimming. Two orange pylons marked off a section of beach, and a man in a black fireman's uniform held the end of a rope that led into the water. He walked with the rope between the two pylons. About twenty yards out, a diver surfaced, lifted his mask, shook his head. They were dragging the bottom. Kayla was so spooked by this that it took her a moment to notice a Jeep sitting alongside the fire department's Suburban. Kayla blinked, confused. The Jeep. And then she saw him, sitting on the front bumper, his face hidden in his hands, his shoulders heaving.

Her baby crying.

It was Theo.

Theo

"Baby. Oh, baby, oh, baby, baby."

Like his worst nightmare, or maybe as an answer to his prayers, he felt arms around him and over the arms he saw Antoinette's face, or almost. The arms and the voice belonged to his mother, that much he knew instinctively. He wanted to throw the arms off, lash out: *What the fuck are you doing? Leave me alone!* But instead he let himself get pulled in. His mother's arms. She loved him. She must know about everything by now, and yet she loved him. His whole life she'd told him that she was a safe place to go, that no matter what he did she would forgive him, and that he never had any reason to be afraid. And yet the last eight, nine hours he'd been very afraid as he watched the diver sweep the bottom of the ocean floor looking for Antoinette's body. He'd cried and watched and prayed to the God he wasn't even sure existed. Thinking that if they did find her dead he would drown himself, too. Because how could he live without her? Now he was in his mother's arms looking through tears at a face that was almost Antoinette's, but not. He let himself cry.

"I love her," he said. "We're going to have a baby."

"Ssshhh. Ssshhh." His mother's hand ran through his hair. She knew, and she wasn't angry. He had been sure his mother would be angry; he was sure the news would devastate and scandalize everyone—his mother, the rest of his family, the island of Nantucket. Antoinette had thought so, too, and that was why she had wanted to get an abortion—because of what his mother would say. And so, he despised his mother and he loved her. His emotions were tangled, knotted like a fishing net. It was too much for a kid of eighteen. Too fucking much.

Theo had known Antoinette his entire life. In the green vinyl photo album there was a snapshot of Antoinette holding him as a baby. She was twenty-seven years old and a complete fox in a black leotard and a black leather miniskirt. In the photo she looked strangely sad, a little like the *Mona Lisa,* he thought. Theo removed the snapshot from the family album—it was the only photograph of her in existence, she said. Theo placed it on Antoinette's nightstand. He sometimes looked at it when they made love.

"That picture makes me feel old," she said. "Elderly."

But he liked it. It proved they had a shared past.

Theo had known Antoinette his entire life. And so there was nothing to hide. She baby-sat once when he was thirteen and certainly old enough to baby-sit his sisters and brother himself. Except that his parents were going off-island, to Boston for a long weekend. Antoinette slept on the sofa under an afghan that Theo's grandmother crocheted, and she slept in the nude. Theo got up in the middle of the night to pee, and he sneaked down to the living room, and there was Antoinette asleep on the couch, covered with the afghan, her clothes in a pile on the floor. It was dark, but his parents kept a light on over the kitchen sink at night and so Theo saw part of her shoulder, a slice of her ass, and what he thought was a *nipple* poking through one of the holes in the afghan. His penis grew so hard it actually hurt, and he hurried back to his bedroom and stroked himself until he came. Antoinette was his fantasy for a long time after that.

But it wasn't an obsession or anything. Because before this past April, Theo had been a normal kid. He did well in school, he played third base on the varsity baseball team, he had friends and girlfriends. The summer between his sophomore and junior years, he'd had sex with two girls—Gillian Bergey from his class, and a summer girl named Ashland. He'd told his dad about both girls. His dad asked if Theo had used a Trojan, and Theo said, *Of course.* (Though a couple of times with the summer girl he'd forgotten, but she'd sent him three perfumed letters the following fall, and there was no mention of any problem.) His dad had said, *"Sex is healthy and highly enjoyable, but I always want you to be smart. And considerate. Do you hear me?"*

Theo had known Antoinette his entire life, but she didn't *enter* his life until the April evening when he bumped into her at the Islander Liquor Store.

Nearly every night after baseball practice, Theo shuttled his teammates Brett and Aaron (catcher and left field) to the Islander to get Cokes and chips and Slim Jims, and Theo—the only one of them who was eighteen—bought scratch tickets and a tin of Skoal for Brett, who was addicted to the stuff. They sat on the curb outside the store and opened the Cokes and the bags of Doritos and pork rinds, they scratched the silver film off their scratch tickets with quarters, and when nobody won anything, they flipped the tickets into the trash bin near the front door. Theo was well-deserving of this hour and its pleasures: the hot shower in the locker room, the blaring radio in his Jeep, the soda, the chips, the cold curb under his rump as he turned his baseball hat backwards and shot the breeze with his friends.

The night Theo saw Antoinette, he gnawed a Slim Jim, and Brett spat nasty brown loogies into the parking lot. Aaron talked about his job that upcoming summer as a beach boy at the Cliffside Beach Club and how he would date all the hot nannies.

"Nanny," Theo said. "There's something twisted about that word, man. It's like something you would call your *grandmother*."

"I call my grandmother Gramma," Aaron said.

"I call my grandmother Mimi," Brett said.

"What about Granny?" Theo said. "Rhymes with *nanny*."

"You know, the foreign chicks aren't technically nannies," Aaron said. "They're *au pairs*."

"You need to find an *au pair* who's got a pair," Brett said.

Antoinette rode her bike into the parking lot while they were laughing about that. It was getting dark, but there was no mistaking Antoinette—curly hair, wearing a black leotard and leggings and black Chuck Taylors. Brett let out a low whistle. Theo bowed his head. Because he wasn't exactly elated to see one of his *mother's friends* as he sat on the curb outside a liquor store. Antoinette didn't see him. She leaned her bike next to the trash bin and went into the Islander, the bells on the door jingling.

"That woman is fine looking," Brett said.

"I love black women," Aaron said. "Like Naomi Campbell? I would definitely do it with Naomi."

"Fuck you guys," Theo said. "I know that woman."

"You do not," Brett said. He spat.

"She's a friend of my mother's," Theo said.

"You're *kidding*," Aaron said. "I wish my mother had friends like that."

The bells jingled again a few minutes later, and Antoinette came out. She pulled three bottles of wine from a paper bag, tossed the bag into the trash bin, and slid the bottles into the black leather backpack she was carrying. Theo watched her, trying to decide whether or not to say hello. Antoinette didn't look their way; she wasn't the kind of person to pay attention to teenagers. She threw one graceful leg over her bike. Then Brett spat and Antoinette glanced over. She locked eyes with Theo, but in a way that let him know she wouldn't say anything unless he did. Aaron knocked Theo with his knee.

"Hey, Antoinette."

"Theo."

That was all she said, just his name, but it brought back a host of tucked-away feelings. Her voice was deep and throaty.

"Do you want a ride?" he said. "I have a car."

She laughed. Immediately, he felt like an ass. "No thanks," she said. "You guys just keep on keeping on."

"Bob Dylan," Aaron whispered.

Brett spat again—he claimed the urge to spit with tobacco was uncontrollable—but it was disgusting. Theo reddened.

"Antoinette," he said. "These are friends of mine from the baseball team. Maybe you want to come see one of our games sometime?"

She laughed again and pedaled away.

"Damn," Aaron said.

That very night, the phone rang. Almost always the phone was for Theo or Jennifer, but this time when his mother answered, she kept talking. Theo was upstairs in his room with the door cracked, half reading *The Scarlet Letter*, half listening to his mother's voice. When she hung up, she said to Theo's father, "That was Antoinette. She wants to come with me to Theo's next game."

And so, truth be told, it wasn't Theo who did the pursuing. Had Antoinette not called, he probably would have forgotten all about her.

"You wanted me, didn't you?" he asked her, months later. "You wanted my ass."

She shrugged, said nothing.

Antoinette came to the game against Nauset High School. She stood out in her black T-shirt, black jeans, Chuck Taylors; she looked like she belonged on a street corner in New York City asking for change. Theo's mom on the other hand looked like the other moms: blue jeans, white turtleneck, lilac fleece vest. Antoinette was her eccentric friend in tow. Everyone stared at her, including Brett and Aaron, who whispered something about *your mom's hot friend, smoking hot* as they sat on the bench waiting to bat. Theo felt the need to impress just as he did when some chick was there to watch him play. When his turn came at the plate, he tapped the bat against the insides of his cleats, knocking off clumps of dirt. His mother clapped and said, "Come on, Theo!" Antoinette said nothing as far as he could tell. (He was too self-conscious to look her way.) Theo stood for four balls in a row and then trotted to first base, where he got stranded.

Theo kept his attention resolutely on the game, although as a rule he hated when guys on the team acted too absorbed in the game to say hello to their own mothers. He knew his mother had three other children and better things to do with her time than

sit on a wooden plank on a chilly afternoon watching
him play baseball, and yet, because Antoinette was
there, he didn't go over to say hello. He was nervous, embarrassed; he had *butterflies.* His second
time at bat, he popped up to Nauset's first baseman.
Theo did make one great play on defense—catching
a line drive and then nailing the runner on second.
Everyone clapped and his mother yelled, but Theo,
who occasionally took a bow after making a good
play, didn't even smile. His third time at bat, he
walked again.

His team won, 1–0.

After the game, Theo listened to Coach Buford's
speech about who needed to work on what at practice the next day (*"the whole team, batting . . . the batting in this game left something to be desired . . ."*).
Then he put on his letter jacket, tucked his glove
under his arm, and trudged over to where his mom
and Antoinette were waiting for him. Antoinette had
goose bumps on her arms, and she wore no bra. Her
nipples poked out like hard little pellets.

"Hey," Theo said.

"Great double play," his mom said. "I can't wait
to tell Dad."

"Thanks," Theo said. He took a deep breath and
smiled at Antoinette. "What did you think?"

"You're quite an athlete," she said.

"The batting wasn't very good for either side,"
Theo said, gazing out at the now-empty field.

"I enjoyed it," Antoinette said.

Theo's mother hitched up the strap of her purse
and checked her watch. "Listen, I have to pick up

Cassidy B. in town in like five minutes, and then go home and get dinner. Can you do me a huge favor, mister, and give Antoinette a ride home?"

"You don't have to," Antoinette said. "I can walk."

"Walk? To Polpis?" his mother said. "Theo will drive you. He loves to drive."

"I'll drive you," Theo said, looking at the ground, embarrassed and thrilled. "Just let me shower. I'll be fifteen minutes."

"You sure?" Antoinette said.

"Sure."

He got ribbing from Brett and Aaron when he told them he couldn't hang out at the Islander because he had to drive Antoinette home.

"Holy shit," Brett said. "You lucky dog."

Aaron rubbed Speed Stick under his arms and pulled a gray T-shirt over his head. "You'd better fuck her," he said, "or we'll never forgive you."

The locker room smelled like feet and clanged with locker doors opening and closing. Mist from the showers gave everything a shimmer.

Theo dropped his bag and collapsed on the wooden bench. "Man, I wish you hadn't said that."

"Why not?"

"Because that's not how it is," Theo said. "She's a friend of my mother's. This is an errand, you know, like going to the store."

"I'd like to go to that store," Aaron said.

"Me, too," Brett said. "Anyway, how about we

come along? This lady lives on Polpis, right? We'll
hit the Islander on the way back."

"No," Theo said.

"Why not?" Aaron said. His black hair stood up
from his scalp like porcupine quills. "You said it was
like going to the store."

"I don't know what it's like," Theo said.

Because the truth was, it felt sort of like an errand
for his mother, but sort of like a date, too. Or not a
date, but giving a girl a ride home. Antoinette was
waiting in the parking lot, leaning against his Jeep,
her arms crossed tightly over her chest.

"You can get in," he said. "You look cold."

"I'm all right."

He threw his bag in the back, dug his keys out of
his front jeans pocket, and started the engine. Antoinette closed her door and stared straight ahead.
Theo worried what he must smell like—what if he'd
carried out the stench of the boys' locker room? The
radio was on way too loud, and he quickly turned it
down. Why was he so nervous? He left the parking
lot.

"You used to have a Jeep like this, didn't you?"
he asked.

"I had a CJ7," Antoinette said. "Drove it until it
fell apart."

"And now what do you drive?"

"I don't," she said. "As you saw the other day, I
ride my bike."

"Oh. Isn't that tough, though, I mean, living out

on Polpis? What about the store and stuff? Or if you have to go to town?"

"I call a cab," she said. "Or I hitchhike."

"You hitchhike?"

"Sometimes."

"Well, if you're ever in a pinch for a vehicle, I can give you a lift. Dad and I split the cost of this thing on the condition that I'm at their beck and call at, like, any given moment. So, if you need a ride . . ."

"Okay," she said. "Thanks."

But he could tell she thought he was an idiot.

He said nothing else and neither did she. She wasn't like his mother's other friends, who always had a question for him: How was school? Who was he taking to the prom? Had he given any thought to college? Antoinette, he was sure, cared nothing for his little life. He didn't even know why she was friends with his mother. They were nothing alike. His mother was so normal. They'd been friends a long time, though, since before he was born, and Theo respected that. He understood that in certain instances, time could fill in for common ground.

As he turned onto the dirt lane that was Antoinette's driveway, Theo allowed himself a glance at her chest. He remembered her nipples poking through the holes of the afghan, and it was an arousing thought. So he looked to see if her nipples were still erect from the cold, and she caught him. He averted his eyes slightly to make it seem like he was looking out her window—but no. He'd been caught checking out her tits as surely as if he'd reached over and touched one.

Antoinette smiled out the window.

Theo hit the gas, and the Jeep went shooting up the driveway to the house. He braked and turned on his lights; it was starting to get dark.

Antoinette sat quietly, making no move to get out.

What was she waiting for? Was she pissed off? Did she expect an apology?

Theo coughed. "My dad built this house for you, didn't he?"

"Yes," she said. "Yes, he did."

"Thought so—"

"Theo—"

They both spoke at once and Theo laughed. "I'm sorry, what?"

"Do you want to come inside?"

"No, I'd better get home."

"How old are you, Theo?" she asked.

"Eighteen," he said. "I'm eighteen."

"You're graduating, then?"

"No," he said. "I'm only a junior. I repeated third grade because I had mono."

"Mono. The kissing disease." Antoinette smiled again, and Theo reached for the gear shift. She didn't make a move to get out or anything, so Theo shifted into reverse.

"Whatever," he said. "I'm a year older than everyone else in my class. I used to hate it, but now it's kind of cool. I have my license and stuff."

She touched her lips and studied the front of her house. "You know, I think I remember that year you were sick. I definitely remember when you were born. Can't believe eighteen years have passed. I must be getting old."

"You're not old," Theo said.

Antoinette opened her door and hopped out. She raised an eyebrow at him. "Oh, but I am," she said.

He saw her again a few days later. Life was funny that way—he hadn't given Antoinette a thought in five years, and now all of a sudden, she was everywhere he looked. He was at baseball practice, standing at third base while the assistant coach, Ned, who had hit .325 for the University of Arizona and had biceps the size of grapefruits, smacked balls to all the infielders. Theo had just caught a line drive that was so hot it burned the pocket of his mitt, when he noticed something out of the corner of his eye: a woman wearing a long black raincoat, riding a bike. Kevin Shaw, the shortstop, saw her, too, and he said, "Oh, look, the Wicked Witch of the West." It was Antoinette.

Brett, who was leaning against the backstop with his catcher's mask secured on top of his head, said, "Theo, man, there's your girlfriend."

The rest of the team turned around, and Big Ned sent a ball past Joey Mackenna at first base. Theo felt his face get hot. He shot Brett the finger, shielded from Ned's view by his mitt. Theo heard the squeal of brakes, and he could tell without turning around that Antoinette had stopped just on the other side of the fence.

Please go away, he thought. Though a part of him was soaring—*Antoinette had come to see him!* It changed his whole day, and even after Ned barked out, "Gentlemen, pay attention!" and even after Theo heard the clickety-click of Antoinette's bike chain resume, he glowed with the fact that she'd sought him out. Ned sent him a choppy grounder, which he plucked out of the air and aced to Mackenna on first.

"Theo on fire," Brett said.

He started taking the long, long, long way home from the Islander so that he could drive by her house. An exercise in futility, because he couldn't see the house from the road, only the first twenty yards or so of dirt driveway. Theo began to look for tire tracks. Did they seem fresh? Had she just gotten home? Was she still out somewhere on her bike?

One evening, he stopped right there on Polpis Road in front of her driveway. He wanted to pull in, but he was too afraid. He'd nicked a can of WD-40 from his father's toolbox, thinking that he could stop by and offer to oil the brakes of her bike. He waited for about thirty seconds, listening for another car, which, if he didn't get moving, would rear-end him and probably kill him. His father had lectured him for almost an hour about being a safe driver—one accident and the car got taken away, blah, blah, blah.

Then, without warning, the passenger door opened and Antoinette climbed in. Wearing black jeans and a silky black blouse, holding a long stick.

Where had she come from?

"Hi," he said. "I was just . . ."

"Waiting for me?" she said.

"No. I, uh . . ."

"Too bad," she said. "I went for a walk in the woods just now and I saw your Jeep. I thought maybe the reason you were peering down my driveway was because you wanted to see me."

Theo's eyes were drawn to the way the material of her blouse lay against her chest. Black material, brown skin.

"Do you need a ride somewhere?" he asked. "I can give you a ride."

"How about you drive me home?"

"You are home."

"Up the driveway," she said.

His heart sailed like a home run. Going, going . . . He shifted into first and zoomed up the driveway to her house.

"Do you want to come inside?" she said.

As soon as she asked, he got an erection, a definite indication that his answer should be no. *You'd better fuck her or we'll never forgive you.*

"No, I can't. I have to get home."

Now it was her turn to look—her eyes targeted the crotch of his jeans, the thickening there. Could she detect it? She reached out one of her long bronze arms, her slender fingers, and stroked him back, forth, like she was painting him. Theo groaned. The touch was feathery light, in honesty he could barely feel it, but the whole idea of Antoinette stroking him made him turgid. What was happening?

"I think you'd better come inside," she said.

He followed her into her cottage, noticing only peripherally what his mother referred to as "Antoinette's cool stuff": the funky, hand-painted furniture, the African drums, the colorful candles knotted and twisted like magician's balloons. He would see all that later. That first time, he followed Antoinette into the bedroom, where she stripped her clothes, casually, as though she were going to shower. She was a woman like none he'd ever seen. Like a flute carved from a single piece of wood.

Somehow he, too, undressed and sat on the bed, and Antoinette knelt before him and took him in her mouth. Sucking and stroking him as he watched the perfect arc of her spine and willed himself not to explode. He wanted to touch her, but he couldn't. His hands were propping him up.

She climbed on top of him and his hands were pinned again, this time above his head. She was holding his wrists together as she slid up and down. Up and down, up and down, until she moaned and Theo knew it was no use holding back. He was gone, cut loose into a part of the world so wonderful he could never have predicted its existence.

Afterwards, he lay on his back, agitated, his mind floundering like a freshly caught fish. He thought of his father first and that led dangerously to thinking about his mother. His mother. Oh, shit.

Antoinette lifted herself off him and went into the bathroom, shutting the door, turning on a light. The rush of water. The flush of the toilet. Theo lay back, terrified to move and yet tense with the understanding that he had to get out of there. He had to go home. Go *home*? How would he be able to go home and eat dinner with his parents and his sisters and *Luke*, for God's sake, when he had just had sex with Antoinette? He thought of running away, and maybe if he'd lived on the mainland, he would have called home and told his mother a lie about staying at a friend's and then he could have driven to another town and eaten quietly at a diner and taken steps to make himself feel more like an adult—drunk coffee, smoked cigarettes. Collected himself. Because he felt scattered, like he'd been broken into pieces: an ashamed piece, a scared piece, an intrigued piece. But since he lived on this island, where there was no place to hide, he'd have to put on his clothes, get in his Jeep, and hope that five miles of cool air through an open window would do the trick.

He dressed. Then the bathroom door opened, and there was Antoinette, still naked, standing before him, backlit.

"Would you like a glass of wine?"

He thought she was making fun of him. Maybe the whole thing was a joke, then, some kind of Mrs. Robinson–type thing to her. Seducing her friend's teenage son. Nothing about this scene was original— at least he had that much straight. Older woman, younger man. Much younger. Twenty-six years younger. It happened, probably, all the time.

"No, thanks. I gotta go."

"Your mom makes dinner every night?"

"Pretty much, yeah."

"So you should go."

"Yeah."

"But tomorrow you'll stay for a glass of wine?"

"Tomorrow?"

"You're busy tomorrow? Well, come back whenever you're not busy. I have something I want to show you."

"You can show me now."

"No, next time." She stepped back into the bathroom and was lit up again. Her skin was the color of dark honey. She stood in front of the mirror and wiped a fingertip under each of her eyes.

"Okay," Theo said. He busied himself with his shoes, then he stood up, checked for his car keys, but was pretty sure he'd left them in the ignition. He didn't know what to say. *That was amazing? Thank you?* "Listen, I'm going to go."

She didn't look his way. "Okay," she said. "Bye."

Theo rode home with both windows open, the stereo thumping. The moon was rising pale and round, and Theo howled at it. He felt okay, didn't he? He felt great! For this moment, he let himself feel great.

He arrived home at a quarter to eight. Late for dinner, which was always at seven. Okay, so he would have to tell his mother he stayed late at the Islander with Brett and Aaron. He would get yelled at, and possibly even lose his Islander privileges for a few days; his mom didn't like him hanging around there, anyway.

But things at home were odd, different. Instead of a regular family dinner—everyone sitting around the dining table, bright and chattery—the dining room was lit only by candles, and it was just Theo's parents and Jennifer eating shrimp scampi from the fine china, drinking wine from the crystal. The three of them smiled at him when he walked in. His place was set.

"Would you like a glass of wine?" his father asked.

"What?"

"Your mother made scampi, and you're old enough to enjoy it with some chardonnay," his father said. "Trust me, it'll wake your palate right up."

"I'm having some," Jennifer said proudly.

Theo shed his jacket and took his seat at the table. He watched his father pour golden wine into the glass. His mother passed him the linguine, then the scampi, then Caesar salad. He piled his plate high. He was starving.

"Where are Luke and Cass?" he asked.

"They wanted to eat hot dogs in front of the TV," his mother said. "So I let them." She shrugged. "I figured if they wanted to eat like kids, then the four of us could eat like adults."

"I wish we could do this every night," Jennifer said.

"I guess," Theo said. He sipped his wine and the taste exploded on his tongue. He hadn't kissed Antoinette, not once the whole time. He picked up his fork—heavy, the silver—and ate.

"I hear you've been playing some terrific baseball," his father said. He reached into the salad bowl for a crouton. "I promise I'll make it to the next game."

"Me, too," Jennifer said.

Theo looked at his parents and his sister. Their faces glowed orange in the candlelight.

"You all look really beautiful," Theo said.

No one seemed surprised by this. His mother smiled at him. "So do you, sweetheart," she said. "So do you."

That dinner was a divine gift. A sign. He didn't feel alien in his house at all; he'd made love to Antoinette and then he'd gone home and drunk chardonnay and eaten scampi by candlelight with his parents and his sister. It all seemed part of a contiguous whole. He was eighteen years old. An adult.

So why not go back the following day? The only obstacle was Brett and Aaron, and they were thrown off track like a couple of stupid dogs.

"I can't go anywhere after practice," Theo said. "I have to take my sister Cassidy to the *library*."

Brett and Aaron winced in sympathy.

Theo reached Antoinette's at a quarter to six; he had an hour, which seemed like plenty of time. He was glad for the parameters. When he pulled into her driveway, he allowed himself the luxury of looking around. There was a half-moon window high up on the front of the house, a deck off the back with built-in benches, an outdoor shower. Patterned shingling, a crisp brick chimney. A neat pile of wood was stacked next to the house and leaned against it, a red-handled hatchet. Did she chop her own wood? The lawn around the house was greener than it should have been in April, and freshly edged around clumps of daffodils. Did she mow her own lawn? Theo had the urge to pick a daffodil and take it inside, but then he ridiculed himself. He was an ass.

The main door stood open and Theo peered inside. The living room was growing dark. Two candles on the coffee table were lit. Theo took in the details of the room: the fireplace, the bookshelves crammed with books, the jewel-colored Persian rug. Theo stepped in and closed the door behind him. The half-moon window threw a shape of fading light onto the wood floor.

And then he heard music, a flute, and Antoinette appeared. It was like she grew out of the floor. She was reaching and stretching and waving her arms, kicking her legs in long, fluid arcs. She was dancing. Theo held his breath. She moved her body in amazing ways, bending backwards while her arms fluttered forward. She wore black leggings and a man's white undershirt. No bra. The T-shirt was threadbare; it was as good as wearing nothing at all, and when she bent backwards he was reminded of the night before and how she'd taken him.

He stood where he was, feet planted on a bamboo

doormat until finally she collapsed in a heap on the floor, breathing hard. Theo wasn't sure what to do; he didn't know if she'd seen him or not. He wanted to think the dance was for his benefit, but he sort of doubted it, and he didn't want to scare her or have her think he was spying on her. He waited until she composed herself, and then he retreated a few steps and knocked on the inside of the door. She turned her head slowly to him, her face unsurprised. So she had known he was there, after all.

"You said you had something to show me," he said.

"Did I?" she said. Her hair was wild around her face, and she tried to secure it in a bun held together by what looked like a chopstick, but strands sprang free. She plucked the T-shirt away from her chest and wiped the back of her hand across her forehead. "Do I? Maybe I do. Would you like a glass of wine?"

"Sure," he said, afraid to move. He watched her take two crystal glasses out of the cabinet and a bottle from the fridge. "Is that chardonnay?"

"It is," she said. "Do you like chardonnay?"

"Yeah."

"Well, good." She nodded at the sofa. "Let's sit down."

Theo moved to the sofa. He tried to breathe, to relax. "I liked your dance."

"Did you?" she said, in a way that made it sound like she couldn't have cared less. He wished he had a word to describe how it made him feel. Well, *aroused*, it aroused him, but he couldn't tell her that.

Antoinette handed him a glass of wine and he took a long swill. He looked at her books. Could she really have read them all? "I'm reading *The Scarlet Letter*," he said. Then he remembered Hester Prynne and the *A* for *adultery* and he closed his eyes. Why had he said that?

"Let's have a toast," Antoinette said. "To your return."

They clinked glasses. Theo took another swallow.

"Now, what was it I wanted to show you?" Antoinette said. "Oh, yes, it was something in the bathroom. Come with me." She pulled him up by the hand.

The bathroom was huge and fancy with a green floor. Theo saw her toothbrush, her baking soda toothpaste, a pink disposable razor. One of her dark hairs curled on the rim of the sink. Theo tried not to look any further. Being in the bathroom with her embarrassed him.

Antoinette lifted a seashell off the back of the toilet and handed it to him. "Do you know what this is?"

"It's a shell," Theo said. "A whelk shell." It was white as a bone with a perfect crown, and the faintest hint of peach inside.

"You gave it to me," she said.

"I did?"

"A million years ago. I took you and your mother to Tuckernuck Island, and you found that shell on the beach. Your mother asked you what you wanted to do with it, and without hesitating you marched through the sand and gave it to me. You were only three years old."

"And you kept it?" he said.

"I hadn't gotten a gift like that in a long time. Nor have I gotten one since." She touched his lips and then she kissed him. She tasted smoky and sweet, and the word *persimmon* came to his mind, though he had never eaten a persimmon, or even seen one, for that matter.

They made love again, and Theo thought of his little boy self on the beach at Tuckernuck, handing the thing most precious to him at that moment to Antoinette, and in thinking about that he felt even more like a man.

He returned again the next day, and the next. At first it was as if his hour with Antoinette were pure fantasy, a visit to another planet where there were no rules, where nothing mattered except their attraction to each other. But then, as more days passed, the opposite became true, and Theo's life at school and at home turned into the fantasy—a false life, a lie he was living until six o'clock came and he was driving along Polpis Road toward Antoinette's house.

Baseball season ended. At the awards banquet, held upstairs at Arno's, Theo was named "Outstanding Infielder." His parents glowed with pride, and Theo walked to the front of the room as everyone applauded. He took the trophy from Coach Buford and saluted the crowd with two fingers, but his heart wasn't in it. It was like he was watching himself, or wondering what Antoinette would be thinking if she were watching. He'd won an award at a stupid high school sports banquet where they'd eaten stuffed chicken breasts and ice cream sundaes. So what? He left his trophy on the table on purpose—it was too childish to take home—but his father noticed it and carried it out to the truck for him.

Theo took Gillian Bergey to the junior prom. Her parents belonged to Faraway Island Club, so that was where they ate—in the club dining room that smelled as damp and mildewy as the hull of a ship. They double-dated with Gillian's friend Sara Poncheau and Sara's date, a kid named Felipe from Marstons Mills. The rest of the people eating at Faraway Island were older, the age of Theo's grandparents, and they smiled kindly at the prom couples. Theo sweated in the white dinner jacket he'd rented from Murray's. Two months earlier, going to the prom with Gillian and eating at the Faraway Island Club had seemed like a good idea. Now he couldn't wait for it to be over.

During the shrimp cocktail, he asked, "Do you think this club has any black members?"

Felipe, who was Hispanic, said, "Shit, no, man! Don't you see all these granddaddies looking at me like I'm the busboy?"

Theo nudged Gillian with one of the black plastic shoes that came with his rented tux. "What do you think?"

Gillian was a pale blonde whose skin looked translucent next to the electric blue satin of her dress.

Two red circles surfaced on her cheeks. "I have no idea, Theo. I'm sure everyone is welcome."

"I'm not sure," Theo said. "I mean, look around. Everyone is white."

"Everyone on Nantucket is white," Gillian whispered. "Please don't make an issue of it. I'll be embarrassed."

"Well, I wouldn't want to embarrass you," Theo said. He wondered how he had ever found Gillian attractive enough to have sex with. She was so pale you could see her veins. Theo pointed the tail of a shrimp at her. "And FYI, baby doll, *not* everyone on Nantucket is white."

Theo danced with Gillian three times at the prom; then he drove her out to the post-party at Jetties Beach. She changed her clothes in the passenger seat of the Jeep, and that would have been the time to make his move—when she was out of her dress but not yet into her shorts and T-shirt—but Theo waited politely outside the Jeep, standing guard, wishing he smoked cigarettes, wishing that he was not at his prom at all, but with Antoinette instead. He took Gillian home without kissing her or feeling her up or anything. Gillian seemed disappointed by that and on Monday she told her girlfriends that he was a jerk, but Theo didn't care. All he cared about were his afternoons with Antoinette.

In June, after school ended, Theo started his job at Island Airlines, and he fell into the habit of stopping by Antoinette's on his way home. The only conceivable danger was his mother showing up unannounced. But at that time of day, she was busy with other things: chauffeuring one of the kids, making dinner. She did ask him once, "You're not still hanging out at the Islander, are you, Theo? After work? You know I don't like it."

"Not the Islander," Theo said. He had a foolproof answer all prepared. "I've been exploring the island. Looking at the architecture. I want to study architecture when I go to college, and I thought I might as well get a head start." He pulled a book out of his backpack titled *300 Years of Nantucket Architecture*; he'd checked it out of the Atheneum with his sister Cassidy's library card. "So I've been driving around, studying."

His mother thought he was a wonder. She told his father about the book over dinner.

His father perked up when he heard the word *architecture,* but otherwise seemed distracted. He was busy, especially after he got Ting in June, and Theo understood his father would never notice if he disappeared for an hour each day.

In this way, it was surprisingly easy.

What wasn't as easy was being in a relationship with an actual woman. With Antoinette.

At first, it was just sex. Seeing her, Theo would get a stubborn erection and Antoinette would make love to him until he cried out, or just plain cried, so grateful was he for the incredible pleasure, a pleasure bordering on pain. Sex made him feel alive, and feeling alive brought on a new fear of death. When he drove, he always fastened his seat belt.

By the time school ended, the sex wasn't enough. Theo wanted to *know* Antoinette, he wanted her to talk to him, he wanted her to listen to him. Theo worked his job at the airport—loading luggage onto planes, taking luggage off planes, telling passengers to follow the green walkway—and he became distraught at how little he knew about Antoinette. He looked around her house each night and picked up an object and studied it, hoping for clues. He memorized a few of the titles on her bookshelves and bought them from Mitchell's Book Corner: *Go Down, Moses,* by Faulkner, *Continental Drift* by Russell Banks. He read these books, wondering what they meant to Antoinette, what she gained from them. He didn't tell her he was reading them.

He started asking her questions at the end of their hour together, simple things.

"What did you do today?"

"What did I *do*?"

"Yeah, you know." He propped himself on one elbow on her bed. "What do you do in a normal day? You never talk about it. You must have a routine."

"Oh, Theo," she said. And she laughed.

"What's so funny?" he said. "I want to know what you do. Is that so odd? To want to know what my—" He almost said "girlfriend," but when the word was on his tongue he realized how wrong it would sound. "—my lover does all day?"

"How does it feel," she asked, "to be an eighteen-year-old with a lover?"

"It feels great," he said. "But you're avoiding my question."

"What question is that?"

"See?" he said. He punched one of her feather pillows like it was someone's face. He felt himself losing patience. "What the hell do you do all day?"

She got out of bed and put on a plain black cotton sundress with skinny straps.

"I do what everybody else in this world does, Theo. I try to survive."

"What is that supposed to mean?"

"Okay, look, I eat, I dance, I read, I satiate my sexual desires."

"Do you want to know what I do?" Theo asked. "Do you want to know how my day at work went?"

Antoinette batted her eyelashes. "How was your day at work, honey?"

"Never mind," he said.

"Exactly," she said.

There were funny little things about her. Like, for example, she had no photographs of herself. No pictures of her family. When Theo brought the snapshot of her holding him as a baby, she gazed at it for a long time. "That's me," she said finally, as if there had been any doubt.

"Well, yeah," he said. "How come you don't have other pictures?"

"Pictures of what?"

"Of yourself."

She looked truly puzzled. "Why would I have pictures of myself? I already know what I look like."

"What about your parents, then?" Theo asked. His

voice was thick and nervous. It wasn't fair—she had known him since the day he was born. "Are they still alive?"

"I have no idea," she said.

"What does that mean?" Theo asked.

"You sure ask a lot of questions," she said.

He asked a lot of questions but received no answers. Maybe there were no answers, Theo thought. It was as if Antoinette were a mirage, a phantom who had no past and whose likeness couldn't be captured on film. He tasted her skin, he sniffed under her arms, he tangled his fingers in her coarse, curly hair to reassure himself that she was real.

He was brave enough to bring up Antoinette with his mother only once. Just after school ended, he was helping in the garden and he said, "I saw Antoinette on my way to work today. Riding her bike."

"Oh, really?" his mother said. She was kneeling in the dirt, staking her tomato plants; it was Theo's job to hold the plants against the stake while his mother tore strips from one of his father's old white T-shirts and tied the plants up. "I should call her, I guess."

Theo stared at the earth, as rich and brown as chocolate cake. "What's Antoinette's story, anyway?"

His mother looked up at him. "What do you mean?"

"I don't know," Theo said. The sun was hot against the back of his neck. "She's just so . . .

weird. How did she end up here? Was she born here?"

"No," his mother said. "She came from New York City the same summer I moved here. We lived together. You know that."

"What did she do in New York?" Theo asked.

"Ballet," his mother said. She moved on to the next plant and Theo followed. "That's really all I can tell you."

"How come?" Theo said. "Is her life, like, classified information?"

His mother ripped his father's shirt down the middle in a way that seemed almost violent. "Yes," she said. "It is."

One evening in mid-June, Theo told Antoinette that he loved her. They had finished making love, and Antoinette was bleeding a little. She had her period.

"Ugh," she said. "Sorry about that."

"I don't mind," Theo said. "I love you."

Antoinette disappeared into the bathroom, closing the door. Theo could hear her opening a drawer, rummaging around. He sank his head back into one of Antoinette's feather pillows. He'd never told a woman that he loved her before. He never said the words, not even to his mother and father. *I love you.* It was an overused phrase, but that was how he felt, that was who he'd become—someone who loved another person. He felt vulnerable, exposed, scared. He put on his clothes.

"I love you, Antoinette," he said to the closed door. "Are you listening?"

Oddly enough, it was his father who caught him. One night, the week after the Fourth of July, Theo sat in his Jeep at the end of Antoinette's driveway. He saw a red Chevy coming from the north, but there were a lot of red Chevys on Nantucket—and besides, his dad was working in Monomoy, which was to the west. But then the driver flashed his lights. Theo threw the Jeep into reverse and backed up ten feet, bent his head, and closed his eyes, praying that the truck would pass. Instead, when he looked up, the red truck was stopped right in front of the driveway, and there was his father, window down, staring at him.

"What are you doing here, Theo?" his father said. "Did your mother send you to get something?"

What could he say? He clawed around for some likely reason for being in Antoinette's driveway.

"I was out exploring," he said, "and I made a wrong turn."

His father stared at him. Theo willed another car to come along and end the issue, but none did. Then his father waved a hand.

"Follow me," he said. "I want to show you something."

Theo pulled out behind his father, reviewing the lie in his head. He'd made a wrong turn while exploring. He'd forgotten it was Antoinette's house until he pulled up, and then, because it looked like she wasn't home, he'd turned around. Nothing wrong with that.

They drove to Monomoy, to the Ting house, such as it was, barely framed out. Still, the views across the water were incredible. Theo climbed out of the Jeep; he was sweating.

"No wonder you're never home," Theo said to his father. "It's beautiful here."

"It's beautiful at home," his dad said. "This is nothing but work."

"Yeah, well. Huge house."

"Biggest house on the island."

"Yeah," Theo said.

They walked inside—the walls weren't completely up yet—and headed toward the front of the house where giant windows overlooked the harbor. The wooden floors were littered with tools, nails, an electric sander. The sun was still up above the steeple of the Congregational Church. Seagulls cried. Theo's hands were shaking.

"So tell me again," his father said. "What were you doing at Antoinette's?"

"I made a wrong turn," Theo said. How long had it been since he'd lied to his father? He couldn't look his father's way, but with a view like this, there was no need. Theo focused on the sailboats, which looked like bits of confetti scattered across the water. "I was hunting for a certain dirt road, and I drove up Antoinette's driveway accidentally."

"The roads back that way are confusing," his father said. "I got lost a few times myself when I was building that house."

It had been two weeks since Theo had told Antoinette he loved her, and she'd said nothing in return. Okay, then, she didn't love him back. Did he really expect her to?

Theo looked at his father. His mother always said his father was a lucky man. "I've been seeing Antoinette," Theo said. He kicked a nail across the floor. "We're sleeping together."

His father's eyes closed and opened again. Brown eyes flecked with gold, like Theo's own eyes and the eyes of his brother and sisters. "No," he said. "I don't believe you."

"You have to believe me," Theo said. "It's true."

"What the hell are you telling me?" Theo recognized the expression on his father's face—he was holding back his anger, keeping himself in check. When Theo's father was a teenager, he'd flown out of control all the time—started fistfights, punched holes in walls, broke legs off dining room chairs. But not anymore. "Theo," his father said, in a voice so low Theo could barely hear it. "What's going on?"

Theo spewed forth the story, an edited version, from the baseball game forward, up to the part where Theo now knew himself to be in love—only instead of the kind of love that made things bright and clear, this kind of love obscured things, confused them. This was the kind of love that was like walking through the dark woods alone, terrifying, unknown.

"I haven't told anybody else about this," Theo said. His voice broke. "I want her to love me back, Dad."

His father put his arm around Theo and squeezed hard.

"Trust me when I say you're in over your head. And what about your mother?"

"What about her?"

His father turned Theo's face by the chin. "What am I supposed to do? Keep this from her?"

"Yeah," Theo said. "I mean, you can't *tell* her."

"Well, then, you shouldn't have told me."

"Except you're my father."

"That's not going to work, Theo. I'm not getting warm, fuzzy father-son feelings about this conversation. Because what you're telling me spells danger for you and for your mother. You especially. You're going to get creamed in this, I promise. Antoinette is too old, too sophisticated, too goddamned complicated. But mostly too old. Do you hear me? Now, I understand wanting to get laid. I understand that part just fine. But not Antoinette." He put his hands on the windowsill and leaned through the empty window. "What the hell is that woman *thinking?* You're just a kid."

"I'm an adult," Theo said. "Eighteen, right? Old enough to go to war and all that."

"It's wrong," his father said. "What Antoinette is doing is *wrong.*"

"It's not her fault," Theo said. "Please don't say anything to Antoinette."

"Well, it's over now. I'm making it over." Theo's father blew air out his nose, like a bull ready to charge. "You're forbidden from going over there again."

"You can't forbid me to do anything."

"I sure can. I'm your father."

"What about you always telling us to make our own choices, to develop our independence? What about that? Was that all bullshit?"

"This isn't a sound choice, Theo."

"Just let me deal, okay? I told you because, well, because I needed to tell somebody, and you asked. Whatever, just let me make this mistake if that's what this is." He poked his father in the back. "If you tell Mom, I'll kill you."

"Don't threaten me, mister."

Theo kicked some more nails, then a hammer. What he needed was some *help*, some *understanding*. Didn't his father see that?

"Just forget it," Theo said. He left the house, got in his Jeep, and headed home.

Theo studied his mother for any sign of change and saw none. So there was that. Either his father respected his decision or he was too afraid to tell Theo's mother the truth. His father was cold with him, distant, and that hurt because his father wasn't home that often anyway, and so Theo went from getting a small amount of his father's attention to none at all. So what could Theo think but, *Fuck him*? All his father cared about was building some huge house that—according to the principles of *300 Years of Nantucket Architecture*—would ruin the character of the island forever.

• • •

And then, Antoinette missed her period.

She'd been irritable for a few days—if a person who almost never communicated could be called irritable—she didn't want to be held or kissed. She slapped Theo across the face while they were making love. She pretended like it was an act of passion, except that it hurt, and tears came to Theo's eyes. When it was over, he said, "Why did you hit me?"

She rolled away from him on the mattress. "Sorry, I was letting out some frustrations."

"What kind of frustrations?" This was what ate away at him: Antoinette had frustrations and he didn't even know about it. "Frustrations with me?"

She stood up and looked him over.

"I missed my period."

"Oh, shit," he said. They had never used condoms because Theo figured Antoinette would take care of herself—the pill, IUD, menopause for all he knew. "So you think you're pregnant, then?"

"Well, it's been a while, but it feels the same."

"Wait a minute. What feels the same? You've been pregnant before?"

"I have a daughter," Antoinette said. "Or I had a daughter. Twenty years ago."

"You're kidding," Theo said. "You have a daughter who's older than me?"

"I gave her up for adoption," Antoinette said.

"Really?" Theo said. "How come?"

She sighed. "It's a long story."

"Tell me," Theo said. "You never tell me anything." He touched his cheek where she'd hit him and wondered if she'd left a mark.

She sat down on the edge of the bed and gazed out the window into the woods. "Let me ask you a question," she said. "Why would you want to know about an old woman's life? What could it possibly mean to you?"

"I want to know you, Antoinette," Theo said. "I show up here every day and we . . . we screw and I don't know the first thing about you. I don't know anything about your family, your parents, this daughter. Just tell me about the daughter, okay?"

"It's old stuff," Antoinette said. "Old and sad."

"Please," Theo said.

"You're going to be shocked," she said.

"I won't be shocked," he said, although he felt completely shocked—Antoinette thought she was pregnant, and she'd been pregnant before. "I promise."

Antoinette wound a strand of black hair around her finger. "I got married right out of college," she said. "My husband and I lived in Manhattan, and my husband was a consultant for Pricewaterhouse. He had projects in California, so he was away a lot, but that didn't bother me. I was getting my master's in dance at NYU, I had a great apartment on the Upper East Side to decorate, I was busy exploring the city. Then, after a year or so, I discovered I was pregnant."

"Okay," Theo said.

"I was a twenty-three-year-old dancer whose husband was all but living on the West Coast. There was no place in my life at that time for a child. I wanted to terminate the pregnancy."

"Get an abortion?" Theo said.

"Get an abortion. But my husband talked me out of it. He *wanted* the baby. *'It's going to be great!'* he said. *'We're starting a family!'* He convinced me to leave school, which I did, and in return I asked him to leave the project in California and take a project closer to home. So he did. He took a project in Philadelphia and he was less than two hours away by train. He was home every weekend. He walked with me in Central Park, he took me to see *Aida* at the Met, he went out in the middle of the night to get me watermelon from the Korean deli." Antoinette tightened her fists and brought them to her ears, like she was trying to block out an awful sound.

"Then what happened?" Theo asked. Here was Antoinette's history, her real history, that even his mother might not know.

"One day when I was pretty far along, seven months or so, I found myself down at Penn Station, and I decided to surprise him. I got on the Metroliner and walked from the train station to his hotel. The front desk clerk knew I was his pregnant wife. He gave me a key to his room; he was happy to do it."

Theo felt like he was standing on a cliff where he was drawn to the edge, yet afraid of falling. "And?" he said.

"And I walked in on him having sex with two women. Monica, who was his consulting partner and another woman, their client. The three of them were so . . . involved with each other, they didn't even notice me standing there until finally I thought to scream. They all noticed that."

Antoinette was openly weeping, wandering the room like she was looking for something. A tissue, maybe. She disappeared into the bathroom and emerged with a hand towel.

"His name was Darren." Antoinette blew her nose into the towel. "I haven't spoken that name in over twenty years. Darren Riley."

"You still use his last name," Theo said.

"I loved my husband. I loved him desperately. He was one of those special people who everybody loves—men, women, dogs, babies. He was charming, dynamic, funny. And that was his downfall. Women fell over themselves for him, they allowed themselves to be degraded. Monica later told me that there had been other threesomes, in other cities, in California, and before that, even."

Theo thought he might vomit. He grabbed a pillow and pressed it to his crotch. "What did you do?" he asked.

"I went back to New York, alone. Darren didn't bother trying to get me back. I guess he knew he blew it. He gave me a quick divorce and lots of money. But it was like he didn't even try. He didn't apologize, and suddenly it seemed he didn't want the baby after all. When she was born, I couldn't make myself feel anything but anger. I couldn't feel any love for her; I couldn't even give her a name."

"So what happened?"

"I tried to kill myself. I took pills. My neighbor found me unconscious, the baby screaming in her crib. I hadn't fed her in, like, twelve hours. Social services took the baby away and by the time I was released from the hospital I realized I couldn't raise her. I didn't want to raise her." Antoinette pressed her thumb and forefinger to the bridge of her nose and threw the towel into the corner of the room. "What has stayed with me after so many years is how Darren made me love that child and then he stole that love away. It is the cruelest thing I've ever known anyone to do." After a few seconds, Antoinette straightened into perfect posture. "After the baby was gone, I moved away and started over."

"You came here?" Theo said.

"I constructed a life that allowed me to survive day to day. Minimal interaction, no one to care about but myself. Here in the woods on this island thirty miles out to sea. This is it, Theo. This is my life."

She retreated into the bathroom. Theo dressed quietly; it was past time for him to go, but he couldn't bring himself to leave. No information for months, and now a deluge.

"So now you think you're pregnant again?"

She stood with her hands on either side of the sink, staring into the mirror. She nodded.

Here was the one thing that Theo had been afraid of ever since he knew enough to be afraid of it, and now he wasn't afraid at all, he was excited. Thrilled. Antoinette, pregnant.

"It's okay," he said. "If you're pregnant, it's okay."

"It's anything but okay," Antoinette said. "God is punishing me."

"For what?"

"For you," Antoinette said. "For sleeping with an eighteen-year-old."

"I want to have a baby with you," Theo said.

"No, you don't. We'll do what's easiest for both of us. If I'm pregnant, I'll have an abortion."

"But I love you! I've been trying to tell you I love you for weeks, but it's like you don't hear me."

"I hear you," she said.

"But you don't believe me."

"I believe you," she said.

"But you don't love me back."

"There's no way to make you understand. You're too young. And so you're just going to have to trust me, Theo." She walked toward him and took hold of his face, her hand resting exactly on the spot where she had slapped him, only now she was gentle, as gentle as if he were a baby himself, and he saw that her eyes were filled with something, and he let himself believe that it might be love.

There was a day or two of reflection. Theo marveled at the power of his own body; he'd created another human being. He ran through scheme after scheme, one more unlikely than the next. He and Antoinette marrying, raising the child. Theo would graduate from high school in a year. He would forgo college and work for his father. Or, if his parents disowned him, he and Antoinette and the baby would move off-island. To California. France. South Africa.

In the evenings, Theo tried to get Antoinette to

talk about her past some more, but she wouldn't. Sometimes she was upbeat, and when he arrived she'd be sitting on the built-in benches of her deck with a glass of chardonnay and a book. Other days he found her in the bedroom with the shades drawn, and when he knocked on the door or tousled her hair, she opened one eye and murmured, "Go away, Theo. Go home to your mother."

Then, on the first of August, a day when his job at the airport had been particularly hellish—all the July people leaving, the August people arriving— she showed him the pregnancy test. It was one of the evenings when she was out on the deck. She poured him a glass of wine, and they sat quietly listening to the birds in the surrounding trees, and then she went into the bedroom and came back with a white plastic stick with two purple stripes. Antoinette held it out to him, turning it in the fading light as though he might want to inspect its authenticity.

"Well," he said. "Now what?"

"I've made an appointment off-island for the Tuesday after Labor Day," she said. "An appointment for an abortion. That gives me four weeks to think it over."

"Don't have an abortion," Theo said. "Please."

"I don't see any options," Antoinette said. "You, my dear, are in no position to think about being a father. Not at eighteen."

He no longer felt eighteen, and he said so.

"Well, then, what about Kayla?" Antoinette said. "This will devastate her. Your mother's one of my few friends in this world, and I'm not prepared to destroy her, or the rest of your family, for that matter."

"What my mother thought didn't seem to bother you before," Theo said.

"It bothers me now. I've crossed a line." She looked at him with genuine sadness. "I'm sorry, Theo. I'm sorry for starting all this."

"Why did you, then?" he said. "If you don't love me, I mean?"

"Oh, Theo."

"No, really, I'm curious. Was this all about the sex? You came to my baseball game and you liked my body? You figured because I'm only eighteen that I'd be okay with sex, no strings attached?"

"It wasn't that."

"What was it, then?"

"Look at my life, Theo." She gestured to the surrounding woods, which were growing dark. "It's pretty damn solitary. I don't believe in other people. Not after what happened to me."

"Why did you let me into your life, then?" Theo asked.

"Because you're young, you haven't acquired a lot of the crap that older men carry around with them. You're clean, you're honest. You're good. You're Kayla's son, and Kayla is one of the people I feel safe with."

Theo set down his wineglass and leaned over the railing of the deck. Fireflies lit up the woods. "First you tell me you want to abort our child because of my mother and then you tell me the reason you slept with me in the first place is because I'm my mother's son and therefore a safe harbor for you? What I would really like is for you to forget about my mother. Our relationship, our *baby*, is about you and me."

"I wish that were true, Theo." She finished her wine and disappeared into the house. Maybe she wanted Theo to follow her, but he wouldn't do it. He hopped the railing and strode across her soft, green lawn. When Theo got into his Jeep, he saw it was nine o'clock.

"Where were you?" his mother asked when he got home. She was alone in the kitchen, drying the dinner dishes. "This exploring of yours is getting a little suspect." She got in his face and sniffed his breath. "Have you been drinking, Theo?"

He stared at his mother. She had a tan and her hair was lighter now that it was summer. When he was a little boy, he always told her how pretty she was. Now, he wanted to slap her.

"Fuck you," he said. He breezed past her and went up to his room.

Hating his mother gave him focus; he funneled all his anger, his hurt, his frustration into dealing with her. She had been a good person to him his whole life, and he had tried to return the favor. But now he couldn't look into her face without thinking of the abortion. His child, the only thing he had ever created, ripped from Antoinette's body and discarded. It was his mother's fault.

Hating his mother transformed him. His anger swirled around him like a wind, blowing his mother—and father and brother and sisters—away. His mother was afraid of him now, he could see it in her eyes, and that made him hate her more. *"Fuck you,"* he said. *"Please just shut the fuck up, and lose some fucking weight while you're at it."* He left the house without explanation. He shunned his chores. And on one night when Antoinette had refused to sleep with him, saying it would be best if they *cooled things off,* he drove his Jeep through his mother's garden. He threw the Jeep into four-wheel-drive and ran over the puny wire fence she put up to keep rabbits out. He drove back and forth over her herbs and vegetables, breaking zucchini and cucumbers, squashing tomatoes, until every plant was mangled and the garden was marred by deep tire ruts. *Fuck you,* he thought. *Fuck you and your stupid garden.*

He kept expecting to be punished. He expected his father, at the very least, to say something. But his parents steered clear; they let him go, his anger trailing behind him like a stench.

As Labor Day approached, Antoinette grew more distant. When he stopped by, she no longer offered him wine, and making love was out of the question. Seeing her still aroused Theo—and once he excused himself to her bathroom, where he masturbated into one of her hand towels. He didn't care if she knew what he was doing.

When they had a week left, he asked her, "You're going through with it?"

"Of course, Theo," she said. Again, on the deck drinking chardonnay but not offering him any. She looked at him as though he were the paper boy. "Don't you think you should be heading home?"

Then the Friday of Labor Day weekend arrived and Theo knew Antoinette would be going for her annual pilgrimage to Great Point with his mother. Before she left, Theo drove to her house to confront her, because he was sure that spending time with his mother would only convince her further that an abortion was the right thing. He walked into her house without knocking, to show her that he wasn't timid anymore. He wasn't the boy that she'd led inside in April. But he checked all the rooms—no Antoinette. Then he heard a car door and peeked out the window. Antoinette climbed out of a taxi. He met her at the door, even though he could see the girl driving the taxi was Sara Poncheau, from school. Antoinette was carrying a plastic tub of lobsters; he took the tub from her and brought it into the kitchen.

"What are you doing here?" Antoinette asked.

"I don't think you should go tonight," he said.

She laughed. "That's not your decision."

"Still."

Antoinette poured herself a glass of wine. "Well, I'm going."

"I'll have a glass of wine," Theo said.

She stared at him a second, then took out a goblet

and poured him some wine. It was a small, small victory. "You haven't told me what you're doing here."

"Do I need a reason to come by? A man should be able to come by and see his own child when he pleases."

"There's no child to see," Antoinette said. It was true: No sign of pregnancy had manifested itself yet on her body. She was wearing another black outfit: leotard, leggings, Chuck Taylors; and her stomach was pancake flat. "But speaking of one's child, it just so happens that my daughter is coming tomorrow."

"Your *daughter?*" he said. "The one you gave away?"

"That's the one."

"How did she find you?" he asked.

Antoinette drank her wine, and Theo felt a surge of protectiveness for his own unborn child inside her, whom he was helpless to protect. Just a cluster of cells, really—still, with a beating heart, probably, and a sex—and here was Antoinette *drinking wine* because she didn't give a shit. Theo took a deep breath.

"The Internet," Antoinette said. "She hooked up with some group on the Internet that connects children with their birth parents. A representative called me and said Lindsey had been making inquiries and asked if I would let them give her my phone number. With the understanding that she might not use it. But then she did call and we talked. She sounds amazingly normal."

"I'm surprised you let her call you," Theo said.

"I surprised myself."

"But you're still going to kill our baby?" he said. He grabbed her wrist and her wine sloshed.

"Don't, Theo."

He clenched her wrist so tightly that she dropped her glass and it shattered against the kitchen floor. "I'm not going to let you do it," he said. "I'll follow you off-island if I have to. I'll follow you right into the clinic."

"This isn't your decision, Theo," Antoinette said. "God, why don't you just let me be, boy? Let it go? You're young, you'll have plenty of children once you're older, once you're married. This isn't something you want, Theo."

"You're not going to kill our child, Antoinette," he said. "I won't let you."

Her voice was icy. "It's time for you to leave."

He kissed her hard on the lips, leaving behind a fleck of dill from the cucumber salad he'd eaten at home. He tried to wipe it away, but she swung at him. "Get out!" she said. She bent down to pick up the shards of glass but did so with her eyes trained warily on him, as though she were afraid he might attack her. This made him feel powerful—finally, she noticed him, respected him—but it made him feel sad, too.

"I want you to have our baby," he said. "I don't want you to kill it." He pounded his fist on the kitchen counter; it was granite, cold and unyielding against his hand. He felt tears rise. The thought of the little baby, his baby, helpless against Antoi-

nette's will drove him mad. How had he gotten here?
Eighteen years old, in a dangerous love affair, things
spinning so hideously out of his control?

Antoinette held the largest shard of glass out like
a weapon, and Theo thought of her cheating husband
and how that pain made Antoinette stronger, how it
made her think she could do whatever she wanted.

"Antoinette?" he pleaded.

"Leave," she said.

He returned later, when he knew she would be at
the beach with his mother. He ripped her cottage
apart. He swept her books off her shelves, he tore
the clothes out of her closet and dumped the contents
of her dresser drawers onto her bed. He smashed her
wine goblets and snapped her fancy candles in half,
like he was breaking bones. Before he left, he stole
her red-handled hatchet from the woodpile and
climbed in his Jeep, sweating, breathing hard, his
heart pounding. God, was he angry! He drove to the
Ting house. He walked into the living room where he
had stood two months before with his father. The walls
were up now. Theo swung the hatchet into the fresh
plasterboard, leaving huge, garish holes. He could kill
someone, he could! He could chop someone's hands
off with that hatchet, someone's head! He swung the
hatchet until the walls were a pile of powdery rubble
and his arms were heavy and sore. And then suddenly it was as if his anger had drained, he'd ex-
pelled it, and he felt better. When he arrived home,
in the minutes before his mother called from the

Wauwinet, before Theo heard his father on the phone giving instructions, and before his father told him the news—Antoinette was missing—Theo had actually felt better.

"Baby, baby. Oh, my poor baby."

His mother led him to her car, saying they would come back for the Jeep, saying they needed to get him home. The woman who was Antoinette but not Antoinette—her daughter, Theo realized—glared at him. A look of hatred. What could he think but that it was Antoinette looking at him? Hating him so much that she had disappeared.

"What am I going to do, Mom?" Theo said.

"You'll do what the rest of us are doing," his mother said. "You'll wait."

Theo crawled into the backseat of the Trooper, and miraculously, his mother produced a blanket and beach towels. She created a nest for him.

"You must be exhausted," she said. "Try and sleep, Theo."

Theo watched the diver surface and shake his head—no, nothing. "But my baby—"

His mother put a hand on his back.

"Lie down," she said.

He lay down. The towels and blanket smelled faintly of fish. The engine started, and the car bounced over the sand, rocking him to sleep.

Kayla

As they drove off Great Point, Lindsey asked Kayla to take her to the airport.

"I've seen enough," Lindsey said.

Kayla was relieved; more than anything, she wanted Lindsey out of her car. No, not more than anything. More than anything, Kayla wanted to travel back in time. She wanted Antoinette safe; she wanted Theo erased from the picture. Theo, her own child, involved with Antoinette. Not Raoul at all, but Theo. Her baby, her first baby, having his own baby with her best friend. So this was Antoinette's confession. Kayla wanted to vomit, scream, spit fire. She thought of Raoul smoothing the dirt in Antoinette's driveway. Clearing Theo's tracks. Because he knew! Kayla was ready to kill someone, but she settled for getting Lindsey Allerton out of her car. Kayla drove to the airport silently, avoiding all thought, the layers of hurt and betrayal that she would eventually have to peel back and examine.

Things at the airport had quieted. Kayla pulled right up in front of the terminal, and only when she retrieved Lindsey's bag from the back did she see the black Jaguar squeeze in behind her. When she

turned to hand Lindsey her bag, she saw John Gluckstern get out of his car. He was still wearing his shirt
and tie, and a pair of dark suit pants. Val once told
Kayla that the man didn't own a single pair of jeans.
"A character flaw, right?" Val said. *"He can't relax."* There was no way that John's presence here
was a coincidence. He must have followed them.

Kayla's instinct was to get out of there as soon
as she could. "Lindsey, I'm sorry," Kayla said. The
words clinked cheaply; they meant nothing in the
face of all that had happened. Kayla wondered if she
should offer to call Lindsey when she had news.
Would she want to know if her mother was alive?
Dead? Kayla couldn't bring herself to exchange
phone numbers for this purpose. If Lindsey wanted
information, she would find a way to get it.

Before Lindsey could respond, John Gluckstern
was upon them. He took Lindsey's elbow. "Can I
have a word with you before you go?" he said.

"What do you want to tell her, John?" Kayla
asked.

"None of your business."

"How can you say that?"

"Antoinette is my client, Kayla. This woman is
Antoinette's daughter. There are some things she
ought to know."

"Like what?"

John smirked. "Once again . . . " he said. Then to
Lindsey, "Can I buy you a cup of coffee?"

Lindsey looked from Kayla to John. "I just want
to get home."

"Let the girl go home, John," Kayla said. "She's been through enough."

"I'll walk you to your plane," John said.

"God, John, give it up."

John led Lindsey toward the terminal. "If I were you, Kayla, I'd get myself a lawyer."

Kayla stood by the side of her car and watched them walk away. From the back, especially, Lindsey looked like Antoinette, and Kayla was glad that Theo was asleep and did not see.

On her way home from the airport, Kayla listened to Theo's soft snoring. She drove home through the state forest—thick blue-green pine trees on both sides of the road. She passed Barbara Diedrich from her quilting class, who waved. Kayla waved back automatically. She was on her island, on streets she'd driven hundreds of times, but now she felt like her surroundings had transformed. Theo and Antoinette together. The image struck her as so horribly *wrong* that the whole world seemed out of whack. And running into John Gluckstern didn't make her feel any better; God only knew what kind of trouble he could drum up. For a minute Kayla wished that she lived in Kansas, or Nebraska, where it would be possible to drive along indefinitely—the car a kind of womb where she could keep Theo safe.

He was eighteen, though. An adult, technically. Old enough to vote, old enough to go to war, old enough to have sex and father a child. Since his ugly behavior started, Kayla had been reminiscing about

Theo when he was little. The year he got mono he was eight years old. Jennifer was four and Cassidy B. eighteen months, and when Theo got sick, Kayla enrolled them in a play group three days a week so she would have time to care for Theo. They played endless games of Crazy Eights and Battleship— Theo in his pajamas in bed, his eyes glazed over, his face pink with fever. He slept for hours at a time, and Kayla checked on him every fifteen minutes. She read to him from Hardy Boys mysteries; she helped him with the math homework his teachers sent home. Long division. It was the math, though, that held Theo back. Three months of school missed due to mononucleosis, and Theo couldn't make up the math. His teachers recommended that he repeat third grade. Theo screamed and said all the kids would call him a dummy, a retard. He didn't want to be separated from his friends, he didn't want anybody to think he'd "flunked." What to do? In the end, Kayla and Raoul sided with his teachers—boys needed more time to mature, anyway; Theo could only benefit from another year—and he repeated third grade.

The idea of the Midwest intrigued Kayla. Maybe this island was the problem. Nantucket had always seemed like a refuge, but if she lived in a place that had a mall, a cineplex, an arcade, would this have happened? Maybe she was to blame for cloistering Theo away on this gray island where there was nothing to do but cruise the cobblestone streets.

How did parents survive their children? It was all so painful. Far, far more painful than growing up herself, Kayla thought, watching her children grow up.

When Kayla got home, Raoul's red truck was in the driveway, and next to it, a blue-and-white Bronco: Jacob Anderson. Cassidy B. and Luke were in the side yard throwing a Frisbee, the picture of normality. Kayla forced herself to check the backseat. Theo was curled up in the fetal position, sound asleep among the beach towels. The poor kid. But now things were starting to make sense: Theo's behavior of the last few weeks was due to this mess.

Kayla put down the windows and shut off the engine. She would let Theo sleep.

She stood in the yard watching Cassidy B. and Luke toss the Frisbee. They knew she was watching, and so they tried extra hard. Luke furrowed his brow and concentrated on holding the Frisbee just so before he sent it sailing through the air with a slight wobble. Cassidy B. caught it flat between her palms, a trick. Two children, as Theo had once been a child. And so, Luke and Cassidy B., too, would have to face adulthood and all its dirty surprises. That made Kayla sadder than anything else. She had no power to protect them, just as she'd had no power to protect Theo from Antoinette.

What were you doing, Antoinette? Kayla thought. Sleeping with Theo. Pregnant with his baby.

Kayla couldn't think of a better reason to disappear.

Inside, Raoul, Jacob Anderson, and Val were at the dining table eating nacho chips and drinking Coronas with limes. They stopped talking when Kayla came in. Kayla just stared. She hated them.

"Does anyone know where Theo is?" she asked.

Raoul remained cool, but Val's face fell. Kayla's mind flashed back to: *Antoinette, why don't you tell us about your sex life these days? What's been going on with you?* Raoul and Val talking in the front seat of Raoul's truck. They all knew. Even Jacob Anderson knew, when Kayla saw him at the Tings', when he almost kissed her. They all knew that her best friend was fucking her son and no one had told her.

"He's at work, isn't he?" Raoul said.

"He's asleep in the Trooper," Kayla said. "I found him up at Great Point. What do you suppose he was doing there?"

"Kayla—" Raoul stood up.

"Stay away from me!" she said. "You lied to me, Raoul."

"I didn't lie," he said. "It was better that you didn't know."

"We didn't want to hurt you," Val said.

"You!" Kayla said, pointing at Val. She looked gorgeous, radiant with her adultery, in a sundress of red, crinkled cotton. Her gold chains glinted at her neck. "You lied, too. And what's worse, Val, is that you're a woman. You are my female friend. You, I should be able to trust."

"Kayla, calm down," Raoul said.

Kayla pulled the pregnancy test out of her purse. "Did you know Antoinette is pregnant?" she said. "Pregnant!"

"I didn't know until last night," Raoul said. "Val told me on the way to Antoinette's house."

"And who told you?" Kayla asked Val.

Val bowed her head; under the table, she and Jacob Anderson were holding hands. "Antoinette."

"Antoinette told you? When did she tell you?"

Val shrugged. "Last week. Remember when I told you that we had lunch? Well, it was more than just lunch. Antoinette came into the office to take care of some business. We talked about things, and she told me about Theo, she told me she was pregnant. She signed a new will."

"She signed a will?" Kayla said. This seemed like important information, something Val might have mentioned the night before. "What did it say?"

"It's confidential," Val said.

"I don't care. I want to know. Did she leave everything to Theo?"

"No," Val said. "She put everything into a trust."

"You set up the trust?"

Val twirled her beer bottle by the neck. "I'm the attorney."

Jacob munched a chip.

"Was she going to keep the baby?" Kayla asked. "Was the trust for the baby?"

"She said she had an appointment for an abortion," Val said.

"What about the vandalism?" Kayla said. "It was Theo?"

Raoul led Kayla to the table. He opened a beer for her and squeezed a tiny wedge of lime into the top. "Probably," he said. "You need to try to relax. We're going to sort through this."

"We just called the fire department," Val said. "The divers didn't find anything."

The sliding door opened, and Kayla heard a shriek. "Mommy!"

They all turned around. Jennifer was standing in the kitchen, her face bright red.

Kayla did a mother's scan: no bleeding, no obvious injury to her daughter's person. Her thoughts zipped to Cassidy and Luke outside, to Theo in the car.

"What's wrong?" Kayla said. How long had it been since Jennifer had called her *Mommy*? Three, four years? "Jennifer?"

"A phone call came to the Ogilvys," Jennifer said, "while I was baby-sitting."

Ed Ogilvy was the publisher of the *Inquirer and Mirror*, the island newspaper. More than once, Jennifer had come home with a story before it broke because she had heard it at the Ogilvys' house.

"What kind of phone call?" Kayla asked, though she feared she knew.

"Someone saying Aunt Antoinette is dead. Someone saying you and Aunt Val killed her."

"*Who* said that?" Raoul asked. "Did you get a name?"

Jennifer shook her head so that her long ponytail swayed. "Anonymous."

"Did Ed Ogilvy hear the message?" Kayla asked.

"Is Aunt Antoinette dead?" Jennifer demanded. "Did you kill her?"

"Jennifer!" Raoul said. "What kind of question is that?"

"The caller said it happened at Great Point last night," Jennifer said. "He said you made it look like an accident, you and Aunt Val. He said you and Aunt Val were after her money."

Val snatched her hand from Jacob's. "Don't worry," Val said. "It was my husband who called. And I guarantee you he doesn't know what he's talking about."

"Is Aunt Antoinette dead?" Jennifer asked.

"We don't know, sweetie," Kayla said. "She got lost in the water, and they haven't been able to find her."

"She's dead," a voice said. Luke walked into the kitchen behind Jennifer. Cassidy B. followed him. "Aunt Antoinette is dead."

"Luke? What makes you say that?" Kayla asked.

"She just is. I know it." His voice was calm and serious. "Aunt Antoinette drowned."

Cassidy B. started to cry. Jennifer said, "Mom, what happened up there, exactly?"

Luke said, "I'm telling you . . ." Suddenly, all three of them were making a commotion—until the sliding glass door opened and Theo walked in. Or a boy who resembled Theo, except this boy was bloodless, lifeless. He'd lost his tan, it seemed, overnight; his hair had lost its color. When Theo stepped into the kitchen, the other kids got quiet. They were still afraid of him.

"Mom?" he said. "I'm going to bed."

"Okay," Kayla said.

His brother and sisters cleared the way for him, and he headed past them toward the stairs.

"The poor kid," Val whispered.

Money, Kayla thought. It couldn't mend a broken heart. Theo's or hers.

The phone rang. Jennifer ran to answer it, and in her very adult voice, she said, "May I tell her who's calling?" A beat passed and she handed Kayla the phone, mouthing, *The police.*

"Kayla?" It was Paul Henry. "Can you and Valerie come down to the station, please? We have some questions for you."

"Have you found her?" Kayla asked.

"No," he said. "We checked at the airport and the Steamship first thing this morning. No one saw Ms. Riley leaving the island."

"Well, then, what kind of questions do you have?" Kayla said. "Can't you ask them over the phone? My family . . ." Jennifer, Cassidy B. and Luke were huddled together like orphaned immigrants, all three of them staring at her with Raoul's wide brown eyes. "My family needs me at home right now."

"And we need you at the station," Paul said. "I suggest you and Valerie cooperate. It'll be easier for all involved."

Kayla's eyelids drooped; she was exhausted. She wasn't sure she could make herself get back in the car and drive into town to the police station, but what choice did she have?

Kayla hung up and turned to the table. "They want us to answer more questions," she said to Val. "Let's go. Let's get this over with."

When they got in the car, Kayla said, "You'd better tell me what's going on."

"I don't *know* what's going on."

"You know plenty," Kayla said. "You know much more than you told me last night."

"John is angry," Val said.

"About Jacob?"

"Yes, about Jacob." She fluttered her hand in such a way that made Kayla notice she had removed her huge diamond ring and her wedding band. "I'm leaving him. I told him this morning. He said if I left, he'd go to the police, and I guess he has." Val twisted her gold chains so fiercely, Kayla was amazed they didn't break.

"I saw John at the airport," Kayla said. "About half an hour ago."

"What was he doing at the airport?" Val said. "God, let's hope he was leaving."

"The question is, what was *I* doing at the airport? The answer is, I was dropping off Lindsey Allerton, Antoinette's daughter."

"That's right. Raoul told us you spent the day with the daughter. What's she like?"

"She's like Antoinette."

"Meaning?"

"Meaning . . ." Kayla looked out the window at a young blond woman pushing a jog stroller. Kayla saw the same woman jogging with her baby every single day and every single day the woman made Kayla feel fat and unmotivated. "Meaning she's thin, beautiful, and articulate. She's as confused as the rest of us."

"I bet," Val said.

Kayla took a deep breath and looked at her friend. "So you've known about Theo and Antoinette since last week. You knew about the baby. And you didn't tell me."

"It was told to me under the strictest confidence, Kayla. Not only as Antoinette's friend, but as her lawyer. Please don't get sensitive about it."

"If I didn't get sensitive about this, I'd be cold-blooded."

"Antoinette was dead set against your knowing about Theo or the baby. She said she was going to break it off with Theo before school started, she was going to get an abortion and hope the whole thing blew over."

"How considerate of her," Kayla said. "Breaking it off before school began so that Theo could have a normal senior year. I mean, what was she *thinking?*"

"It was about sex," Val said.

"That doesn't make me feel any better," Kayla said. She wasn't ready to imagine one of her children as a lover—and yet now she was forced to. "Why did Antoinette let herself get pregnant?"

"Yeah," Val said. "You'd think she'd know better."

"Did she disappear on purpose?" Kayla asked. "Did she pull a Houdini?"

"I don't know, Kayla," Val said.

"Why did she want a new will? Do you think she was planning on killing herself? Think back, Val, think back to the beginning. That first Night Swimmers. She was suicidal then."

"She told me she wanted to protect her assets. Which, with her daughter showing up, wasn't a bad idea. Obviously, if I knew more than that, I would tell you."

"Obviously you've kept a lot from me already," Kayla said. "And now we have your husband after us."

"John's also angry because I advised Antoinette to pull her money."

"What do you mean 'pull her money'?"

"Pull it out of his account. His care. I suggested that she transfer her assets to another broker. Now John wants to make it look like I killed her for her money because I'm the only one who knows where she put it. Except he has no evidence. And nobody likes him, especially not the guys at the police station."

The streets were crowded, and Kayla sat at the corner of India and Centre waiting for traffic to pass. "Where did Antoinette put her money?"

"I can't tell you that."

"Val, please."

"Abroad somewhere. That's really all I can say."

"Abroad, like Switzerland?"

"Oh, God," Val said, lurching forward. "There's his car."

Kayla looked where Val was pointing. John Gluckstern's black Jaguar cruised by with Lindsey Allerton in the passenger seat. Of course.

"Shit," Kayla said. "Do you know who that is in his car, Val? That's Antoinette's daughter."

"Where?"

"In the front seat of his fucking car!" Kayla said. Fear passed through her like a cold wind. "He must have convinced her to go to the police after all. Shit. She knows about Theo because she was with me when I found him at Great Point and he said some things. So you can bet John knows now about Theo and the baby. Let's ditch Paul Henry, Val. Let's catch the fast boat to Hyannis and have dinner at Chili's instead."

Val craned her neck. "I want to see the daughter! Follow them, Kayla. There they go. They're taking a right onto Federal."

"I'm serious, Val. Maybe we should leave the island."

"I can't believe I missed her," Val said.

Kayla turned onto Chestnut Street. Miraculously, there was a parking spot across from the police station.

"What do you think they told the police?" Kayla said. "Do you think they told them everything?"

"I guess we'll find out," Val said.

Kayla had lived on Nantucket for nearly twenty years, and she was still discovering things. For example, the police station had a holding cell and an interrogation room. She'd heard about the holding cell years ago—one of Raoul's drunk friends spent the night there—but she'd forgotten about its existence. The interrogation room was a complete surprise to her. After Kayla and Val walked into the station and announced their arrival to the officer sitting behind glass, Paul Henry materialized from behind a heavy door.

"We're going to question you one at a time," Paul Henry said. "Valerie, why not you first? Follow me to the interrogation room."

Kayla watched Val step through the door and disappear down a dark hallway.

"You can have a seat, ma'am," the officer behind glass said to Kayla.

There was a metal couch with mustard yellow vinyl cushions and a small table that had three magazines on it: *Reader's Digest*. Kayla came into the police station exactly once a year to get a beach sticker for her car, and never once had she noticed how ugly it was.

Kayla plopped onto the sofa and leaned her head back against the wall. At least it was air-conditioned. She closed her eyes, opened them, pitched forward and scanned the front of the *Reader's Digest*s. Then she leaned back again. She searched through her purse for her Ativan, but she couldn't find them. In the car. She considered going out and looking for them—she liked the calm they brought her, and if she was going to sit in the interrogation room, she wanted to be calm. But then her fingers found the keys to Theo's Jeep, and next, the sandwich bag that held the pregnancy test. Kayla dropped her purse, closed her eyes. She was exhausted.

She woke up drooling. The officer behind glass paid her no attention; he was typing, and when a voice broke the static of the police scanner, he held his head alert but still, like a cat stalking a bird, and when the call proved to be uninteresting, he resumed his typing. Kayla checked the clock: Val had been in there forty minutes. Paul Henry must have been giving her a hard time. Antoinette disappearing was a bad development for Val—with a new will and a soon-to-be ex-husband out to nail her. Who knew what the police would think?

Kayla tapped on the glass of the reception window. The same cat-and-bird reaction; the typing stopped.

"Yes?"

"How long do you think they'll be?" she asked. "I have a husband and four children at home waiting for me to feed them."

The officer scowled. Kayla thought of Officer Johnny Love, a kid not much older than Theo, playing policeman. She longed for him.

"I have no idea, ma'am."

"May I please use your—" Her question was cut off when the heavy door opened and out came Val, Paul Henry, and the offensive detective. Val was staring resolutely at the floor, her arms crossed in front of her.

"Are you okay?" Kayla said. "What happened in there?"

"We're ready for you, Kayla," Paul Henry said.

"I'm not sure I'm ready for you," she responded.

Val raised her eyes. "You might want to get a lawyer."

"You are my lawyer."

"Not anymore."

"What's that supposed to mean?"

Val headed for the door. "I'll see you later, Kayla," she said.

Kayla trailed Paul Henry down the dim hallway past the holding cell, which looked like any jail cell—bars, cot, sink—and a couple of offices with desks and filing cabinets. And then, the interrogation room. A sign on the door said PRIVATE. Inside was a wooden table, four folding chairs, a water cooler, and perhaps to remind them that they *were* on Nantucket Island, one of the most charming locations in all the world, there was a poster of a Beetle Cat with a green sail breezing around Brant Point lighthouse. Kayla was thinking of Val. She felt bruised somehow by what Val had said. Val wasn't her lawyer anymore? Why not? And Val had left the station. How was she getting home? Taxi? Kayla wasn't even sure where Val considered home. Now that Val had left John, was she living with Jacob? Kayla wanted to run out onto the street after her friend, but there was little hope of that now that she was in the interrogation room. Kayla wondered if the door was locked.

Detective Simpson sat at the table with a yellow

legal pad that was covered with scribblings. "Sit down," he said. Paul Henry paced around by Kayla's right, in the area near the door, as though waiting for a chance to escape. She couldn't blame him.

"We've taken three statements so far," the detective said. "One from Valerie Gluckstern, one from John Gluckstern and one from Lindsey Allerton, birth daughter of Antoinette Riley."

Kayla shook her head. "John Gluckstern and Lindsey Allerton have nothing to do with this. I don't see how statements from them would have any relevance."

"They have relevance," the detective said. "Because what we're interested in here is motive."

"Motive?" Kayla said. "What's that supposed to mean?" She had known Paul Henry for years, and his idiosyncrasies—his crew cut, his cardigans, his quiet intensity—were accepted by all Nantucketers. He and Raoul were in Rotary together; he gave school assemblies on common-sense safety. Kayla didn't exactly like him, but she cared about him. This new guy, the detective, was a stranger, and his arrogance pissed Kayla off. He was just a kid they imported from the mainland and gave a title: detective. Now here he was throwing around words like *motive*. "I don't feel like playing games. My children are at home waiting for dinner. Why don't you tell me what you know and I'll tell you what I know and then I'll go home and you two can get back to the business of finding Antoinette?"

The detective sniffed. "Your children are at home?"

"Yes."

"Your son Theo. He's at home?"

Kayla paused. So they knew. Okay, what did she expect? They knew about the affair, and maybe they thought he was the one who ransacked Antoinette's cottage.

"He was at home when I left."

The detective flipped a sheet on his yellow pad. Kayla saw him write her name and underline it. Then he looked at her with an annoyingly casual expression, as though he was surprised to find her sitting there.

"And you're aware, I assume, that your son Theo was having a sexual relationship with Ms. Riley."

Kayla nodded.

"And you're aware that Ms. Riley is pregnant by your son?"

Kayla glanced at Paul Henry, her mind swirling with the furious tornado of the Nantucket rumor mill and how it damaged lives. Theo would be starting his senior year in three days, and every single kid would know.

"Can you prove she was pregnant by my son?" she said. "I mean, if she's missing . . ."

"We know you found a positive pregnancy test in Antoinette's house last night," Paul Henry said.

"What are you talking about?"

"You didn't find a pregnancy test in Ms. Riley's house last night?" the detective asked.

"No."

"Kayla," Paul Henry said. "We know you took it.

The woman's daughter told us you showed her the pregnancy test."

"You removed a positive pregnancy test from Ms. Riley's house last night," the detective said. "Even after we ordered you not to touch anything."

Kayla pointed at the detective. "You have no right to talk to me like that."

"So you're going on record saying that you did not remove evidence from a crime scene?"

Kayla nudged her purse with her foot and then she pulled out the sandwich bag. She waved it in the detective's face—the pregnancy test jiggled inside—and set it down on the table. He snatched it up.

"Do I need a lawyer?" she said.

"We believe it was your son who ransacked Ms. Riley's cottage," the detective said. "We could charge him with B and E right now. What you need is to start telling us the truth."

"Paul?" she said.

"Would you like to call a lawyer?" Paul asked. "It might not be a bad idea."

Kayla dropped her face in her hands. "Val is my lawyer."

"Well, in that case you're going to want to get another lawyer," the detective said. "I guarantee it."

The interrogation room was air-conditioned, and Kayla was chilly in her sundress. She rubbed her arms. Val was in trouble, then, and that was why she'd acted so strangely. "You have the pregnancy test," Kayla said. "Are there any other questions?"

"Let's get back to the events of last night," Paul

said. "Tell us again about Night Swimmers. What kind of group is this, exactly?"

"It's not a *group*," Kayla said. "It's just three women. Myself, Val, and Antoinette. It's a tradition we have, swimming at Great Point on the Friday of Labor Day weekend."

"You drink champagne and swim in the nude," the detective said. "You understand that's a bit unusual? Why not wear bathing suits like other people? Does this . . . *Night Swimmers* group include any rituals of a sexual nature? Perhaps you're more than just old friends?"

Paul Henry cleared his throat and turned away. Kayla sneered at the detective, although she wasn't surprised. Men would always think what they wanted about what women did when they were alone.

"We drink a little champagne, we eat lobsters, and we swim. That's all there is to it. And last night, at some point, Antoinette went into the water and didn't surface. I called the police from the Wauwinet gatehouse, and you responded. That's the whole story."

"Let's talk about when you called the police," Paul Henry said. "You reached the pay phone and you called 911 right away? First thing?"

"Yes." As soon as Kayla said this she remembered that she'd called Raoul first. Before she could correct herself, the detective stood up.

"You're lying again," he said. "We checked that pay phone this morning. There were three phone calls placed successively to your house before you called 911."

"That's right," she said. "I called my house first."

"You called three times," the detective said.

"I wanted to reach my husband."

"You wanted to reach your husband even though your best friend was drowning?" the detective said. "Why not call 911 first and then call your husband? That's the order that makes sense to me."

"I was scared. I panicked. I wanted to talk to Raoul."

"Those minutes you wasted could have cost Ms. Riley her life."

"It wasn't very long," Kayla said.

The detective shuffled through his papers. "Four minutes. Might not seem like a lot of time to you, but I assure you it was a long time for Ms. Riley."

"I'm sorry," Kayla said. "I was under a lot of stress, I'd been drinking, and I did what I did. I don't know what else I can tell you. My intention was to get help for Antoinette."

Both Paul Henry and the detective were quiet. The detective sat back down.

"At what point did you throw the champagne glasses into the water?" he asked.

"Oh, God," Kayla said. "I see where this is headed—"

"Where is it headed, Ms. Montero?" the detective said.

"Why are you badgering me?" Kayla said. "Why are you making it seem like I am somehow to *blame*? What did John Gluckstern tell you? He has it in for us, you know. He's angry at his wife and so whatever he told you has a very unfair slant. But why would you believe him? He wasn't even there. If I were you, I'd forget everything John Gluckstern told you. It was all lies."

"What John told us is none of your business," Paul said. "It's our business, which we will check out in due course."

"Ms. Riley was sleeping with your son," the detective said. "I would guess that upset you pretty badly."

"It would have upset me had I known. But I didn't find out about Antoinette and Theo until today."

"Kayla, please," Paul Henry said.

"What?"

"You're going on record saying that you had no idea—no hint or clue—that your son was having a relationship with Ms. Riley until today," the detective said.

"That's right."

"And today, when you found out, who told you?"

"Theo told me."

"Your son Theo told you?"

"Yes, he did."

"When did he tell you?"

"This afternoon, at about two o'clock."

"And that was the first you'd heard of it?"

"Yes."

The detective removed his glasses and rubbed the bridge of his nose. "At what point did you throw the champagne glasses into the water?"

"When I got back from using the phone."

"And why did you throw them in the water?"

"I already said I was scared. I panicked."

"Is it true that when Ms. Gluckstern asked why you threw the glasses you said you were 'destroying the evidence'?"

"I can't remember what I said."

"Ms. Gluckstern told us that you said you were 'destroying the evidence.' I wonder what you meant by that."

"I didn't mean anything by it. I was nervous that we'd been drinking."

"Yes," the detective said. "Judging from that bottle of champagne, it would seem the three of you drank quite a lot. How much would you say Ms. Riley had before she went swimming?"

"Two glasses."

"Two glasses? A huge bottle like that, and she only had two glasses?"

"That's right."

"Ms. Gluckstern suggested that it might have been more like four or five glasses."

"Well, maybe. I wasn't counting."

"Who poured the champagne?"

Kayla shifted in her seat. She hated the interrogation room. The atmosphere was stifling, and she couldn't think. There was nothing to focus on except for the poster of the Beetle Cat, and the water cooler, which had those cone-shaped paper cups that looked like little dunce caps.

"May I have some water?" she said.

Paul Henry nodded; the detective huffed with impatience. Kayla filled one cup, drank it down, filled it again and drank it more slowly while she stared at the poster of the Beetle Cat. Who had poured the champagne? She tried to jump a step ahead of them. Why were they asking? Her eyelids felt heavy. By now Raoul would have done something about dinner, ordered a pizza or something. She wondered if he would wake Theo. She wondered if Theo would ever be able to sit and eat dinner with their family again. She crumpled the cup and returned to her seat.

"Val and I poured the champagne," she said. "Antoinette may have poured some for herself, I guess. We all poured it. And there was a lot of spillage, too. I mean, we didn't come close to consuming that whole bottle. We're only three people."

The detective looked at her. "So you poured Ms. Riley's champagne?"

"Some of it."

The detective scribbled something down on his legal pad and ended his sentence with two exclamation points, which he wrote with a flourish—dash, dot, dash, dot. Then he stood up.

"I'll be right back," he said. He left the interrogation room, closing the door behind him.

Kayla leaned back in the folding chair. "Paul, what's going on?"

Paul Henry pinched his lips together and shook his head. Then he drew a breath as if he were going to explain all the secrets of the world to her, but he let the breath go and said, "You need to do a better job picking your friends, Kayla."

It was a strange thing to say. Stranger still because what Kayla couldn't possibly explain to Paul Henry was that she had never picked Val and Antoinette as friends; rather, they'd been brought together in the house on Hooper Farm Road by some larger force—God, fate, the powers that ruled. And Kayla knew from the very first Night Swimmers that she and Val and Antoinette would be lifelong friends. She knew it the way some people knew about love. "I'm furious at Antoinette, Paul, don't get me wrong. But I didn't have anything to do with her disappearance. And neither did Val. I feel like this clown—" she nodded at the door "—wants to hold us responsible."

"John Gluckstern . . . " he said.

"I can't believe you're listening to John Gluckstern," Kayla said. "He's waging a vendetta against his wife. But that's between John and Val. It has nothing to do with me."

"We've received conflicting information," Paul said.

"Because John is lying," Kayla said.

Before Paul could respond, the door swung open and the detective was back. He looked between Paul Henry and Kayla, frowning. Then he chuckled under his breath like a frat boy about to pull a prank. Kayla wanted to slap him. He sat back down across from her, and with the slow, deliberate movements of a magician, he produced a brown pill bottle from his shirt pocket. Kayla thought immediately of the pills in Antoinette's medicine cabinet until he said, "Tell me, do these belong to you?" He pushed the bottle toward her. Her Ativan.

"Where did you get these?" she said. She looked down at her feet where her purse lay. The pregnancy test had been in there, and so, she assumed, was the Ativan. Or in her car. Had he gone out to her car?

"Ms. Gluckstern gave them to us. She said she found them on the beach up at Great Point last night. Your prescription for Ativan, a heavy-duty sedative." The detective put his hands on the back of his folding chair and leaned toward her. "Ms. Gluckstern gave us reason to believe that you slipped one of the sedatives into Ms. Riley's champagne. She said *you* were pouring the champagne. She said you threw the glasses in the water to *destroy the evidence*. She also told us that you mentioned fleeing the island this evening instead of coming to talk to us. And she pointed out that you have a strong motive—your son's relationship with Ms. Riley. I don't know how much more plainly I can put it, Mrs. Montero. We suspect foul play on your part."

"Foul play on *my* part?" Kayla tried to get her mind around what this wicked man was telling her. Val had given her pills to the police? She'd twisted the facts so that Kayla looked like a suspect?

"Let's not forget that you put off calling 911," the detective said. "Why not allow a few extra minutes to be sure that Ms. Riley was swept out to sea?"

Kayla couldn't believe what she was hearing.

"Kayla?" Paul Henry said.

Kayla closed her eyes. *You need to do a better job picking your friends.* First Antoinette, and now Val.

"Val lied to you," Kayla said. "She knows I only found out about my son and Antoinette today."

"She said you made a comment just before Ms.

Riley entered the water. Accusing Ms. Riley of an affair. And Lindsey Allerton's statement corroborated this. She said you told her that you'd accused her mother of an affair."

Kayla wasn't sure how to proceed. Half of her wanted to deny everything. But this was so unfair, so twisted, that she wanted to set the record straight. "I accused Antoinette of having an affair with my husband, not my son."

"You accused her of sleeping with Raoul?" Paul asked.

"*Accuse* is a strong word," Kayla said.

"So now we have a husband and a son sleeping with the same woman," the detective said. "This is better than I thought."

"Sorry to disappoint you, Detective," Kayla said venomously. "But there's nothing going on between Raoul and Antoinette."

"Then why did you accuse her?" Paul asked.

"I was drinking," Kayla said. She could have gone on to explain that she sensed something wrong when she'd looked at Antoinette. But she'd said Raoul's name—well, because that was what came to mind. Not Theo. Never Theo. She drilled her finger into the table. "I had nothing to do with Antoinette disappearing. Val is trying to deflect blame off herself because she's afraid you'll believe whatever her husband told you. She's lying."

"Now everyone's lying," the detective said. "You already lied to us about the pregnancy test and the phone calls. There's no reason for me to believe you over Ms. Gluckstern. She was very up front with us. Cooperative."

"Cooperative about framing me," Kayla said. "I can't believe this. Am I under arrest?"

"Did you put a sedative in Ms. Riley's champagne?" the detective said.

"No," she said. "I had them out because I needed one. I took one. I must have left them lying around."

"I don't believe you," he said.

"I don't care if you believe me," Kayla said. "It's the truth. I had nothing to do with Antoinette disappearing." An anger grew in her that was so vile and so dangerous that she felt capable of killing Antoinette, Valerie, and the detective. "Am I under arrest?"

"No," Paul Henry said. "We're not sure what to think. The detective believes Ms. Riley is in that water, although I'm not convinced. But we have to consider every possibility."

The detective rapped the bottle of Ativan on the table. "And one possibility is that you took advantage of this yearly nude champagne-drinking, lobster-eating adventure of yours to make your friend disappear. After all, she was sleeping with your son! You knew Ms. Riley would be drinking, you knew she would be swimming in risky waters in the dark. You knew everyone would believe that she simply got swept away. But some of us are on to you, Mrs. Montero. Your friend Ms. Gluckstern is on to you, and I am on to you." He smiled. "If we do find Ms. Riley's body in that water, we'll come after you first. And since she was pregnant, well, then there's that life to consider as well."

That life. The baby's life.

Paul Henry guided Kayla down the dim hallway by the arm, and Kayla thought for a minute that he was going to throw her into the holding cell, but instead, he led her to the waiting room, which glowed like a laboratory under the fluorescent lights. Kayla was dizzy with the accusations; her vision was splotchy. She had to go to the bathroom.

"I can't believe this is happening to me," she said.

They stood in the waiting room. The officer behind glass pecked away at his typewriter, and Paul lowered his voice. "We'll call you if we find her," he said.

"Can't you do anything else?" Kayla asked. "Check her bank account or something? Because for all we know, Antoinette could have disappeared of her own volition. She had reasons, Paul. Her daughter arriving today, the pregnancy. Can't you make an effort to look for her?"

"She hasn't even been gone twenty-four hours," Paul said. "We're not conducting a missing persons yet; we're conducting a recovery mission. We have to check with the coast guard, and the fire department, see what they think."

"What does it matter? You said yourself that you don't think she's in the water."

"I don't know what to think," Paul Henry said, and Kayla saw he was telling the truth. Furthermore, she agreed with him. She didn't know what to think, either.

"What about Theo?" Kayla said. "He's supposed to start school on Tuesday."

"He should go to school," Paul said. "Unless we find reason to tell you otherwise." Paul ran a hand across the top of his crew cut. "I'm sorry about Detective Simpson. He's new here."

"He's appalling. I hate him. He's accusing me of terrible things."

"But you have to admit, Kayla, it doesn't look good."

"This is ridiculous, Paul. Val *lied* to you. She set me up. Please tell me you see through this. First, John comes in here accusing Val, then Val comes in accusing me."

"Val was very convincing." Paul said. "She had physical evidence. Being an attorney didn't hurt, either."

"Attorneys lie all the time," Kayla said.

"And the girl," Paul said. "What the girl said didn't help your case."

"Lindsey set foot on Nantucket for the first time this morning," Kayla said. "She doesn't know her ass from Altar Rock."

Paul patted Kayla on the back. "Just go home," he said. "Get your kids their dinner."

Outside, the Labor Day crowds filled the streets. A line was forming at the Dreamland Theater. Kayla stumbled up Chestnut to Visitor Services, where she used the public rest room. She splashed water on her face and dried off with a paper towel. She stared in the smudged mirror, blind, deaf, dumb with the news: Antoinette and Val had both betrayed her. And Kayla had loved them without reserve or exception, like sisters.

So now what? Go home, like Paul Henry said? Get the kids their dinner?

No. Find Val.

There was no way Val had returned to Kayla's house—Jacob or no Jacob—and so Kayla drove out Pleasant Street toward Val's house. She slowed down as she approached because the last person she wanted to see was John Gluckstern, especially if he had Lindsey Allerton with him. But thankfully the only car in the driveway was Val's BMW—with the trunk flipped open. Kayla pulled into the driveway.

Val rushed out of the house carrying clothes on hangers—her expensive blouses, her linen pants. When she saw the Trooper, she hugged the clothes to her body. Kayla watched her lips clamp shut, her jaw lock. Val laid the clothes over the suitcases in the trunk. Without a word, Kayla walked past her into the house.

Val's house was designer perfect; it was the kind of house featured in magazines, a house no one actually lived in. In the brick entryway was a pine table with a lightship basket meant for mail and keys— empty. A gilt-framed mirror hung over the table. In the mirror, Kayla watched Val enter the house behind her.

Val stepped around Kayla and headed down the

hallway into the kitchen. She opened a cabinet door and brought down some cookbooks.

"I have to get out of here," Val said. "Before John gets home."

"You know why I came?" Kayla asked.

"Actually, I have no idea. This isn't a good time."

Kayla peered into the living room—white sofa and love seat, a glass coffee table with a glass vase of pink peonies and Robert Gambee's book of Nantucket photographs. White furniture—what Kayla wouldn't give to be able to have even one piece of white furniture in her house. But this white furniture gave the room a cold, sterile feel, like a hospital. Val and John owned good, valuable Nantucket art—a glorious Illya Kagan hung over the sofa—the view from Monomoy, from the exact spot where Raoul was building the Ting house.

"We've known each other twenty years," Kayla said. "That's a long time to be friends."

"Kayla?"

Kayla turned to look at Val, loaded down with cookbooks—Martha Stewart, Sarah Leah Chase.

"What?"

"You have to leave. I'm leaving. I told you this, remember? Moving out? Now isn't a good time."

"Right," Kayla said. She reached for Val's load. "Let me help you with those."

Val seemed relieved. "Thank you."

Kayla threw the books to the floor. They made a tremendous crashing noise; the gilt-framed mirror shimmied on the wall. "You gave the police my sedatives," Kayla said. "You made them think I drugged Antoinette."

Val knelt and stacked the books primly, like a librarian. "The police have their own ideas about things."

"An idea *you* put into their heads," Kayla said. "You gave them my pills. Why did you do that?"

"I had no choice," Val said. Avoiding Kayla's eyes, she left the house. She threw the books into the trunk. That was it. Val opened the car door. She was going to leave.

Kayla raced outside. "What do you mean you had no choice? That's outlandish! Of course you had a choice. A choice between telling the truth and lying."

"I didn't lie." Val pointed a finger in Kayla's face. "I did not, technically, lie."

"You told them I accused Antoinette of sleeping with Theo."

"I told them you accused Antoinette of an affair. Those were my words."

"But I didn't know about Antoinette and Theo," Kayla said. "They're using that as my motive."

"I know," Val said.

Kayla threw her hands in the air. "I can't believe this. You turned me in to the police."

"I did what I had to do, Kayla, okay? John made this whole huge case about how I murdered Antoinette for her money."

"But he doesn't have any evidence," Kayla said.

"That's right," Val said. "As I was sitting there, I realized that none of the evidence points to me. It all points to you. But that's not my fault. You can't blame me for that."

"You gave them my pills." Kayla closed her eyes. She felt an old sense of hurt—the kind of hurt she hadn't felt since the playground. "Why would you do that to me?"

"Because you can handle it, Kayla," Val said. "It seems pretty bad today, but you know as well as I do that you can survive these accusations. They'll roll off you like water off a duck. But I don't have a loving husband and children to fall back on. As you may have noticed, I'm all alone. All I have is my career, my reputation. I'm an attorney, Kayla. If my name is even whispered in connection with this, I'll lose all my business."

"What about my reputation?" Kayla said. "What about my life?"

"You're a housewife, Kayla," Val said. "I don't mean that as an insult. But let's face it, if you get blamed for this, no one will even notice."

"That may be," Kayla said. "But I had nothing more to do with Antoinette disappearing than you did."

"You upset her," Val said. "What you said about Raoul upset her."

"I didn't put a sedative in her drink," Kayla said. "I didn't know about her and Theo."

"But you can't prove it," Val said. "Unfortunately."

"So that's it, then? You screwed me over because I'm a dinky unimportant housewife."

Val shook her head. "I knew you would blow this out of proportion."

"Out of *proportion*? They suspect me of *murder* because of what you said."

"You're being very dramatic."

Again, dramatic. Kayla felt like she was going to cry, but she didn't want Val to have the satisfaction. Dramatic Kayla. Sensitive Kayla. Housewife Kayla. All these years she'd stood up for Val, protected Val from her *real* reputation as a bitch, a viper, someone other women talked about in the most unflattering ways. Now Kayla felt like telling her about every petty insult ever directed at her. But Val wouldn't believe it. Val thought she was beyond reproach. "How do I know you didn't poison Antoinette yourself? To get control of her money? Maybe John is right."

"The police don't seem to think so."

"Why would you do something like this to me? I thought we were friends."

"We are friends."

"Friends don't treat each other this way," Kayla said.

"Of course they do, Kayla," Val said. She put one of her gold chains into her mouth and sucked on it like a child would. "Friends disappoint and fall short of expectations every day. Now, maybe you have a different idea of friendship. Maybe your idea of friendship is what we do up at Great Point—hold hands, walk in a circle, bare our souls. Do you ever wonder why we only get together like that once a year? Because that's all we can handle. If we shared and gave and loved that much every day, we'd be exhausted, drained, and sick of each other. That's why Night Swimmers is only one day of the year. The rest of the days we have to live our own lives and protect our own interests. That's real life. This, Kayla, this is real life." Val held out her arms to indicate her house, her perfectly trimmed shrubs, her green lawn. *Polished on the outside, rotten on the inside*, Kayla thought. Then in a series of quick, clean movements, like someone folding up a penknife, Val tucked herself into the car, clicked the door shut, and whooshed out onto the street. Drove away.

Kayla stood in the driveway. It was starting to get dark; between the trees across the street, the sky was streaked pink and purple. Did friends betray each other every day? Did they turn each other in to the police? Did they sleep with each other's sons? Did they shatter dreams, destroy happiness? Her friends, yes. Kayla touched her cheek as if she'd been slapped.

At home, Kayla found Raoul and Jacob still at the dining table. They hadn't bothered to turn on any lights; they were two shadowy figures, drinking vodka now. The room smelled of peanuts.

"How did it go?" Raoul said.

"Where are the kids?"

"Theo's still asleep. I gave Jennifer money, and

she walked with Cass and Luke to the Clam Shack."

Kayla felt feverish. She looked at Jacob. "You're still here."

"Val was planning on hashing things out with her hubby," Jacob said. "Not a scene I wanted to walk in on."

"Kayla, what happened with the police?" Raoul asked. His diction was thick and deliberate; it sounded like he'd had too much to drink.

Kayla looked out the sliding glass doors. Theo's Jeep was gone—still up at Great Point. She listened to the ice clink in Raoul's and Jacob's glasses, she listened to their molars grind up peanuts. She turned on the kitchen light and this startled them both. Raoul looked at her quizzically with his golden brown eyes. Eyes that, it had always seemed to Kayla, were flooded with sunlight. He was supposed to be her ally, her last resort, her safe place. And yet he'd betrayed her, too. He'd never said a word.

"Jacob?" Kayla said. "Are you on your way home?"

Jacob emptied his drink into his mouth, crunched the ice cubes, and stood up. "Actually, yeah. I was just going."

"Can you do me a favor?"

"Sure."

"Can you give me a ride up to Great Point? I have to get Theo's Jeep. We left it there. God knows what the police will do if they find it."

"It can wait until morning," Raoul said.

"No, Raoul," Kayla said. "It can't."

"I'll take you," Jacob said. "It's no problem."

"But it's dark," Raoul said. "You're not going up to Great Point in the dark. Not after last night."

"I'm getting the Jeep," she said.

"Okay, fine, then I'll take you," Raoul said.

"You've been drinking," Kayla said.

"So has Jacob."

"It's on Jacob's way home," Kayla said, although Great Point was so out of the way that this could barely be counted as true.

"Relax, man," Jacob said. "It's no problem."

Raoul stuffed his hands into the front pockets of his jeans. Kayla's heart ached with how much she loved him, and with how sorely he'd disappointed her. The luckiest man she'd ever known, until tonight.

Her third trip to Great Point in twenty-four hours was with Jacob Anderson in his 1991 Bronco that smelled of marijuana. Kayla hadn't smoked dope since Theo and Jennifer were small children, but she thought of smoking now with longing, especially since her Ativan was gone, especially since she was steeping in her anger.

Her semi-oldies station was on the radio, continuing with the countdown ("Uncle Albert," "Baba O'Reilly") and Jacob whistled along. He wasn't into conversation, and that was fine with her. There weren't any safe topics tonight, anyway.

When he turned onto Polpis Road, Kayla said, "Do you have a joint?"

He glanced at her. The moon was full, and trees cast shadows on the road.

"Sure." He flipped open the ashtray and produced a fresh joint. "I didn't know you smoked. Raoul, he's so straight . . ."

"We have four children," Kayla said. "That's why he's straight."

"Yeah. But you?"

"Ask Val sometime about my wilder days."

Jacob pressed the cigarette lighter to the tip of the joint. The paper hissed and crinkled as it caught. He inhaled deeply and after he let the smoke go, he held the joint out to her and said, "I always knew there was a wild woman in you somewhere, Kayla."

She smoked the joint down without responding. What did he mean by that? She concentrated on the dope, the fresh green smell, the promise of it in her lungs. Immediately her head felt lighter, like a balloon. Luke's purple balloon. She laughed, and it felt wonderful.

They passed the turn for Antoinette's driveway, but Jacob didn't slow down or look. Antoinette's disappearance meant nothing to him except a day off work, a little excitement, his straight boss's family involved in a small-time scandal. Kayla peered into the dark woods surrounding Antoinette's driveway and she wondered if they had posted a policeman there for the night. Did the town have that kind of extra staffing? That much money? Did anyone at the police station care except for Detective Simpson? No, she guessed that Officer Johnny Love had gone home at the end of his shift with no one to replace him, and now Antoinette's house was dark and unprotected.

"Turn around," Kayla said.

"I thought you wanted to go to Great Point," Jacob said.

"I do," she said. "But I want to take a detour. Is that okay with you?"

The air in the car was sweet with smoke. Jacob pulled a U-turn on the spot; the road was completely deserted.

"Where to?" he said.

Kayla directed him to Antoinette's driveway. The house was still bound up with police tape, but it was unattended, as expected.

"I worked on this house," Jacob said.

"That's right," Kayla said. The front door was closed. Kayla took down the police tape and tried the knob. Locked.

"Shit," she said.

"You know," Jacob said, "I remember this woman." He eyed the front of the house as if Antoinette's image were projected there. "She is one beautiful lady."

Kayla sighed, pressed her hand against the wooden panel of the door. "I can't believe they locked it. How could they lock it without a key? Do you think they found her keys? God, it would be just like the Nantucket police to lock themselves out."

"I can get in," Jacob said. He raced back to the Bronco and returned brandishing a T-square. "Looks like a simple measuring device—but wait and see!"

Jacob wedged the ruler into the crack. Kayla was

so close to him that she could feel the muscles in his forearm tense. He was a typical man, intent on solving a physical problem. Jacob grunted and *voilà*—the door popped open.

"You see?" Jacob said.

"Well done," Kayla said.

Jacob held his arm out. "After you."

Kayla stepped into the house. Everything had been left as it was—the Norfolk pine lay on its side, dirt spilling from it like blood.

"Antoinette?" Kayla called out. "Antoinette, are you home?"

A clock ticked, moonlight polished the wood floors. Kayla tiptoed down the hall toward the bedroom; broken glass crunched under her feet. The Waterford goblets, smashed.

"Antoinette?"

Antoinette's bed was mounded with enough black clothing for a month of funerals. The drawers of the dresser had been emptied; the Tiffany lamp on top of the dresser had a crack in its milky glass. It was Theo, Kayla reminded herself. Theo had done this.

As she stepped into the bathroom, someone grabbed her. Kayla screamed. Then she felt Jacob's face against the back of her neck. He wrapped his arms around her waist and lifted her up. Kayla screamed again. As she struggled to free herself of Jacob's grip, he lost his balance and the two of them tumbled to the ground. Kayla conked her head on the foot of the bed.

"Ouch!" she said. She started laughing. "You clown!"

Jacob held her around the waist. "Why did we come here?" he asked. "You don't think Antoinette is here?"

"No," Kayla said. "I just wanted to look around. I thought maybe if I looked around, things would start to make sense."

"Some things don't make any sense." Jacob said this in the most off-handed way; it was a sentence without any thought behind it, but it rang true in Kayla's head. Some things didn't make any sense. Her child having sex with her best friend. Val turning Kayla in to the police. Antoinette dancing into the water.

Jacob rested his hand on the curve just above her hip. Kayla felt heat rise off her body; she was simmering, a cauldron of water ready to boil. She couldn't find a place inside her to contain her anger—it was too wild, too chaotic. Jacob lay behind her, he growled in her ear. To be funny—but Kayla was overcome with a desire to upset the system. She recalled Val's words from early that morning. *I'd like to do something drastic, something dangerous.*

"Jacob?" she said.

He squeezed her in response.

"We should go."

They smoked the rest of the joint, and by the time they reached the Wauwinet gatehouse, Kayla was hopelessly stoned. She saw the pay phone she had used to call Raoul, then the police, and she giggled. She thought of Detective Simpson and the way his thin, bloodless lips said the words, *"Foul play,"* and she giggled. Jacob had a dreamy smile on his face. She wondered if he was thinking what she was thinking. She was thinking about his hand on her waist.

"You should let your tires down," she said.

He kept driving: past the gatehouse, over the speed bumps, and out onto the path that led to the beach. "We'll be okay," he said. "I come out here all the time. On Sundays? Just me and my pole." He pointed a finger at her. "My fishing pole, that is."

They lumbered over the dunes to the ocean, and Jacob hit the gas. They flew up the beach, sand spraying from the tires. Because it was Labor Day weekend Kayla figured they might see people barbecuing or enjoying the full moon, but the beach was deserted. Maybe word had spread that someone had drowned. Kayla gazed out at the silver water, the gentle waves. It looked just as it had the night before.

"I can't believe Antoinette is out there," she said. "Can you believe it?"

Jacob shook his head. "Man."

"Does Val ever talk about me, Jacob?" she asked.

"About you? What do you mean?"

"Does she ever say she thinks I'm a good friend or that she likes me, or that I'm someone she can trust?"

"She brings up your name sometimes," Jacob said. "I mean, I know you two are friends. I knew you were friends when I started seeing her. But I can't remember anything she's said, like, specifically."

Kayla popped the cigarette lighter and lit the roach, smoked it until it was nothing but a tiny piece of charred paper. She flicked it out her window.

"I think Val hates me," she said. "She might not even realize it, but she does."

Now it was Jacob giggling. "I don't understand women."

"No," Kayla said. "Me, neither." Because only one day earlier Kayla had ridden up this beach with her two dear friends, friends of twenty years— friends who it turned out were her enemies. She pointed at Theo's Jeep in the distance. "There it is. Up there. Good, nothing happened to it."

As Jacob approached Theo's Jeep, the sand got softer, deeper. He downshifted and eased the Bronco alongside the Jeep.

"Door-to-door service," he said.

"Thanks," Kayla said. "I appreciate the ride, and the smoke. I needed it."

"My pleasure, madam," he said. He smiled at her, an incredibly gorgeous smile, and Kayla hesitated. The idea of her and Jacob together was powerful, tempting, and because of all that had happened, maybe even reasonable. Kayla had never intentionally hurt anyone in her life; the feelings she had now were so foreign she didn't know what to make of them. The best thing, she thought, was to go home and sleep.

"Good night," she said. She got out of the Bronco and fished Theo's keys from her purse. She climbed into the Jeep. There was a hatchet on the passenger seat. What had Theo been doing with a hatchet?

In her rearview mirror, Kayla watched Jacob swing the Bronco in a circle. She started the Jeep and lurched forward. When she checked her mirror a moment later, Jacob had stopped. She hit her brakes; he flashed his lights. *Are you okay?* she thought. Then she saw his tires spin, they bit into the sand. Jacob got out of the Bronco and ran toward her.

Kayla pulled the parking brake, put down her window. "Don't tell me."

He grinned. "I'm stuck."

Kayla slogged through the sand toward the Bronco. Jacob knelt by his front left tire to let out air. She started on the back tire with the key to the Jeep. The air coming out made a sharp, satisfying hiss and smelled of rubber.

Kayla closed her eyes and listened to the waves and the hiss of the air. A cool breeze swept off the water, and Kayla felt rooted to her place in the sand, like she was a heavy, old piece of driftwood. She couldn't even think about Night Swimmers without feeling hurt and foolish—she believed in the rituals, in the magic of it. But she had believed alone, like the last kid to find out about Santa Claus or the tooth fairy, the last one to realize that the adult world didn't contain magic of any kind.

Jacob walked over to check on her progress. Kayla tugged on the leg of his jeans.

"Hey," she said.

"How's it coming?"

"Sit here with me a minute," she said. A slow fear spread through her as she spoke the words. She pictured the detective pulling the bottle of Ativan from his shirt pocket. And then Paul Henry: *You need to do a better job picking your friends.*

Jacob plunked onto the sand next to her, and they watched the waves roll onto the beach.

"Sorry I got stuck," he said.

"It's okay," she said. "Actually, it's kind of nice out here tonight." She took a deep breath. "So . . . Val's moving in with you, then?"

Jacob rested his arms on his knees, the tire gauge dangled from his fingers. "Looks like it."

"That's good. You two are serious."

"Val's serious," he said. "I can't believe she left her husband."

"John's an asshole," Kayla said. "He deserves to be left."

"I guess," Jacob said. "I mean, I was content to let things be, but Val, you know, she wanted to make the whole thing legitimate. Because she's a lawyer and she doesn't want to damage her reputation." Jacob turned to her. He hadn't shaved, and dark stubble was growing in on his chin. "I'm just a dope-smoking carpenter," he said. "And I'm still pretty young. Do you think she expects me to marry her?"

"She might," Kayla said.

He clenched the tire gauge in his fist. He was scared; Kayla could see it. She thought of Val giving the police her pills, letting them stack the clues against her: Ativan, champagne glasses, phone calls. And then pretending like it was no big deal, like it happened every day. Kayla thought of Raoul getting up each morning to work at the Ting house with the knowledge that Theo was sleeping with Antoinette. Her own husband knew and didn't tell her. Kayla thought of Antoinette holding her arms in a wide circle before she pirouetted into the water. It was clear now what the circle meant—she had been telling Kayla that she was pregnant. Which of these betrayals was the worst? Kayla couldn't decide. What was clear was that all three people knew how to deceive her.

Kayla looked at Jacob sitting inches from her. She raised her hand to touch the back of his head, but she was too afraid, and she dropped her hand into the sand. Raoul. Oh, God, Raoul. Kayla started to cry.

Jacob turned to her, his green eyes growing wide with surprise. He put his arm around her shoulders. "Hey," he said. "Hey, Kayla, don't cry."

But she had been waiting to cry all day, waiting to surrender to her sadness. She sobbed into Jacob's shoulder, and somehow Jacob's shoulder became Jacob's mouth, hot and searching against her own. His lips, his tongue. They kissed like a couple of hungry teenagers, Kayla's heat rising to the surface of her skin, an aching between her thighs. Jacob reached into the front of Kayla's sundress, and she moaned. A man other than her husband touching her breasts, fingering her, tonguing her nipples. It felt amazing. Was this why people broke the rules, turned the world upside down—because it felt this good, this electric, because it made them feel this alive?

Kayla fumbled with the buttons of Jacob's jeans.

She tore her mouth away from his so that she could
see what she was doing. His erection strained
through his jeans, long and hard and perfect, and
although Kayla wanted him more than she had ever
wanted anything that was bad for her—more than a
cold beer at the end of the day, more than a cigarette
when she was drunk with her girlfriends in a smoky
bar, more than hot, liquid butter on her popcorn—
although she wanted this thing to happen, she
stopped. Rolled away from him.

Raoul. No, thinking about Raoul wasn't good
enough. Her children: Theo, Jennifer, Cassidy B.,
Luke. She thought about her children.

"I can't," she said.

She noticed that he'd torn one of the spaghetti
straps of her sundress, and she fruitlessly tried to
secure it back into place. Jacob stared at her, confused. Then, slowly, he removed his T-shirt.

"I have wanted you for so long," he said. "You
know that, right?"

Kayla nodded, mute with terror over what she'd
set in motion. She thought of him touching her lip
the day before at the Tings'.

"Just let me kiss you again," Jacob said. "I will
die if I don't kiss you one more time."

It flashed through Kayla's mind that Jacob knew
just how to trick her, too. Because who could turn
in the face of those words? Who could resist Jacob,
bare-chested, leaning over her for just one more
kiss? His curly head blocked the moon as he came
toward her. The moon was her only witness. They
started kissing again with even more heat, and Kayla

surrendered. She undid Jacob's jeans and guided him inside her.

As they made love, Kayla's world became nothing more than strokes and skin and lips and tongues. She was nobody's wife, nobody's mother, nobody's friend. Kayla closed her eyes and listened to the water surge and recede, surge and recede. The endless repetition of waves that had carried Antoinette away was now carrying Kayla away.

So this, Kayla thought, this was drowning.

Raoul

He'd always believed that everything one needed to know in life could be learned by building a house. Start with the basics: sturdy foundation, solid walls, a sound roof. Move on to esthetics: light, air, creativity. And finally, make sure the details are done correctly. Raoul's workers cursed at him when he complained about cabinets set off an eighth of an inch over six feet, but Raoul wanted every surface in his houses to be plumb, square, level. That was what made him one of the best. Raoul built houses people could actually live in—breathe in, make love in, dream in. He built houses to last.

Following these same rules, he raised his family. He married the most nurturing woman he had ever met, and they produced four children, two boys, two girls. He and Kayla brought up their kids with love and discipline, with respect for each child's individuality. That was the Montero family: sturdy, solid, plumb, level. Built to last.

Raoul tried to tell Kayla about Theo and Antoinette three times, and three times he failed. The first time was in early July, the very evening Theo confided in him at the Ting site. Raoul raced home from Ting, steaming and incredulous. His son sleeping with a forty-year-old woman. It was perverse, sickening, and he blamed it on Antoinette and her heightened sexual desire. Theo was easy prey for her, Raoul supposed, an easy lay. In some sense, it was a bio-logical match—two people at their sexual peaks. But it was wrong, and even though Theo was eighteen, Raoul was going to put a stop to it. He was going to tell Kayla.

When he got home, he found Kayla in the kitchen hulling strawberries. A platter of hamburger patties rested on the counter next to her. Jennifer sat on a bar stool combing out her long, wet hair, talking to Kayla about how she was saving her baby-sitting money to buy a really expensive pair of shoes from Vanessa Noel. Purple suede sandals, she said, with a three-inch heel.

"They sound pretty exotic," Kayla said. "Can I see them before you buy them?"

Jennifer shrugged. "Sure," she said. "You'll like them. They're tasteful."

Raoul surveyed the kitchen. "Jennifer, can I talk to your mom alone for a second?"

"Why?" Jennifer said.

"Why?" Kayla said. "Is something the matter?"

"Everything's fine," Raoul said, although his voice had a serrated edge. He focused on Kayla's hands, which were stained with pink strawberry juice. "I just need to talk to you alone for a minute."

"We don't really have a minute," Kayla said.

"The kids want to go to the movies tonight at eight, and they need to eat first. I was hoping you could light the grill. Theo should be home any second."

As if on cue, the Jeep pulled into the driveway, and Raoul closed his eyes, listening to the *schluff*ing sound of Theo's flip-flops as he entered the kitchen.

"Hi, people," Theo said jauntily, as if the scene at the Ting house with Raoul had never happened.

"Theo, honey, can you start the grill?" Kayla asked.

"Sure, Mom," he said. He nudged Raoul aside as he retrieved the long matches from the drawer. "Hi, Dad. How was your day?"

Raoul nearly slapped the kid for his boldness. *Go ahead and tell her*, Theo was saying. *I dare you.*

I'll tell her later, Raoul thought. *I'll tell her when we're really alone.*

Later that night, Raoul tried again. The kids went to the movies and Theo offered to go as well so he could drive. Kayla stood at the sliding glass door as they pulled out. "Do you know how lucky you are to have such good kids? You are so lucky. They love you and they love each other." She put her arms around his neck and kissed him. "Lucky, lucky man."

"And they love you," Raoul said.

"And they love me."

"Kayla," Raoul said. "There's something I have to tell you."

"Let's leave the dishes for later," she said. "Do you know how long it's been since we've been alone in this house?" She ran her hands up the inside of his shirt. "You're always working."

"I know," he said. "I'm sorry. But Kayla . . ."

"Make love to me," she said.

He followed her upstairs and they made love sideways on their king-size bed. Raoul thought of Theo and Antoinette engaged in the same act, and he was ashamed at how it excited him. The idea of their lust made him lustful. He made love to Kayla as he hadn't in a long time. It was the best sex he'd had all year, in several years—with their naked bodies sweating, sticking together, pulling apart, sticking together. Kayla cried out as loud as she could without alerting the neighbors through the open windows, and Raoul groaned his pleasure. Sex—that's all this thing with Theo was about. The kid was eighteen, having fun.

When it was over, Raoul collapsed in a heap. His legs were shaking.

"Heavenly," Kayla said. "I love you."

"I love you, too," he said.

Lucky, lucky man. his whole life, people had been telling Raoul that he was lucky. He was the only child of Ignacio and Sabrina Montero, who had money and good connections. They loved Raoul, and they loved each other. Lucky. Raoul graduated from Syracuse University, he spent a year in Breckenridge, Colorado, skiing bumps, and he moved to Nantucket at the start of the building boom. Lucky. He was lucky in small, funny ways, too. He once

bought a scratch ticket at Hatch's on his lunch break
and hit for ten thousand dollars. He always seemed
to have sunny weather when he needed to build outside and gray weather when he needed to sit in his
office doing bills. He always found a parking spot;
he never missed a flight or ferry. He won door prizes
and raffles; he won the Super Bowl pool three years
in a row. The one time he visited New York City,
he sat next to Mick Jagger on the subway and they
talked about *Beggars Banquet* and Mick took Raoul
to a bar and bought him a beer.

He was lucky.

Raoul tried to tell Kayla about Theo and Antoinette
a third time a few weeks later, after Theo started
acting out. Raoul figured the love affair must be running out of steam, frustrating his son. Kayla was so
upset by Theo's foul words, by his staying out late,
that she made an appointment with Dr. Donahue,
who prescribed her sleeping pills. Round pink pills
that looked like candy. Kayla took one each night
before she climbed into bed. She fell asleep before
Raoul turned off the light and slept without stirring
until after Raoul left the house at quarter to six in
the morning.

Dr. Donahue also prescribed dinner out, just the
two of them—and so one night Kayla persuaded
Raoul to leave the site early and they ate at Company
of the Cauldron on India Street. This was Kayla's
favorite restaurant—candlelit, decorated with copper
pots and dried flowers, and graced by a harp player.

Raoul wore his navy blazer, which he hated; it made him feel like some dumb yachtsman. But the food was delicious, and Kayla looked happy again.

Over the appetizer—roasted corn chowder with smoked salmon, poured into their bowls table-side—Raoul said, "You should be careful with those pills."

"They help me sleep."

"Yeah, no kidding."

"I can't deal with Theo like this," Kayla said. She sipped her merlot and lolled her head back. "He's so angry all of a sudden. He hates me. I keep wondering if I've done something, said something, you know, unintentionally. But he won't talk to me."

Raoul stirred his soup. "What's happening with Theo has nothing to do with you, Kayla."

"How do you know?"

"Because I know." Raoul collected himself. Now was the time to tell her. They were alone, Kayla was relaxed. Maybe here among the lilting notes of the harp, the news wouldn't seem so bad.

"What are you staring at me like that for?" Kayla asked. "Do you know something that I don't?"

His path was clear.

Tell her, he thought.

But he was afraid. What if she made a scene?

Besides, Raoul told himself, Theo was an adult.

If Raoul ignored the situation, it would clear up on its own.

He was doing Kayla a favor, really. Sparing her pain.

And he had always been lucky.

"No," he said. "Of course not."

• • •

Regret was too mild a word for what Raoul felt now. He should have told Kayla the truth, that was all there was to it. Never in a million years could Raoul have predicted the turn of events: Antoinette missing, Theo hiding in his room, whimpering with pain, and Kayla somehow caught up in the middle of the whole thing.

As soon as Kayla and Jacob left the house for Great Point, Raoul began to think about sleep. He'd drunk a six-pack of Corona, and then Jacob coaxed him into switching to vodka, and now he actually felt kind of drunk. But Raoul waited until Jennifer and Cass and Luke got home from the Clam Shack before he went to bed. He'd made them walk in the dark because the exercise would do them good, and they liked to do adult things like have dinner by themselves. When they got home, they were bickering and irritable. Cassidy B.'s face was shiny with perspiration and food grease. Luke scratched a mosquito bite on his ankle until it bled.

"You should have reminded us to wear Off!" Luke said. "I got seven more bites."

"You counted?" Raoul said.

"Jennifer didn't eat," Luke said. "She's keeping her share of the money to buy makeup."

"You didn't eat?" Raoul said.

Jennifer swatted Luke on the side of the head. "Brat." She took a rubber band out of her dark hair, releasing her ponytail. Her hair rained down her back and into her face. Such pretty hair, Raoul thought. She would be his next worry, and in the none-too-distant future. "I'm upset about Mom," Jennifer said. "Plus the food at the Clam Shack is so greasy."

"I had a hot dog," Cassidy B. said. "That wasn't greasy."

"Do you know what they put in hot dogs?" Jennifer said. "Ground up pigs' ears. Anyway, you had fries."

"Shut up," Cassidy B. said. She looked at her father. "Where's Mom? Is she home from the police station?"

"She got home from the police station a little while ago," Raoul said. "She went to run an errand." He checked the clock, thought of Kayla out at Great Point again tonight. She must be exhausted, delirious even, and he hoped she didn't do anything stupid. "Okay, so . . . you guys get ready for bed. I'm about to turn in, myself."

"What would you like us to do about washing?" Luke asked.

"Whatever you normally do." Raoul was embarrassed to not sound more authoritative. He hadn't been home to supervise bedtime in months.

"Jennifer showers in the morning," Luke said. "Cassidy and I take baths at night. But not together. We take separate baths. Mom tells us who goes first."

"Who went first last night?" Raoul said.

"Whoever's dirtier goes first," Luke said.

"You can go first tonight, Luke," Cassidy B. said. "I might shower instead."

"It's only nine o'clock, Dad," Jennifer said. "Okay if I watch TV?"

"Saturday night," Luke said. "Mom says TV is okay on Saturday night until ten."

"I know that," Raoul said.

"What's up with Theo?" Jennifer asked. "Is something going on?"

"Is he being punished finally?" Luke asked. "He disobeys Mom all the time and never gets punished."

"Theo isn't being punished," Raoul said, although of course Theo *was* being punished, in the worst kind of way. "He's just tired and he doesn't feel well."

"Was he out drinking?" Jennifer asked.

"No, he wasn't out drinking," Raoul said. "Anyway, it's none of your business." He and Kayla needed to come up with something better than that, but for the time being—well, that was all the information they were going to get. "Jennifer can watch TV and you two work out your baths. As for me, I'm going to bed. Knock on the door if you need me."

Raoul went into his bedroom, stripped to his underwear, and crawled in between the sheets, which smelled of Kayla. He heard the rush of water, the buzz of the TV, and fell asleep.

He woke again an hour later. No Kayla. He kept his eyes open long enough to consider driving up to Great Point after her. He listened to the house; the TV had been shut off. He should at least check on the kids to make sure they'd gone to bed. And Theo, he should check on Theo. But his head ached with the alcohol, and the house was dark and quiet, and Raoul fell back to sleep.

He woke when Kayla crawled into bed. His mouth was dry, his eyes caulked shut with sleep. Where had she gone again? It took a minute to remember. Great Point.

"Did you get the Jeep?" Raoul asked. The sentence was barely intelligible to his own ears.

Kayla was crying. God love her, she'd had a hell of a day. Raoul tried to sit up, but it was like his head had been nailed to the pillow. Were his eyes open? He could just barely make out the figure of Kayla sitting next to him cross-legged on the bed.

"They'll find her," Raoul said. "The police and Jack and all those guys, Kayla, they're doing the best they can."

"Things are so screwed up. Oh, God, my life is over."

"Your life isn't over, Kayla."

Suddenly, Kayla flipped on the light. Raoul shielded his eyes. "Whoa," he said. "I wasn't ready for that. Hold on." He gave himself a second for his eyes to adjust; meanwhile Kayla moved off the bed and paced the carpet between the bed and the door.

"What's wrong, sweetie?"

"You didn't tell me!" she said. She burst into a fresh round of tears. "You knew about Theo and Antoinette, and you kept it from me. And we agreed long ago to operate as a team. Didn't we?"

Raoul tried to focus. At first he fixated on the soft marks Kayla's footprints left in the plush, light green carpet. Ghost footprints. Then he raised his eyes. She was wearing a dress, the same dress she'd had on all day, only now the dress was wrinkled and one strap hung loose. Her hair was tangled. Her nose and eyes were red.

"We did," Raoul said. "Listen, you look tired. Will you please come to bed?"

"You lied to me, Raoul!" She was practically shouting, and Raoul wondered if she would wake the kids. This wasn't like her. "You and Theo and Antoinette and *Val*!"

"Kayla?" he said. "What happened at the police station?"

"Today was a living nightmare," she said. "I can't even begin to explain."

"All right, let's talk about it in the morning," Raoul said. He began to visualize the light switched off, his head hitting the pillow. "Things will be better tomorrow."

"I won't be able to sleep," she said. But she disappeared into the bathroom and Raoul heard water, the toilet flush, Kayla's noisy sobs. He thought he smelled marijuana. When she emerged, she shut off the light. Raoul succumbed to gravity and lay back down.

The phone woke Raoul in the morning. His cell phone, which chirped like a shrill, annoying bird. Raoul's head was throbbing, but he managed to put two feet on the floor and stumble to the chair where he'd left his clothes in a pile. The cell phone was in the pocket of his jeans. Kayla was still fast asleep, so Raoul took the cell phone into the bathroom and shut the door. He lifted the toilet seat and peed.

"Yeah?"

"Raoul, man, it's Carter."

Carter, his tile guy. Who was lagging behind—with the Tings' indoor pool and seven bathrooms, it had been only too easy to fall behind. Carter told Raoul he was going to make up time this weekend, finishing the master baths. God, Raoul hadn't thought about the cathedral in twenty-four hours, some kind of record.

"What's going on?" Raoul asked.

"Man, I just thought you should know . . . something happened here."

"Spit it out, Carter."

"The place has been wasted, man. I mean, mostly just the living area? But it's ugly. Looks like someone took an axe to the walls. The walls are history."

Raoul flushed and sat down on the toilet seat. His brain ached. "Vandals?"

"I guess," Carter said. "I mean, yeah, vandals. Shit, yeah. You'd better get out here, Raoul. You're going to want to see this for yourself."

"I'll get there as soon as I can, which might not be for an hour or two. I have family obligations." Raoul thought of Theo. Theo, Theo, Theo. Theo hacking away at Ting. "I have to go, Carter," Raoul said. He punched off the phone and threw it at the side of the bathtub with all his strength so that it busted into several pieces. Damn that kid! Raoul pulled on a pair of jeans and a shirt and walked down the hall to Theo's bedroom. As much as Raoul wanted to rip Theo apart limb by limb, he stopped, took a deep breath. *It's only a house. One hell of a house, but still only a house.*

Raoul knocked. "Theo?"

There was no answer. He could be dead, Raoul thought. Or he could have slipped out in the night. Raoul knocked louder. "Open the door, Theo." His voice was controlled fury. He couldn't imagine any of his children defying this voice. Raoul listened. Just as he was about to try the knob, he heard a rustling, and a few seconds later, the door opened.

Theo's was the face of heartbreak. His eyes were swollen, he had gray streaks on his face from tears. His hair was a mess, he wore an old bathing suit and a wrinkled NANTUCKET BASEBALL T-shirt. Theo's shoulders started to shake.

Raoul took his son in his arms. His child, who had chosen Raoul to confide in, and what had Raoul done with that confidence? He'd ignored it. Raoul could have stopped this whole thing from happening. If he'd said the right thing, if he'd dealt with it head-on. But no—every morning, off to build the cathedral. No wonder Theo had hacked away at it. That house had stolen away his father, when his father had been his only hope.

"You vandalized the Tings' house?" Raoul said. "You vandalized my project?"

Theo clung tighter to Raoul. "I'm sorry, Dad."

"Yeah," Raoul said. "Me, too, Theo. I'm sorry, too."

• • •

For his family's sake, Raoul gave the morning his best shot, although the situation at the Tings' nagged at him like a crying baby. He was going to have to tend to it sooner rather than later. Raoul insisted that Theo shower, and then he checked on the other kids. Jennifer was still asleep, Cassidy B. and Luke were playing Connect Four in Luke's room. Raoul stuck his head in. God, he'd had that game when he was a kid.

"Come down to the kitchen," he said. "I'm making waffles."

He stood outside the door to his own bedroom, listening. Then he walked in. Kayla was making the bed. Raoul watched her smooth the sheets, tuck them under the mattress. She plumped the pillows, set them in place, and then turned, saw him, and sat on the bed.

"How are you doing, sweetie?" he said. "Do you feel any better?"

Her eyes were droopy, and she had marks embedded on her face from the pillow. She didn't answer.

"Can you tell me what happened at the police station?" he said.

"I don't want to talk about it right now."

"Okay," Raoul said. He hated to admit it, but he was grateful. He wanted to get breakfast on the table and then leave for work as soon as he could. He didn't have the heart to mention the vandalism to

Kayla. "I'll be downstairs making waffles," he said. "Is there bacon?"

She stared at him blankly. "Yes," she said. "There's bacon."

He leaned over to kiss her and again noticed the smell of marijuana. "Good." Before he left their bedroom, he said, "Did you smoke last night?"

"No," she said quickly, in a way that let him know she was lying. She fell back on the bed. "Yes. I did. With Jacob. We smoked a joint on the way to Great Point."

"Oh," he said. "Well, you might want to shower. I smell it on you."

Raoul went downstairs and set about making breakfast. Flour, milk, a couple of eggs in a bowl. Dust off the waffle iron, plug it in, and let it get nice and hot. Cass and Luke took out the dishes and silverware, and the butter, syrup, and orange juice from the fridge. They set the table as quietly as professional waiters. Raoul felt funny, bothered, and he realized he was angry that Kayla and Jacob had smoked a joint. Why the hell had Kayla done that? And why had Jacob offered it to her? He knew Raoul hated the stuff. Of course under the circumstances, he supposed a little adolescent behavior wasn't unreasonable. Still, it bugged him.

"Are you excited about starting school on Tuesday?" Raoul asked Luke.

"No."

"How about you, Cass? Are you excited about school?" He had to stop and remember what grades they were going into. Kayla chastised him every time he got it wrong. "Junior high? That's going to be a big change."

"Change is excruciating," Cassidy B. said.

Raoul laughed. He mixed up the batter, turned a few strips of bacon. "Well, I guess you're right. Change can be excruciating. And junior high in particular can be excruciating. But not for you. You're a survivor. We're all survivors, aren't we?" Raoul heard the water shut off upstairs—Theo out of the shower. If Kayla were smart, she would shower next, before the kids smelled the smoke on her. Or in case she had to go back down to the police station. Raoul poured batter onto the hot waffle iron and lowered the lid. The iron hissed and batter leaked out the sides. Raoul turned down the heat on the bacon and walked to the bottom of the stairs. "Breakfast in five minutes for anyone who wants it!" he said.

A noise came from his bedroom. His cell phone again. Kayla appeared holding the phone, which she must have put back together. She descended the stairs slowly, like a beautiful ghost, an unfamiliar expression on her face, and she handed the phone to Raoul.

"I don't want to talk to anybody right now," he said.

She shrugged and slipped the ringing phone into the pocket of her robe.

"Dad," Luke called from the kitchen. "The waffles."

"Coming," Raoul said. He pulled out the first-batch of waffles, burning two fingers, and drained the bacon on paper towels. The phone kept ringing. Raoul turned to see Cassidy B. hugging Kayla as if her mother had returned from some faraway country after a long absence.

"Give me the phone," Raoul said. "And here, these waffles are done. Luke, here you go." Raoul took the phone from Kayla and walked into the living room, where he could have some quiet.

"Yeah."

"Raoul? It's Micky."

Micky Glenn, his foreman. "Micky. Listen, I know what happened. I'll be out there as soon as I can. I have a situation here with my family."

"You've seen the paper?"

"What paper?"

"The *Cape Cod Times*. About the missing woman? Kayla's name is in it, and yours. And Ting's. It sounds pretty incriminating, Raoul."

"Oh, Christ."

"Do you want me to read it to you?"

"No, we have delivery. I'll read it myself."

"Okay, whatever. You'll be here soon?"

"Soon as I can."

Raoul flew out the front door. It was hot already, and the air smelled of grass and dirt and the nearby ocean. Raoul walked barefoot through the front yard to the end of the driveway where the fat Sunday edition of the *Cape Cod Times* lay in a plastic bag. Raoul looked around at his neighbors' houses— quiet. Raoul slid the newspaper out of its plastic and scanned the front page. At the bottom in the right-hand corner was the headline: WOMAN MISSING OFF NANTUCKET'S GREAT POINT. Raoul moved slowly up the driveway, reading.

NANTUCKET, MASS.-

A woman disappeared off the coast of Nantucket Island early Saturday morning, Nantucket police officials said. Antoinette Riley, 44, longtime island resident, was swimming with two friends: island attorney Valerie Gluckstern and Kayla Montero, wife of construction baron Raoul Montero, builder of the Ting home in Monomoy. Mrs. Montero alerted police at 1:40 A.M. that Riley was missing. She told police that Riley danced into the water after consuming a significant amount of alcohol, and was apparently swept away by the riptide.

Detective Dean Simpson of the Nantucket Police Department said no body had been found, although the coast guard and Nantucket Fire Department had dispatched search parties based on information given to officials by Montero.

"We haven't ruled out the existence of foul play," Detective Simpson said. "These women call themselves the 'Night Swimmers' and they've been practicing dangerous and unorthodox rituals for years—skinny-dipping in tricky waters, drinking champagne. Suspicious circumstances surround Ms. Riley's disappearance, although we haven't brought formal charges against Mrs. Montero or anyone else yet."

The detective went on to say that according to the coast guard's mathematical formulas, had Riley swum with her full strength, her body would most likely have been recovered. Thus officials feared she was hurt or poisoned before entering the water.

"There is an extensive and complicated past be-

tween these three women," Detective Simpson said.
"And especially between Mrs. Montero and the
missing woman. Some questionable factors have
come to our attention, and we feel Ms. Riley's disappearance requires further investigating."

Citizens with information about the disappearance should contact the Nantucket Police Department.

Raoul threw the paper into the front seat of his
truck. He had to keep the article out of Kayla's
hands for as long as he could. He wondered what
exactly had happened at the police station. It
sounded like they were trying to pin this on Kayla,
and Val, too, though Raoul couldn't imagine Val
tolerating that. He would have to get the whole story
later. As soon as he made his excuses inside, he was
off to the Tings'.

Somehow Kayla had finished making both the waffles and the bacon, and three out of four kids were
sitting at the table eating. Jennifer had joined Luke
and Cass; she was chewing a dry waffle one square
at a time. Kayla, who was always so concerned
about Jennifer's eating habits, didn't even seem to
notice. She sat at the breakfast bar, watching the kids
eat, but it was obvious to Raoul that her mind was
somewhere else.

"Where's Theo?" Raoul said.

"Upstairs in his room," Luke reported. "He said
he's not hungry."

"What's going on, Dad?" Jennifer said. "Did they find Aunt Antoinette?"

"No," Raoul said.

The phone rang. Jennifer stood to answer it.

"Don't you dare," Raoul said. "This morning nobody answers the phone. Not even Mommy."

"What if it's Amy?" Jennifer said. "We're supposed to go to the beach today."

"If it's Amy, she can leave a message and you can call her back," Raoul said. He looked at Kayla. "Okay, Kayla? Don't deal with anybody until I get back."

"Get back from where?"

"I have to go to Monomoy."

"For God's sake, Raoul . . ."

"This isn't optional. I have to go check on a problem that's come up, and after I've dealt with it, I'll come home. Okay? In an hour or two?"

Kayla said nothing, though Raoul could tell she was pissed. Her day was only going to get worse, but she didn't have to know that yet.

"Home soon," he said, grabbing his truck keys. "Don't answer the phone."

Raoul was hungry, starving, and he wished he'd eaten one of those waffles. He pulled up in front of Island Bakery. He'd get a couple of doughnuts and a cup of good coffee.

Tanner Whitcomb, owner of the bakery, saw Raoul as soon as he walked in. Tanner was Raoul's age, skinny, a former cocaine user who was still constantly nervous and antsy. He wore a Red Sox hat and a long white apron smeared with lipstick-pink icing. Raoul had remodeled the bakery for Tanner fifteen years earlier during the height of Tanner's drug habit; it was one of Raoul's first big jobs, and so he didn't mind when Tanner was late paying him. Behind the counters were built-in baker's racks. Raoul had sanded each shelf of those racks by hand while Tanner and his buddies hung out in the back, sniffing lines off of cookie sheets.

Raoul smiled. "Tanner."

Tanner looked past Raoul out the door. "Is the murder suspect out there in your truck?"

Raoul paused. Tanner's voice was good-natured, playful—so maybe that was how folks on the island would treat this, as a joke. A silly assumption made by the overzealous police, who had nothing to do in the summertime but write parking tickets and break up high school beer parties.

"No, she's at home," Raoul said. "Sharpening knives." He gazed down into the glass cases. There was a whole section of doughnuts iced with the garish pink. "Three bear claws," he told the flame-haired Irish girl behind the register. "Three of those cream horn things, and a chocolate éclair." He turned back to Tanner, who gawked at him.

"I was kidding, Tanner," Raoul said.

Tanner stuffed his hands in the large front pocket of his apron. "I don't know, Raoul," he said. "It sounds like Kayla got herself in a heap of trouble with the law."

Raoul paid the girl, dropped his change and an extra dollar into the tip jar, and took his bag. Then he squeezed Tanner's arm hard enough to show him that it would be easy to break.

"You, my friend, shouldn't pass judgment on anyone," Raoul whispered. He let go of Tanner's arm and strode out to the truck. He pulled away as quickly as he could, and then he realized that he'd spaced the coffee.

At the Ting house, there were three trucks in the driveway: Micky's Durango, Carter's sorry-looking Toyota pickup, and Jacob's Bronco. Technically, his crew had the day off. Holiday weekend. Carter had tiling to do, and Micky was there to check out the vandalism, but Jacob? Why was Jacob around? The person they needed was Colin Freed, the plaster guy. Not Jacob.

As Raoul walked into the house, he stuffed a cream horn into his mouth. "Hello!" he cried out with a mouthful of icing. "Micky?"

"In here." Micky, Carter, and Jacob stood in the living room gaping at the damage. The walls of the living room were gouged open so that the joists were exposed. The drywall lay in ragged sheets and crumbling piles. It would all have to be torn out and redone.

"What I can't figure out," Micky said, "is why anyone would want to do this. Do you think it was somebody from another crew?"

Raoul looked at Jacob. The night before as they drank the vodka, Raoul had sworn Jacob to secrecy about Theo and Antoinette. He wondered if Jacob suspected this vandalism was Theo's. Raoul felt guilt clog his throat. He needed something to drink. "Listen, guys. I know who did it."

Carter sucked in his breath. He looked like such a goof, wearing his safety goggles over his glasses. Raoul tried to remember why he had ever hired Carter in the first place. His work was good, but he was very slow. "Who?" Carter said.

"Theo," Raoul said. "My son."

"Well, shit," Micky said. "In that case, I wish I hadn't called the police."

"You called the police?" Suddenly it felt like Raoul had eaten a pastry filled with cement. "Does anybody have any water? Or coffee?"

Jacob held out a Coke. "Here."

"Thanks," Raoul said. He swilled some down. "I can't believe you called the police. Why the fuck did you do that? You should have waited until I got here."

"I think a better question is, Why did Theo knock the walls in?" Micky said.

Again, Raoul looked at Jacob. Jacob had his arms crossed in front of him and was staring at the floor. "Have you called Colin?" Raoul asked. "He's going to have to come in and fix it."

"Colin?" Micky said. His freckled face reddened. "You'll excuse me for saying so, Raoul, but you should be the one to fix the walls. You or Theo, but I'd say you, since you're the one who knows how."

Raoul glared at Micky. The guy was Irish, and Catholic, and he went to Mass every Wednesday before work. He had a conscience, and that was why Raoul made him foreman so many years ago. Now

Raoul wanted to punch him. Except that he was right.

"Fine," Raoul said. "I'll fix the walls myself. But it's not going to happen today, and it's not going to happen tomorrow. I have to get home to my family. So, Micky, you take a couple of days off, and Carter, you get your ass in gear and don't leave until bathroom number three is finished. Do you hear me? Finished!" Raoul's anger was mounting—the vandalism, the newspaper article, Micky—and his head hurt. Suddenly, Raoul was left alone in the room with Jacob. Jacob, who thought it was okay to get high with Kayla.

"Come out to the truck with me," Raoul said. "I want to talk to you."

"I want to talk to you, too," Jacob said. "That's why I showed up today."

Raoul got a bad vibe from the sound of Jacob's voice. "You go first, then. What's going on?"

"I have something difficult to tell you, man. I don't even know how to say it."

They moved outside into the sun. Raoul's head felt like it was splintering apart. "Can you just break it to me gently, please?" Raoul said. "I've had one hell of a weekend."

"I know. I really don't want to add to your worries, Raoul, but I've got to tell you this one thing."

"Tell me."

Jacob took a deep breath. "I quit."

"I'm sorry?"

"I'm moving away, actually. I decided last night."

Raoul grabbed his truck bed to steady himself. "How long have you worked for me?"

"Eight years."

"Eight years, and you're the best finish guy I have, and now you're telling me you decided in one night that you're quitting and moving away."

"That's right," Jacob said. "Sorry, man."

"Why?" Raoul said. "Are you going somewhere with Val?"

"No." Jacob turned his baseball cap forward, then backwards again. He looked up into the sky. "Actually, we broke up."

"You broke up?"

"Yeah," Jacob said. "Last night."

"So you're moving away because you broke up with Val?"

"Not exactly," Jacob said. "I'm not going to explain the whole thing to you, Raoul. And believe me, you don't want to know. But basically, now that she's left her husband she wants me to marry her, and I can't. I don't want to. It's time for me to get out of Dodge. Trust me."

"I was going to yell at you for smoking a joint with my wife, but I don't think I'll bother," Raoul said. "It sounds like you had more on your plate last night than you needed."

"Right."

"So. So you're moving away. Where will you go?"

"I'm not sure. Maybe to live with my brother. He works on a good crew."

"In Arizona?"

"Uh-huh."

"And you're sure about this? You're really fucking sure?"

"Yep."

Raoul glanced into his truck and saw a bottle of Advil on the floor of the passenger side. "Give me your Coke," he said to Jacob. He downed three Advils and finished the rest of the soda, wondering how long it would be until he felt better. "Okay, come see me in the office on Tuesday, then. To get your check. We'll have to figure out what you want to do with your retirement account."

"Can you just send me that stuff in the mail?" Jacob asked. "I want to leave today."

"Today?" Raoul was overwhelmed. Nothing was working the way it was supposed to. But before he could figure out what was going on, really, with Jacob, a car screeched into the dirt driveway. It was a BMW. Val. Raoul moved for the driver's side of his truck. The last thing he wanted was to get in the middle of some crazed, jilted-lover scene between Jacob and Val. He needed to get home.

Raoul waved to Val and then climbed into his truck. "Come see me Tuesday," he said to Jacob. Raoul started the engine, but Val pulled right up to his front bumper, blocking his way. He cursed at her under his breath. Now he was stuck.

Val got out of the car and marched to Raoul's window. When she lifted her sunglasses, Raoul saw that her eyes were puffy and red. She had the hiccuppy breathing of someone who'd been crying for a long time.

"Did he tell you?" she said.

"Yeah," Raoul said. "He did. I'm sorry."

"You're sorry?" she said. "You're *sorry?*" She glared at Jacob, who just stood there, balanced on the balls of his feet like he was ready to dart away. "Frankly, I'm surprised you didn't beat him bloody."

"It's really none of my business," Raoul said. "I'd rather not get involved."

"None of your business?" Val said. "He slept with your wife, and it's none of your business?"

At that moment, Jacob dashed for his Bronco. He drove into the brush to get around the BMW. In a matter of seconds, before Raoul could process the words he'd just heard, Jacob was gone.

"Coward," Val said. "So I guess he didn't tell you."

Raoul opened his mouth, but the sounds he made weren't words.

"They slept together, Raoul," Val said. "Last night, at Great Point. When Jacob came home, I smelled her on him. And he admitted it. He flat out said he'd had sex with Kayla."

"He was lying to you," Raoul said. "He was lying to get out of the relationship. Because you scared him, Val. You fucking scared him."

"I smelled her on him, Raoul," Val said. "She's my best friend. She wears Coco Chanel, and that was what Jacob *reeked of* when he got home last night."

"Get out of here," Raoul said. "Get your car out of my way."

Val started to cry again. "We were just trying to protect her. I can't believe she'd do this when we were only trying to protect her from the truth."

"Val!" Raoul shouted. "Aw, fuck it." Raoul started the truck and he, too, drove into the brush to get around the BMW. Once he was on the road, he felt better. But God, what to do with this news, where to go? Jacob having sex with Kayla, his wife? The mother of his children? Of course it was a lie, a hysterical, dramatic accusation dreamed up by that lunatic woman. As Raoul drove toward home, he tried to remember what Kayla had been like the night before. Crying, insisting that her life was over, the strap of her dress torn, the distinctive scent of marijuana. And Jacob, quitting, leaving the island today without even his last paycheck, running like a fugitive from the law.

Raoul screeched into the driveway. When he stormed into the kitchen he found Kayla, showered and dressed and smelling of perfume, cleaning up the breakfast dishes.

"Where are the kids?" he said.

"Theo's still in his room. Jennifer's getting ready to go to the beach. Cass and Luke are outside. The phone has been ringing like crazy."

Raoul watched Kayla rinse the last sticky plate and put it in the dishwasher. She pulled off her rubber gloves. Raoul was trembling.

"We're going for a ride," he said.

She turned and looked at him. Saw his face and knew. Knew that he knew, after nineteen years of marriage, and without a word. It was true.

Raoul took the keys to the Trooper and the Jeep—he didn't want Theo going anywhere—and he led

Kayla out to the truck, tears blurring his eyes. *Jacob inside his wife.* It disgusted him. Kayla had let Jacob touch her. Raoul couldn't believe it. Not Kayla. They had been married nineteen years, some years better than others, but never once had Raoul questioned Kayla's fidelity. It had always been the other way around. Kayla was sensitive about Raoul and other women; she had some loony idea that Raoul was one of these contractors who seduced his female clients. But Raoul had played it straight his entire marriage. There was one woman in 'Sconset, Pamela Ely, who pursued him, maybe. She used to lie on her deck in a bikini, straps untied, while Raoul and his crew worked around her. When Raoul was nearby, she would lift her head and her shoulders so that he would see her bare breasts; she did this all the time, and Raoul's crew couldn't stop talking about it. *She wants you, man, that woman wants you.* One night, Pamela kept Raoul hanging around after his crew went home, saying she needed an estimate on one more project—in her bedroom. She gave Raoul a cold Beck's and preceded him up the stairs with her bikini bottoms riding up her cheeks. He'd had every opportunity to screw her. It was just the two of them in the bedroom looking at a hole in the plaster (her ex-husband had punched the wall, she said). But what did Raoul do? He gave her a fair estimate for the plasterwork; then he guzzled the rest of his beer and left the house immediately. Because as appealing as Pam Ely might have been, what was more appealing was what waited for him at home: a strong marriage, good kids. The real thing.

Kayla was silent as they drove. Raoul took dirt roads until they popped out onto a deserted section of beach between Nobadeer and Madequecham. Raoul didn't know if Kayla would remember, but this was where they used to make love the summer they started dating. Raoul had met Kayla at the Chicken Box. She was very thin back then, and she wore pedal pushers without any underwear. She had Farrah Fawcett hair, she listened to Earth, Wind & Fire. Their first date was a picnic of American cheese sandwiches and Fritos that she brought to him on the job site. She liked it when Raoul tossed tiny pieces of bread to the seagulls. During those first few weeks Raoul didn't call her often and occasionally, when he told her he would meet her out at a bar, he stayed home instead. But then the unexplainable happened. She cut the legs out from under him, and he fell. In love with Kayla. He brought her to this very beach and peeled off her pedal pushers and made love to her on a skimpy towel that was no match for the two of them. They jumped into the waves afterward and washed sand out of the uncomfortable places.

It sounded idyllic, too good to be true, and that was how Raoul remembered it. The summer ended, Kayla decided to stay, and they moved in together for the winter. They lived in an old, rickety cottage out in 'Sconset where the only source of heat was the fireplace. Kayla chopped wood every afternoon, and they ate, slept, made love, and watched TV in front of the fireplace. Occasionally they ventured into town, once to the Gaslight Theatre to see

Stripes, and it was so cold in the theater that they could see their breath every time they laughed. Kayla bought three rounds of hot toddies, and by the time the film was over they were silly drunk. To this day, it was the funniest movie Raoul had ever seen. Living with Kayla that winter had been living with love day in and day out; it was that simple, that clear cut. When the first daffodils bloomed in the 'Sconset Rotary on the second of April, Raoul asked her to marry him.

Then things moved quickly—a June wedding and Theo born ten months later. Reality, yes, they'd had nothing but reality since then: diapers, mortgage, incorporation, school conferences, chicken pox, big jobs falling through, big jobs not falling through. And then this weekend.

Raoul shut off the engine. "I'm going to ask you a question, and I need the truth. I need to hear the truth from your mouth. Did you—?" Raoul wasn't sure he'd be able to speak the words. "Did you have sex with Jacob last night?"

"I need to explain—"

"No," Raoul said. "No. I don't want you to explain. I want an answer. Yes or no. Did you sleep with Jacob?"

Silence.

Raoul was angry enough to hit her, but instead he slammed his hands against the steering wheel, inadvertently hitting the horn, which sent a flurry of seagulls into the air around them. "Yes or no?"

"Yes."

Raoul extracted his keys from the ignition and

tucked them into his jeans pocket. He climbed out of the car, removed his shoes, and sprinted down the beach in his bare feet. He ran as fast as he could, keeping just above the shoreline. He ran over stones and shards of clam shell, he pumped his arms and forced himself to go even faster. When he started to tire, he slowed to a jog, but he kept going. He wanted to go as far as he could; he wanted to be miles away. And then, when he was completely exhausted, he stopped. He was alone on a stretch of beach on his island; the truck was just a red dot in the distance. It was hot, and Raoul was thirsty. His headache was back. He wanted to have a life like Jacob's that he could run away from, that he could leave with only a day's notice. But for Raoul, there was too much at stake: his kids, his house, his company, his work. Raoul trudged through the sand toward his truck. And his wife.

To his surprise, she wasn't crying. She was sitting in the truck bed with her head propped up against the cab, eyes closed. She looked peaceful, although Raoul doubted she was actually asleep. He fought off the urge to slap her. He grabbed her arm.

She started, banged her head. When she saw him, her eyes filled. "How did you find out?"

Raoul watched the waves pummel the shore. He was parched. "Val told me."

"Val?"

"Jacob told her last night, I guess, and she came to the job site this morning and informed me."

"So Val knows."

"Yes. Are you going to explain what happened?"

And so, Kayla told him the story. About John Gluckstern and Antoinette's daughter, Lindsey. About Val turning the tables to get herself out of trouble, giving the police Kayla's pills. About how Kayla confronted Val at her house and yes, Val admitted to steering the police in Kayla's direction because Kayla was a housewife and therefore it didn't matter if Kayla took the blame.

"I was so furious with her last night, Raoul, I could have killed her. And you. Because you knew about Theo and Antoinette. You knew and you kept it from me. I was so mad, and Jacob was just there. He was revenge on two fronts. But I regretted it as soon as it happened." Kayla's eyes without makeup looked very small and sad. "I'm sorry."

"This isn't something you can apologize for. You let Jacob fuck you." The words were so offensive, Raoul had to lower his head and suck in some air. He needed water. "You broke your marriage vows."

"Huh!" she said. "As if you haven't broken them yourself."

"I haven't," he said. "And believe me, there is *nothing* I would like better than to tell you right now that I *did* screw Pam Ely, but I didn't. Because I am a married man. I believe in marriage, Kayla. At least I did until right now."

She sat with that awhile. He could see every nuance that crossed her face. *You didn't sleep with Pamela Ely?* Suspicion, then relief, even happiness. Then guilt, her defenses resurfacing. "You lied to me, Raoul. You lied about Theo."

He remembered sitting across from her at Company of the Cauldron, sweating with the secret. It was an instance when he understood his two choices and he chose the easy solution over the right one. "I was trying to protect you."

"Well, look where we are now. Theo had an affair with Antoinette and got her pregnant. He ransacked her house. Antoinette might be dead and somehow *I* am a murder suspect. Do you think *that* upsets me?"

"No one will believe it, Kayla."

"Everyone will believe it!" she said. "I heard the messages people were leaving on the machine at home. I know there was an article in the paper."

"The police have no evidence."

"They have all they need: the pills, the champagne glasses, the belated phone calls. I should have called 911 right away."

"I told you that," Raoul said. "And there's something else you should know. Theo destroyed the living room of the Tings' house with an axe."

"There was an axe in the Jeep," Kayla said.

They were both quiet for a while, watching the violent waves.

"Where *is* Antoinette?" Raoul said.

"I wish I knew," Kayla said. Her voice softened. "She was carrying our *grandchild*, Raoul."

Raoul stared at the beach. He could picture the freckles across Kayla's nose that first summer, the white straps of her bikini crossing her back in an *X*. Suddenly, his stomach didn't feel so good.

"I can't deal with this thing about Jacob," Raoul said. "Maybe I'm being macho, maybe I'm being overly sensitive, but I can't have Jacob hanging around in our marriage. The idea of Jacob, I mean. I'm thinking . . . about separation." Raoul couldn't bring himself to say the word *divorce*. Divorce, as far as Raoul understood it, was something that happened to other people—people who thought it was okay to give up, walk out, try their luck elsewhere. It didn't happen to Raoul and Kayla.

"How can I blame you?" Kayla said. She buried her face in her hands. "I ruined everything." She sniffled. "These last two days have been awful. And now I've contributed to the mess. I wanted to contribute! I wanted to be as bad, as lawless, as everybody else."

"You succeeded," he said. "I'm going to need some time and space to think about this, Kayla. Time alone."

"So you want me to move out?" Kayla said.

"No," Raoul said. "Yes. Maybe. A vacation, maybe. You could go on vacation."

"I don't deserve a vacation," Kayla said. "You should go on vacation."

"I have work," Raoul said.

"I don't want to go on vacation," Kayla said.

"We don't have to decide right now," Raoul said. "Let's just go home." He had to believe that dealing with this would be easier under his roof, within the walls that he himself had constructed. "Let's go home and help our son."

At home, Kayla went upstairs to check on Theo. Raoul poured himself a tall glass of water and found Luke and Cassidy in the living room, parked in front of the TV. A show about hot-air ballooning.

"Where's Jennifer?" Raoul asked.

"Beach," Luke said.

"Did anyone call?" Raoul asked.

"The phone rang," Cassidy B. said. "But we didn't answer."

"Thank you. You two can go outside and play."

"Do we have to?" Luke said.

"Yes."

Reluctantly, they picked themselves up off the floor. Raoul shut off the TV.

Kayla yelled down from upstairs. "Kids, where's Theo?"

Luke and Cassidy B. were quiet. Luke scratched a mosquito bite. Raoul checked the driveway—all the cars were there.

"Tell us where he went," Raoul said.

Luke stared at his father, cold and calm. "He went to the police station."

"The police station?"

"He called them," Cassidy B. said. "They came and picked him up."

"He called *them*?" Raoul said. "You're sure about that?"

Cassidy B. put her index finger to the corner of her mouth as though she had to scan the far reaches of her memory. "He called to see if they'd found Aunt Antoinette. And when they said no, he asked if they could come get him. He said he had things to tell."

"They came in a squad car," Luke said. "We saw. But no lights."

Kayla descended the stairs, looking pale. "You two go outside," she said. "I'll be out in a minute to throw the Frisbee."

"I'm sick of Frisbee," Luke said. But he and Cassidy obediently tied their sneakers and left the house through the sliding glass door.

"I'll get Theo," Raoul said. "I'll find out what's going on."

"Thank you," Kayla said. "I can't deal with that detective again."

Raoul's cell phone rang. The phone was there on the coffee table where he'd left it. He and Kayla stared at it.

"Leave it be," Raoul said. "I'm going."

At first, the police officer who sat behind the glass at the front desk wouldn't tell Raoul whether Theo was there.

"Listen, I'm his father. I don't know how much more plainly I can put it to you. Do you want me to bribe you?" Raoul slid some money underneath the glass. "Here, take this. It's all yours if I can see my son."

The officer eyed the money disdainfully. He stopped filling out his piddly, unimportant form, smoothed the front of his blue uniform shirt, and disappeared into the back.

Raoul took a deep breath, looked around. The place was a dungeon. They should remodel. Put in some windows.

A door clanked open, and Paul Henry stuck his

head into the waiting room. "Raoul?" he said. "Follow me."

Raoul trailed Paul Henry down the hall. It smelled medicinal, like Ben Gay. Or maybe that smell was coming from Paul Henry. Raoul wished he hadn't drunk so much the night before. He wished he'd never hired Jacob Anderson. The thought of Jacob made Raoul's stomach swoop. *Jacob inside his wife. Theo,* he thought, *what have you done?*

Behind a door marked PRIVATE, Theo sat at a long table, wiping his eyes with balled-up tissues. When he saw Raoul, he cried harder. It embarrassed Raoul to watch Theo cry in front of the other men. *Buck up*, Raoul wanted to say. *Be strong.* Except that wasn't how he and Kayla had raised Theo at all; they'd raised him to express his emotions honestly. Raoul put his hands on Theo's shoulders.

"It's okay, buddy," he said. "It's okay."

"This is all my fault," Theo said.

The detective sat across from Theo, writing on a yellow legal pad. He raised his head, pushed his glasses up his nose. The guy who had yelled at Raoul for kicking dirt around in Antoinette's driveway. The guy who had bullied Kayla. There wasn't an ounce of emotion in the guy's face. But that wasn't exactly true—the detective looked interested. This was just one hell of an interesting day at work for him. Raoul narrowed his eyes.

"What's going on?"

The detective leaned back in his chair, scratched his head with a pencil. "Theo, here, was explaining a few things."

"Such as?"

"He admitted to ransacking Ms. Riley's cottage. He admitted to vandalizing a work site out in Monomoy with a hatchet." The detective paused. "You know about that? It's your work site."

Raoul nodded.

"Yes," the detective said. "One of your crew called to report it. Theo also told us that Ms. Riley was in fact pregnant and that she had an appointment to get an abortion on . . . Tuesday, right, Theo? This coming Tuesday?"

Theo put his hands over his face. He broke into high-pitched, breathless sobs and for a minute, the men listened to the sound of Theo's crying. Raoul closed his eyes, tightened his grip on Theo's shoulders.

The detective cleared his throat. "Theo told us that he was against Ms. Riley getting an abortion, and he thinks she may have disappeared on purpose—to carry out her plans without any interference from him."

"She wanted to get away from me," Theo said. "Because she knew I would do anything to keep her from killing our baby." Theo looked at Raoul, and Raoul remembered him vividly as a little boy. Tough, funny, afraid of nothing. When he was only a year old, he used to sit inside his toy box and row it like a dinghy. When he was learning to talk, he repeated words again and again, and one week he said nothing but "backhoe loader." As the oldest, Theo had taught Raoul everything he knew about being a parent. He broke all the new ground. Even now.

"Theo wants us to place him under arrest," Paul Henry said quietly. "He feels he needs to be punished."

"I wish I were dead," Theo said.

Raoul squeezed Theo's shoulders. Nausea overcame him, an urgent sense of personal shame. He was going to vomit. "Is he arrested?"

"No," Paul Henry said. "In fact, I think you should take him home right now. We'll deal with the vandalism charges later."

Theo started crying again. "They're not even going to look for her, Dad. They're not even going to try."

"We're looking for her, son," Paul Henry said.

"The divers are going back out this afternoon," the detective said.

Theo shot up. "She's not in the water!" he said. "I know she's not. She's not dead and my baby *is not dead*!"

Raoul backed away; the other two men were quiet. Raoul studied the detective's face. It was strained, and Raoul realized that the guy was trying to suppress a smile.

"You think this is funny?" Raoul said. "You're looking at an eighteen-year-old kid crying over a woman who's pregnant with his child and that *amuses* you?"

The detective let out a giggle, and the giggle turned into a laugh.

Paul Henry tried, but he could not contain Raoul.

No, not Raoul who had woken up that morning to find that his wife had cheated on him, his son had vandalized his workplace, and the whole island thought his wife was a murderer. Raoul jumped over the table, and before he could think better of it he had the detective jacked up against the wall, his glasses half-cocked, his face blanching. Raoul held him there a minute—this was the time to say something meaningful—but Raoul had nothing to say. Raoul hit the detective as hard as he could. It was an odd, sick feeling, connecting with another human being in that way. The detective's face gave like a piece of overripe fruit. It caved in, smashed, smooshed, soft and wet. There was blood everywhere, but before Raoul could truly appreciate the damage, and before he could pull his arm back to hit the motherfucker again, there were other officers in the room, and Raoul was facedown on the table, hands pinned behind him. There was a lot of shouting, and the cold steel of handcuffs pinching his wrists.

Raoul raised his head. Theo was standing against the wall watching the men shackle Raoul. But he wasn't crying. He was shaking his head in disbelief, admiration even, and Raoul smiled at him. A real smile. Raoul was crazy—this wasn't a good example for his son at all, this wasn't the way he'd brought his children up to act. But hitting the detective had felt honest, and Raoul smiled.

Theo smiled back. *Thank you*, he mouthed. *Thank you.*

They put Raoul in the holding cell and let him sit there for hours, or so it seemed. Raoul vomited—finally, gratefully—into the toilet. The blasted cream horn. He lay down on the cot and drifted in and out of consciousness. In his mind he hit the detective over and over again. He wondered what would happen to him. Would he have to go to court? Probably. The prick detective would press charges; Raoul's name would be smeared across the police blotter of the *Inquirer and Mirror* on Thursday. This was a downward spiral, worse following bad. How would it end?

The sound of Kayla's voice roused Raoul from his dream-sleep.

"Raoul?"

Raoul lifted his head from the dirty mattress, which had probably absorbed the bodily fluids of dozens of drunks. Kayla stood on the other side of the bars, her blond hair glowing in the faint light of the hallway. "Come on," she said. "We're going."

Raoul signed papers at the reception desk, papers diligently typed by the officer behind the glass barrier. Kayla had paid $105 to spring Raoul from the cell; he had a court date in six weeks. He needed a lawyer.

Before they left the police station, the detective appeared on the other side of the glass. His nose was mottled and misshapen; he had half a black eye. He pointed at Raoul, and when he spoke, it sounded like he had a bad cold.

"You, sir, are going to pay for this."

"Feel safer behind glass, Detective?" Raoul asked.

The detective sneered at him and Kayla. He touched his nose gingerly and shook his head. "You two are quite a pair," he said. "You two deserve each other."

"I'm sorry," Raoul said when they got in the Trooper. "I was out of line. None of us needed that."

"I'm glad you hit him," Kayla said. "I hate that man."

"Well, it won't look very good. I'm going to need a lawyer."

"You'll get a lawyer."

Raoul noticed she said *you* instead of *we*.

"Should we stop for pizza or something?" he said. "For the kids?"

"Sure," Kayla said. "Theo won't eat. He's locked himself in his room again. Jennifer was still at the beach when I left. But Cass and Luke will like pizza. I'd like pizza."

"Me, too," Raoul said. His stomach was sour and empty. The thought of bubbling cheese and a thick, doughy crust appealed to him. Plus, the normalcy of it: he and Kayla walking in together with a hot pizza. They might be able to distract the kids with food until this whole thing blew over.

Kayla drove to the Muse. She went in to order the pizza while Raoul waited in the car. He closed his eyes and tried to relax. Tomorrow, Monday, was a holiday, but he'd make an appearance at work. Fix the damaged walls himself. The lawyer thing would need to wait until Tuesday. Val had handled all Raoul and Kayla's legal matters until now; that would have to change. She didn't handle criminal cases, anyway. *Criminal cases*—Raoul's heart steeled itself against the new names that would be coming his way. His son was a vandal, his wife a murder suspect, and he, Raoul, was a criminal case.

Suddenly, Kayla flung open the door. She was sniffling.

"I saw Marty Robbins in there," she said. "Theo's boss? He said he read about me in the paper. 'What did you do to that woman?' he asked me. 'Rumor has it you poisoned her.' " She handed Raoul the piping hot pizza box; the car filled with the smell of the pizza, and Raoul's stomach tensed with expectation. Kayla slammed her door shut. "*Rumor has it?* Everyone knows, Raoul."

"Well, yeah," Raoul said. "They know what they read, but no one knows what actually happened."

"What actually happened doesn't matter!" Kayla said. "Word is out." She sped down Surfside Road toward home. "Everyone's talking about it, Raoul. You know how when something bad happens to someone and everyone you meet whispers to you about it? And you end up knowing the gory details of someone else's private life, someone you barely even know? That someone is me. People are gossiping about me."

"That's why you need to go on vacation," Raoul said.

"So people can say I'm running away? So people can say you kicked me out of the house?"

"No one will say that, Kayla. Two weeks from now the only people who will remember this happened is us."

"My life is ruined, Raoul."

"Yeah, well, mine's not looking too rosy, either."

This made her cry. She cried until they pulled into the driveway. Raoul held his open palms against the burning bottom of the pizza box. He was ashamed to say he was glad Kayla was being punished, even if it was for the wrong crime.

Inside, Luke and Cass were sitting at the breakfast bar playing Crazy Eights. Raoul heard music coming from Theo's room upstairs.

"I have pizza," Raoul said. "Cassidy, will you get plates and napkins, please?"

Neither kid moved. They were watching Kayla cry. She ripped a paper towel from the roll, blew her nose, and then dropped the towel in the trash can.

Cassidy B. stared at Raoul. "What's wrong with Mommy?"

Before Raoul could formulate a believable answer, Luke spoke up.

"Mom killed Aunt Antoinette," he said.

"Luke!" Raoul said. He wheeled Luke into the living room, where they were alone. "What in God's name made you say that? Did you overhear something?"

Luke eyed his father. He was a judgmental little bugger—it was his legacy as the youngest. He'd watched the other kids screw up and he learned how to keep himself in a safe, cool place where he could do things like accuse his mother of murder and get away with it. "You told us not to answer the phone, and we didn't," Luke said. "But we heard the messages."

Raoul looked at the red light on the answering machine blinking like crazy. Seventeen messages. "What have people been saying?"

Luke crossed his arms over his chest. "That they heard Mom was in trouble for killing Aunt Antoinette. And someone called Mom a lesbian."

"Go eat your pizza," Raoul said. "Right now."

Luke stomped into the kitchen. A wave of exhaustion crashed over Raoul. And he was hungry. But he turned the volume down on the answering machine and listened—there were five or six hangups, but the rest of the messages lit a fiery panic in the pit of Raoul's stomach. Ed Ogilvy from the *Inquirer and Mirror* asked Kayla for an official statement. Joyce Shanahan, Fran Dunleavy, Denise Grover—all friends of Kayla's—called to see what was going on. Was what the paper said true? Kent van Bonner, the guidance counselor at the high school, called to say he'd heard Theo had been charged with B and E—news to Raoul. A few unidentifiable voices called saying Kayla should be sent to jail. The minister of their church, Albert Froman, called to see if there was anything he could do to help. And John Gluckstern called three times—in increasing states of intoxication—labeling Kayla a fraud, a lesbian, an accomplice to murder. Raoul erased every message, and when he was through, he held his head in his hands and listened to the sound of his own breathing.

"Everyone knows." The room was dark, but Raoul made out Kayla, perched on the back of the sofa. How long had she been there? "They think the worst because they want to think the worst, Raoul. Everyone on this island has been looking for a reason to hate us for years."

"No," Raoul said, shaking his head. "I don't accept that. We're good people."

"That's why they hate us," Kayla said. "Because we're good. Because we're lucky."

"Our luck has run out," Raoul said.

"Yes."

Cassidy and Luke went up to their rooms without baths or TV. They were bewildered. Raoul and Kayla finished the pizza in silence. When Jennifer came home, she slammed the sliding glass door so hard that the walls of the kitchen shook; the dishes rattled in the cabinets. Raoul stood up.

"What's the big idea, young lady?"

Jennifer's skin was dark brown from her day at the beach. Her ponytail was stiff with salt, and she had sand halfway up her calves. Raoul checked the clock; it was almost nine.

"I heard what happened," Jennifer said. She threw Raoul and Kayla a killer look, the kind of look that could only cross the face of a fourteen-year-old girl who was angry at her parents. "It's disgusting."

They waited. She said nothing else. Raoul cleared his throat. "What did you hear?"

"About Theo and Aunt Antoinette *sleeping together?* And Mom poisoning Aunt Antoinette so that she fucking drowned?" Her voice hit the work *fucking* like a hammer. "What's going on in this family?"

Kayla cleared the pizza box from the table. "Have you eaten?"

Jennifer stared at her mother. "*Excuse* me?"

"If you want something, there's stuff for sandwiches. We ate all the pizza. Sorry." She opened a cabinet. "Oh, and there's soup. New England clam chowder." She picked up the can. "Twenty-three grams of fat. I guess not, huh?"

"Mom? Is it true?"

"Yes, yes, true. All of it true."

"Kayla," Raoul said. They should have thought of something to tell the kids. But now—well, they'd believe everything they heard from everyone. "Maybe we should explain."

"Explain?" Kayla said. She turned to face them, a look in her eyes like an empty room. "What could we possibly say that would explain what has happened this weekend?"

"Wait a minute." Jennifer dropped her straw beach bag to her feet and sand sprayed across the tile floor. Raoul watched Kayla reach instinctively for the broom. "So Theo was having sex with Aunt Antoinette? That is so gross. She's, like, twice his age."

"Then add ten years," Kayla said.

"It's your brother's business," Raoul said. "Who told you all this?"

"Some kids," Jennifer said. "Everyone's talking about it." She put the back of her hand to her fore-

head in a gesture of mock distress, only Raoul could
see that for Jennifer, it was real. "What am I going
to do? I'm going to have to run away from home."

"That's a good idea," Kayla said sincerely. "I
wouldn't want to live here with the rest of us."

"Are you going to jail?" Jennifer asked.

"No one's going anywhere," Raoul said. "Except
to bed."

"Can I sleep at Amy's house?" Jennifer asked.

"No," Raoul said.

"Yes," Kayla said.

"No," Raoul said. He wanted all his children at
home, under his roof, where nothing else could happen to them.

"Let her go, Raoul," Kayla said. "If she doesn't
want to sleep in this house, she shouldn't have to."

Jennifer softened. "Thank you, Mommy." She
hugged and kissed her mother. "I don't think you
killed Aunt Antoinette. You didn't, did you?"

Kayla shook her head. She was crying again.

Jennifer glanced at Raoul uneasily, like she might
cry herself, but instead she picked up her beach bag
and disappeared into the night.

"There you have it," Kayla said. "Our own daughter."

Raoul thought that Kayla might offer to sleep downstairs on the sofa, but she climbed into their bed and
fell asleep almost immediately. Raoul considered
sleeping on the couch himself, pretending for the
kids' sake that he fell asleep in front of the TV, but

in the end, he didn't want to sleep in the house at all, and so he went out to his truck. The moon was full again, shining like a polished pearl. Raoul wanted to drive away, but he was too tired, so he put his seat back, gathered up all the bad news of the day, and sank with the lead weight of it to the bottom of his dreams.

Raoul woke the next morning to the sound of his cell phone ringing. Groggily, Raoul reached for it, and when his arm hit the gear shift he remembered where he was. In his truck. His legs were cramped and his back hurt and his mind was heavy with the question of what to do about Kayla. She had to go away, for a while at least. It would give him a chance to breathe, to think, without having her around when he got home. *Please forgive me, everyone hates me, I ruined everything.* Raoul had to admit, though, he had a hard time imagining her on vacation by herself, without the kids. He couldn't picture her existing anywhere except for in this house.

Raoul snatched up the phone. The sun wasn't even completely up yet, and no one in the neighborhood had started to stir, which was a good thing. He hated to imagine the rumors if someone saw him sleeping in his truck.

"Hello?"

"Mr. Montero?"

Raoul wished he'd checked the clock. The only person who addressed him as Mr. Montero on his cell phone was Pierre Ting.

"Hello, Pierre."

"Mr. Montero, we have a problem." Pierre Ting's voice sounded distant and manufactured. Ting was in the construction business himself; he brokered scaffolding. He'd provided scaffolding for the Statue of Liberty, the Bank of Hong Kong, the Arc de Triomphe. He could be calling from anywhere.

"What kind of problem?" Raoul said.

"My name in the newspaper connected with some woman's disappearance? And today I'm looking at ruined walls in the living room. They tell me your son did this damage. What's going on, Mr. Montero?"

"You're *here*?" Raoul said. The beauty of working for the Tings was that they had never shown up to check on his work. Not once all summer. Raoul had Micky snap photos with a digital camera and they sent pictures of their progress to Ting's e-mail address.

"I flew in last night," Ting said. He sounded a thousand miles away. "And I've been bombarded with dismaying news since I arrived."

"Okay. I'll be right there. Give me five—"

"Don't bother," Ting said. "I'm replacing you. You're fired."

"Wait a second," Raoul said. "Pierre, please." There was silence on the other end. What should Raoul say? He was a grown man who had spent the night in his truck. Raoul fidgeted with the spare change he kept in the console, then the keys to the Doyle house that they'd finished in May, then the bottle of Advil, the contents of which Raoul would empty into his mouth as soon as he got off the phone. "Pierre, you can't fire me. We have a contract."

"I'm breaking the contract. I'll pay what I owe you for the work you've done so far, but no more. I'm hiring someone else." Raoul could hear Ting's footsteps against the wooden floors of the empty house. He wondered if anyone from his crew was there listening. He wondered who had called Ting to alert him in the first place. Micky, presumably.

"You won't be able to find anyone else," Raoul said, hoping this was true. "Besides, Pierre, that house is my design. Those are my plans. No one else will know how to execute them."

Ting laughed. "Ha! We'll see."

Raoul nearly wept at the thought of his cathedral being built by a crew of hackers, dope smokers, these guys who flew over from Hyannis each morning with no regard for the architectural integrity of Nantucket. "Please don't do this, Pierre."

"Are you going to fight me?" Ting asked.

"No," Raoul said. He didn't want to fight anyone else. He shut off the phone and stared at the front of the house, which caught an orange glow from the rising sun. What waited for him inside? Nothing anymore. A wife who cheated on him, the job of a lifetime ruined. He began then to understand how Theo must feel—the most important things in his life gone, washed away, irretrievable.

Theo

He didn't manage to make it back to school until Friday, and by then it was too late. Sara Poncheau, summer cab driver and best friend of Gillian Bergey, told everyone that she had seen Theo at Antoinette Riley's house. This was the story as Theo finally heard it: Ms. Riley had been a frequent fare for Sara, a huge tipper, and Sara wondered about her. A beautiful black woman with a ton of cash living back in the woods off Polpis; it was intriguing. Then, on Friday afternoon, she saw Theo standing in the doorway of Ms. Riley's house; she saw him grab her arm like he owned her or something. Sara assumed they were sleeping together. Which she reported to Gillian Bergey ASAP—and then two days later it hit the newspaper that the woman, Ms. Riley, was *missing* and Theo's mother was somehow involved. Covering up for Theo, maybe. Theo confessed to two counts of vandalism, which meant Theo probably killed the woman, probably hacked her to bits with an axe and buried her body parts in the woods. And his mother took the blame. Everyone knew Theo's parents spoiled him—his own Jeep, for starters, and spending money from his father who made all kinds of sick cash building huge houses for Chinese people. Yes, Theo was guilty of murder. Why else would anybody miss the *first three days* of senior year? That was insane, social suicide, and so there had to be a good reason.

Theo heard this from Aaron, just after first period, calculus—where the teacher, Mr. Eviasco, had started on derivatives and Theo stared helplessly at the numbers on the blackboard, unable to concentrate. As soon as the bell rang, dismissing them, Aaron yanked Theo into an empty classroom and told him the rumors that were going around.

"Man, is this the woman we saw at the Islander? And at the game? Your mom's friend?"

"Shut up, Aaron. I don't want to talk about it."

"I'm asking because I care about you, man. There's some serious shit going around. Perpetuated by Gillian and those bitches. They're saying you *killed* her, man."

Theo looked into the empty classroom at the rows of desks. He felt so alien here, like an impostor at his own high school. He didn't belong anymore.

Aaron ran a hand across the top of his spiky black hair. His neck started to splotch the way it sometimes did when he stood at home plate on a full count; he was nervous. "Man, is it *true*? Did you kill her?"

Theo grabbed the front of Aaron's T-shirt and pressed his lips against Aaron's ear. "Get one thing straight," he whispered. "That woman is not dead."

* * *

By lunchtime, Theo sensed the other kids moving away when he walked through the halls. Mrs. Waverly, his English teacher, giggled nervously when she called his name for attendance—and she had been his teacher since sophomore year. She liked him. But she squeaked when she said his name, as if noticing for the first time that he had three arms or something. They all thought he'd killed Antoinette. Or that his mother had killed her.

Because he was a senior, he had off-property lunch privileges, and Theo watched the other kids in his class fly out the doors when the bell rang. The guys from the baseball team—Aaron and Brett among them—stripped off their shirts. Theo heard them say they were going to Surfside Beach to eat at the snack bar. They didn't ask Theo to join them, although Theo figured he would still be welcome—for a price. He'd have to throw them a bone, a lie or something about Antoinette, his mother, the vandalism. He wasn't up to it.

Grief flooded Theo as he sat in the lunchroom, alone, with the egg salad sandwich that his mother had packed for him despite everything. His sister Jennifer sat at a table of ninth-grade girls, but even she wouldn't make eye contact with him. Last year her friends had all been gaga over him; now they thought he was a psycho. Theo's vision blurred and the tables of other kids decked out in their new clothes melted into a horrible stew. His old life decomposing.

He couldn't eat. He shoved his sandwich back

into the brown paper bag and left the cafeteria. He walked out to the parking lot, climbed into the Jeep, and drove away.

He ended up at Antoinette's house. The police car was gone, but the yellow tape remained. Theo took down the pieces of tape over the front door and let himself in. The place was pretty much as Theo had left it—Antoinette's books all over the floor with the wine bottles, the sofa cushions, the broken candles. Theo picked up a wine bottle and wandered through the house holding it like a club. A cocktail napkin was secured to the refrigerator with a magnet—in blue ink it said, *L., Cape Air, noon Sat.* Theo stared at the napkin—her daughter, he realized after a minute. Lindsey. Had Antoinette really meant to pick up Lindsey, or was this just a decoy? When Antoinette's body didn't turn up in the coast guard search, his suspicions were confirmed: Antoinette had been planning to disappear during Night Swimmers for a long time. But that napkin. It bothered Theo. He folded it carefully and put it into his jeans pocket.

He moved through the house touching all the things that Antoinette might have touched, the light switches, the doorknobs. He'd dumped her clothes in a pile on the bed and that's where they remained—a mound of black T-shirts and black jeans and black sundresses. He buried his face in one of the dresses, rooting for her smell, but he couldn't identify it. The dress smelled like fabric softener. He swept the clothes off the bed and turned back the sheets, looking for a stain from their lovemaking or one of his hairs, something to prove that he had lain with Antoinette in this bed, he had created a child here. But the sheets were clean, crisp even, Antoinette's Egyptian cotton sheets.

In the bathroom, Theo saw pills on the countertop divided into neat, colorful piles. Theo checked himself out in the mirror—he looked awful, like a sick person, a dying person. He had dark half-moons under his eyes, and his lips were cracked. His hair stuck out all over the place. That napkin was a bad clue. That napkin said: *I am planning on being around Saturday. I'll see you at noon!*

So she drowned.

Or, it was a trick. An Antoinette trick.

What Theo wanted the napkin to say was: *I love Theo Montero and I love our baby.* What he wanted the napkin to say was: *Meet me in Newport, Rhode Island, noon Sat., and we'll run away together.* What he wanted the napkin to say was: *I am thinking of you, Theo.* Yes, even that, only that. What had she expected him to do? How had she expected him to feel? Did she really expect him to survive the love affair and then the pregnancy? He was only eighteen. His heart had been broken and entered, ransacked, robbed.

Theo studied the piles of pills. *Take them*, he thought. *Wash them down*. It might be as easy as falling asleep.

As Theo picked up the first pill, the whelk shell caught his eye. It sat on the back of the toilet. Here was what Theo had been looking for—a piece of himself in this house. He cradled the shell in his hands as though it were a small animal. He kissed its smooth, cool surface, and then he brought the shell to his ear and listened to the ocean.

Even though it was the middle of the day, both of Theo's parents were at home. His father had lost the Ting job, although he insisted it wasn't Theo's fault. It was because of the newspaper article, that prick detective. Theo's father went out to Ting to gather his sawhorses and his tools, the Dumpster, the vans. He fired two men from his crew—Micky and Carter, saying that he wanted to pare down the operation. Mainstream. Montero Construction had projects lined up for the next thirty months with people who needed a builder so desperately that a mere accusation of murder wouldn't deter them. Losing Ting was a blessing in disguise, Theo's father said with false cheer. Because really that house was preposterous. That cathedral.

But Theo's father hadn't started on any new projects yet. He'd been at home trying to find a lawyer to defend him against the assault charges. Theo's mother hadn't left the house for errands or shopping because she was afraid to see anyone she knew. "They all think I'm a murderer," she said. "My own children think it."

Theo didn't think his mother was a murderer. He longed to climb into his mother's arms and say, *It's my fault. Blame me.* But both his parents insisted on protecting him. He wasn't even going to get in trouble for the vandalism. He'd gotten off scot-free—

except for Sara Poncheau. But now that Theo thought about it, he was glad Sara had told everyone at school about him and Antoinette. It made his pain real. Sara had seen them together only a week before. She had seen that it was real.

When Theo opened the sliding glass door, he heard his parents yelling. He wondered if this had been going on all morning while he was at school—his parents home alone in the empty house, screaming.

". . . you're throwing me out!" his mother said.

"Call it what you like, Kayla. I need time alone. I need time to think."

"You want to get rid of me," his mother said. "You hate me."

"I'm angry," his father said. "I'm hurt. But this is for you, too. You need to get off the island for a while."

"I won't know what to do," Theo's mother said. "The kids, I'll miss the kids."

"The kids will be fine. I'll take good care of them."

"What about Theo?"

Theo tensed. He locked his knees and pressed the soles of his Nikes into the kitchen tile.

"What about Theo?" his father said.

"He'll need a counselor. He has to have time to grieve."

"We'll take care of that."

"You'll find another woman while I'm gone," his mother said. "Someone to replace me."

"Are you listening to yourself, Kayla? You sound ridiculous."

"Okay, fine, you want me to go, I'll go."

"It'll be good for both of us," Theo's father said.

"I doubt that."

There was silence. Theo thought to stomp his feet or otherwise make himself known, but before he could move, his mother said, "Theo?"

Theo looked around. How did she know he was there?

"I see you," she said. "In the picture frame. What are you doing home?"

Theo walked into the living room, where his parents were pacing like a couple of caged animals.

"I left school," he said. He collapsed on the sofa. "The kids . . . whatever, everyone thinks I'm a psycho."

"Well, you're going to have to rise above that," his father said.

Theo shook his head. "No can do," he said. "Not going back."

"Oh, Theo," his mother said.

"What? I don't see you two running out to face the general public." He remembered the piles of pills. "I want to kill myself," he said. "I want to be dead."

His parents exchanged a look.

"And what were you two yelling about?" he said. "Are you getting a divorce?"

Another look. His mother at his father, as if to say, *This one's all yours.*

"Mom's taking a vacation by herself," his father said. "Just for a month or two."

"I want to go with you," Theo said. "Mom, please?"

"The idea is for your mother to have some time by herself. A change of scenery."

"I need a change of scenery," Theo said.

His parents were quiet. His father tousled Theo's hair the way he hadn't done in many years. "We'll see about getting you some help."

"I don't want to see any counselor," Theo said. What came to mind was some cinder-block room in the school. Being forced into meaningful conversation with Mr. Permanente, the guidance counselor, who had hair growing out of his ears. "Just send me away," Theo said. "Send me to the moon."

They didn't make him go back to school, and so Theo spent the weekend and the early part of the following week driving around aimlessly in his Jeep with the cocktail napkin that Antoinette had written on in the pocket of his jeans and the whelk shell next to him on the passenger seat. He called the police station each morning to see if they'd found any clues. Most mornings he talked to a Sergeant Webster, who sounded young and bored.

"No news," the sergeant said. "But hey, no news is good news."

The guy was a bonehead, Theo thought. The third time the sergeant fed him this line, Theo responded, "No. Good news would be my girlfriend turning up alive. Got it, pal? Let me speak to Paul Henry."

Most always, Paul Henry was on the other line, or out on a call, or busy organizing the Rotary Scholarship Auction, and Theo was put through to his voice mail. The one time Paul Henry called Theo back, he said they hadn't found a body and they were starting a limited missing persons search. Subpoenaing access to Antoinette's post office box and all that.

"So you think she might be alive, then?" Theo asked.

"Oh, Theo." Paul Henry's tone of voice was just like that of Theo's parents—sad and indulgent. "I haven't the slightest idea what happened to the woman. But we're going to cover all the bases for you. Okay, son? The important thing is for you to go on with your life."

Except that he had no life without Antoinette. "Yep," Theo said. "You bet."

And then, Thursday, thirteen days after Antoinette disappeared, Theo saw her bike leaning against the side of the Glucksterns' house. Theo stopped at the Glucksterns' with a paper bag of Val's things that his mother had asked him to return—some books, a green glass vase, a bundt pan. His mother was finished with Val as a friend, and she couldn't bear to give the things back herself. So she sent Theo to do it—in the middle of the day when no one would be home. As Theo hurried across the lawn toward the front door, anxious to drop the bag off and get out of there, he noticed a bike, which struck him as strange because the Glucksterns weren't the bike-riding type and they didn't have any kids. Then Theo realized it was Antoinette's bike. There was no mistaking it. It was a green Schwinn with a tattered basket on front that was connected to the handlebars by two disintegrating leather straps. Theo felt like shouting. Her bike! He'd never thought to look for her bike!

Theo touched the handlebars and his nose tingled with impending tears. Her hands. God, her hands had touched the handlebars. He put his hand on the black vinyl seat, which was warm from the sun. He let himself remember back to the first night at the Islander when Antoinette had pulled in on her bike. And then later, when she drove by the baseball field. The bike had been an integral part of their relationship, it had meaning, and without thinking twice, Theo walked the bike over to his Jeep and hoisted it in the back.

As he drove away, he wondered what it was doing at the Glucksterns' house. He couldn't very well call up and ask. More pressing was what Theo would tell his parents when they saw it. He decided to tell them that he'd gone up to Antoinette's and taken it as a reminder of her. They wouldn't fight him. As for the Glucksterns, well, they'd probably assume the bike had been stolen. Or they might not even notice. It was just an old bike to them—but to Theo, it was much more.

A few days later, matters were decided. Theo's mother was going to Puerto Rico for six weeks on a vacation that she didn't want to take. And Theo's

parents decided that Theo would live with his grandmother, Sabrina Montero, in Boston. Attend Boston
Hill, a private high school in Cambridge. Start a new
life. Theo packed one huge duffel bag, tucking the
whelk shell, the cocktail napkin, and the snapshot of
Antoinette holding him as a baby among his clothes.
He'd managed to convince his parents to let him take
the bike to Boston. "If Antoinette shows up and
wants it back, I'll return it," Theo said.

"Of course," his mother said quickly, like she
knew that would never happen.

When it was time to catch the ferry, Theo hugged
his sisters and shook Luke's hand. He was leaving
a week earlier than his mother, and so both of his
parents stood with him in the parking lot of the
Steamship Authority before he got on the boat. His
mother was crying, of course. His father wore sunglasses, his mouth a perfectly straight line. Even in
the crowded parking lot filled mostly with tourists,
Theo felt people staring at them. It was hot and his
shoulder grew sore with his heavy bag. He hadn't
let anyone else touch it. Theo kissed his parents
good-bye and was the first person up the ramp of
the boat, walking the bike alongside him. He didn't
wait to watch them wave.

Theo found a spot on the upper deck and lay
down in the sun, resting his head on his duffel. He
stayed awake until the boat passed Great Point, and
then he fell asleep.

Theo's grandmother, Sabrina, did things her own
way. For most of Theo's life she had lived on ten

green acres in Concord, Massachusetts. The house was called Colonial Farm, although it wasn't a farm at all—just a sprawling house and lots of grass and a small pond stocked with fish. It was the house where his father had grown up. When Theo's grandfather died, Sabrina sold the house and bought an apartment on Marlborough Street in Back Bay. Many of her friends were moving into retirement communities, but not Sabrina. She headed right for the big city, like a kid fresh out of college.

Theo insisted on finding the apartment himself. He took the T from South Station and wandered over to Marlborough, hauling his heavy-ass bag, walking Antoinette's bike. The city of Boston was as foreign as Kathmandu. The noise, the rows of brownstones, the throngs of people. The smell of urine in the T station. So different from Nantucket. *I could forget about her here*, Theo thought. *I could forget about everything*.

He had to ring his grandmother before he could get into her building; he remembered that much from previous visits. A loud buzz sounded, and Theo pushed open the door. He locked his bike to the banister for the time being and lugged his suitcase up to where his grandmother stood in the door of her apartment, smiling at him sadly. She wore dangly earrings that looked like very small wooden spoons, and a red-and-purple scarf over her silver hair.

"My poor, dear child," she said. "Come to Sabrina."

Theo put his bag down and hugged his grandmother. She was wiry and strong, and her embrace nearly strangled him. He wanted to thank her for letting him stay, but he was afraid if he opened his mouth he would cry. He wondered how much she knew.

"My grandchild," Sabrina said. "Son of my son. Or should I say sun of my son? Wait until people meet you. No one believes I'm old enough to have a grandchild, much less a grown man like you. Oh, Theo, come in. Come into my life. I'm glad you're here. I can help you."

"No one can help me, Sabrina."

She ushered Theo in. Her apartment smelled like curry and apples. On the walls hung Indian tapestries and a Salvador Dalí print. In the living room was a low, round table surrounded by big turquoise pillows. Theo remembered the table from her other house. It was the table where Sabrina performed séances. Sabrina had psychic powers; she knew how to talk to God.

"Do you still do séances?" Theo asked.

Sabrina smiled at him. She had the same golden brown eyes as his father, only her eyes were surrounded by millions of tiny wrinkles. "But, of course," she said. "In fact, just before you arrived, I asked the Madame what our time together was going to be like, and do you know what she said?"

The Madame—this was how Sabrina pictured God, as an old French peasant woman who collected eggs in a basket and baked her own baguettes. "What?" Theo asked.

"She said it would be transforming. Transforming!"

He had his own bedroom and his own bath. On his bed was a crocheted afghan knit by Sabrina herself, a twin to the one Theo's family used to have, the one he had seen draped over Antoinette's naked body when she came to baby-sit. Theo shoved the afghan into the bottom of his closet. He unpacked his clothes and placed the cocktail napkin and the snapshot of Antoinette in the drawer with his boxer shorts. The whelk shell went on the back of the toilet.

I could forget about her here. How wrong Theo was. In the city of Boston, Theo saw Antoinette everywhere—a long, lean woman with bronze skin wearing black, with dark hair caught carelessly in a bun. She rode the T with Theo on his way to his new school, she lounged under the weeping willow in Boston Commons, she drank coffee at Rebecca's Café near Government Center. When Theo spotted her, his heart banged in his chest until he realized that it wasn't Antoinette at all, but someone else, many someone elses.

Theo's new school was expensive. It sat on a campus of three square blocks of grass and trees across the Charles River, in Cambridge. Boston Hill—there was no dress code, but the senior boys wore soft chino pants or gray flannels, and pressed oxford shirts. They were quiet in the hallways; they were studious. The girls ate hummus for lunch. Everyone listened to National Public Radio. There was no baseball team, only fencing and archery. Theo told the few people who approached him that he came from Nantucket, but no one was impressed. Much of the student body was foreign—they summered in places like Provence and Tuscany. Theo made no friends, but at Boston Hill solitude was popular. There wasn't a lunchroom—students ate alone under one of the trees, reading Rick Moody or Anne Lamott. Theo's English teacher, a man named Geoffrey, assigned a year-long journal project. *"Record your thoughts,"* he said. *"Explore your soul. And read these ten books and compose a reaction to them."* Theo picked up seven of the ten books and a journal at Waterstone's on Newbury Street. One of the books, *A Passage to India*, he'd seen on Antoinette's shelves.

Theo took classical music and art history. He sat in acoustically designed rooms listening to Mozart's eleventh piano sonata spiral through the air. He sat in other dark rooms and stared at slides of important paintings like Seurat's *Invitation to the Sideshow*. Theo thought of Antoinette at the age of twenty-three meandering through the Met in New York, studying the original painting. This made him feel less lost, that they might have gazed upon the same painting or listened to the same Mozart sonata.

In the afternoons before he headed to the T station, Theo watched ballet class. It was held in the school's dance studio, where they had a grand piano played by a white-haired gentleman whose hands trembled when they weren't moving over the keys. Theo watched the dancers go through their stretches at the barre, their pliés, their positions. He appreciated the lines of their bodies as they twirled. Some of the girls noticed him staring, and they scowled, or they smiled. They thought that he lusted after them with normal teenage-boy hormones. They had no idea that when Theo watched them dance he was thinking of the one time he'd seen Antoinette dance, her arms flowing, her back bending. He was thinking of how his mother described Antoinette in the last moment she saw her, up at Great Point. She danced into the water, his mother said.

After ballet class, Theo bought a PayDay bar from the subway kiosk and sat on a bench on the grimy platform of the Harvard T station watching people. Sometimes ten trains would screech into the station and pull out again before Theo finally boarded one. He got lost in his thoughts; occasionally he swam around in his old life, afternoons at the Islander liquor store, a hundred years ago, a million miles away.

Am I transforming? he wondered.

Pregnant women were everywhere in Boston, and Theo saw Antoinette in each one. Antoinette growing soft and round with his baby.

Theo spoke very little to his grandmother and that seemed to be okay. She had plenty of other people to talk to. She'd created a life for herself that seemed to revolve primarily around shopping for dinner. It was very European, she claimed, to make numerous stops, and with each stop, enjoy a conversation. Sabrina chattered away with Joe the butcher, Helen at the bakery, Dominic at the fish store, Nathan with Down's syndrome who bagged at the regular grocery, and a young man named Gianlorenzo who worked in the shop in the North End where Sabrina went to buy cannoli, fresh marinara, and ricotta pies. Sabrina was a great cook and an extravagant wine drinker—she adored the reds of France, which, she told him, were more expensive than his tuition at Boston Hill. *But worth it!* Sabrina poured Theo a glass with every meal—her paella, her osso buco, her Peking duck. Theo started to gain weight. *Am I transforming?* he wondered.

Weekends were the most painful days because he was removed from his school routine. On Saturdays, he slept as late as he could, hoping that when he rolled over, the blue numbers of his digital clock would say eleven or twelve so that at least the morning would be over with. Sabrina made him breakfast—granola, yogurt, strawberries—and always invited him on an excursion—strolling along the Charles, studying the gravestones at Old North Church, visiting the MFA. Theo always said no.

"I don't blame you," Sabrina said. "I'm an old woman. Not much fun."

"You're fun," Theo said. "It's me who's no fun." On Saturdays at home, his mother made him do chores in the morning and then he went to the Whalers games with his friends. Here, in Boston, he had no friends. On Saturday afternoons he rode Antoinette's bike down to the FAO Schwarz on Newbury Street where he waited to see pregnant women, even though the pregnant women Theo found never failed to disappoint him—Diet Coke in one hand, bag of M&M's in the other, puffy-faced, swaybacked and miserable looking.

He allowed himself one fantasy per day: autumn on Nantucket with Antoinette. Theo sitting with her on the back deck, Theo peeling her an apple, slicing a piece of cheese. Listening to the Canada geese pass overhead, Antoinette wrapped in a nubby wool sweater, Theo placing his hand on her stomach and feeling his baby kick.

He masturbated exactly once a week—Saturday night—in the shower. It made him incredibly sad.

One night, when Theo had been living with Sabrina for just over a month, she made an old-fashioned meatloaf slathered with ketchup. It seemed uncharacteristically staid—a dowdy old meatloaf made by a woman wearing a fuchsia pantsuit with a matching head scarf. Sabrina's long, manicured nails clicked against the plates as she set them down.

"This was your father's favorite food growing up," she said.

Theo picked up his fork. "Really?" Sabrina had said surprisingly little about his father since he'd arrived. She hadn't mentioned his mother or his siblings at all. Theo sometimes caught Sabrina staring at him in a way that let him know she was trying to read his mind. He stared back, sending her the message, *Please don't ask, Sabrina. I'm not ready.* But now as Theo ate the delicious, oniony meatloaf, he felt ready. "Has Dad called?"

"Twice," Sabrina said. "While you were at school. Should I have told you?"

Theo shrugged. He was so busy longing for Antoinette that he didn't have the energy to miss the rest of his family, not as he should. "What did he say?"

"He asked how you were doing."

"What did you tell him?"

"I said you were quiet, but that you were doing as well as could be expected under the circumstances."

"Do you know the circumstances?"

"I know that you've learned a difficult lesson," Sabrina said. She put her fork down and moved her hand across the table toward him. "I know that you've lost someone you loved."

"Yes," he said. Tears rose at his grandmother's words. Finally, an acknowledgment of what was really wrong. He'd lost someone he loved—not one person but two—because Theo loved the baby Antoinette was carrying. Loved it with a fierceness that surpassed anything he'd ever felt. "They're lost. Lost. Antoinette and . . . my baby. Antoinette was pregnant."

"Yes," Sabrina said. Her eyes shone with tears. "I know."

"She wanted to have an abortion, and I was trying to stop her. I didn't want her to kill our baby."

"That's understandable, Theo."

"She disappeared to get away from me," Theo

said. "I think. But lately I've been having doubts. I've been wondering, you know, what if it *was* an accident? What if she *is* dead? Because what I picture is her living in Hawaii or something, you know, hiding from me."

"They haven't found her body," Sabrina said. "Your father told me that much."

"So she's still alive, maybe," Theo said.

He and his grandmother ate in silence as it grew dark. Then Sabrina cleared their plates and lit some candles.

"You're going to think I'm nutty," she said. "And you'll be right, of course. But would you like me to ask the Madame?"

Theo squeezed his eyes shut.

"Never mind," she said. "I just thought I'd offer. In case you were a believer."

He *was* a believer of sorts. He had no choice but to believe. "Okay," Theo said. "Ask Her if Antoinette is alive."

Sabrina lit more candles. The apartment glowed with soft light. Outside on the street, Theo heard car horns. On his way home from school that afternoon, he'd smelled autumn for the first time, the smokiness of falling leaves.

"I never make promises," Sabrina said. "The Madame doesn't always feel like communicating. She's an old, old woman."

"It's okay," he said. "I don't expect much."

Sabrina sat down on one of the turquoise pillows and waved him over. "Come," she said. She readjusted her head scarf. "Come and relax."

Theo plopped onto a pillow next to her while she rubbed her small, manicured hands together. "Okay, now close your eyes and take my hands. What I need you to do is think about Antoinette. Really think about her. Picture her in your mind's eye and hold her there. Hold her steady."

Theo framed Antoinette with her arms crossed over her chest, leaning against his Jeep as she waited for him to emerge from the boys' locker room after his baseball game. This was a good picture, a "before" picture: before the sex, before the baby, before Theo fell in love. A moment in time with Antoinette when Theo was still safe. He was just a kid giving his mother's friend a ride home.

"Okay, got it."

Sabrina hummed—not a spooky, mantra hum, but a show tune of some kind. *Try to remember the kind of September* . . . the one that went like that. She massaged his hands and Theo pictured the Madame wearing a red kerchief, carrying her basket of brown eggs. *She's an old, old woman*. Sabrina had been trying to convince Theo and his brother and sisters that God was a woman all their lives. *Think of her infinite compassion*, Sabrina said. *Her nurturing*. Now Theo felt like laughing—his classmates were at home listening to *All Things Considered*—but part of him was anxious. Was the Madame saying anything?

Abruptly, Sabrina stopped humming. "Riley," she said. "A black woman?" Her voice sounded surprised.

"Yes," Theo said. "Yes, yes, she's black." *Calm*

down, he thought. His grandmother probably already knew that. She was teasing him. But maybe not; Sabrina wasn't cruel. "Do you see her? What does the Madame say?" Theo held the picture of Antoinette in his mind and added other pictures of her: Antoinette standing nude in the bathroom after the first time they made love, Antoinette lounging on her back deck with a glass of wine balanced on the flat spot between her breasts, Antoinette slapping him across the face. She had feelings for him, yes, she did.

Sabrina was quiet for a long while. Theo heard her slow, rhythmic breathing and he feared she'd fallen asleep. He was close to sleep himself, so when her words came, she startled him.

"The Madame says the woman is alive. And the baby, too. The baby is alive."

Theo opened his eyes. Sabrina was looking at him with the kindest possible expression.

"She's alive, Theo," Sabrina whispered.

Was she telling him the truth or simply saying this to make him feel better? *Sun of my son. Come into my life. I can help you.* She was his grandmother, and if Theo wanted Antoinette to be alive, she would make it so. This was her way.

That night, Theo wrote in his journal. Because his journal was supposed to have something to do with his reading, he wrote about Antoinette living in India, disappearing into one of the Marabar Caves. So many dark openings, one indistinguishable from the next. Which one was she in? Where was she hiding?

He wrote, *Am I transforming?*

The week before Thanksgiving, Theo saw Antoinette on Clarendon Street, getting out of a cab. It was Sunday and Theo had taken to sitting at the bar of T.G.I. Friday's where he drank Coke, ate chicken fingers, and watched the Patriots game. Sabrina didn't have a TV and Theo liked to sit at the bar with his food and his drink and his anonymity. He liked listening to John Madden and Pat Summerall, he liked the roar of the crowd. His whole family were Patriots fans, and because his father didn't work on Sundays, he used to sit with the rest of them in the living room watching the game, eating potato chips. "These are the good times," his father used to say. "Don't you ever forget it."

At dusk, Theo was riding Antoinette's bike home when a cab stopped a few yards ahead of him, and Antoinette stepped out.

Theo squeezed the brakes. Antoinette in black pants and a black leather jacket. He saw her profile as she rummaged through a backpack for money.

"Antoinette!" Theo called. He ran toward her with the bike before she could hop back in the cab and escape from him. He grabbed her arm. "Antoinette!"

Antoinette yanked her arm free. "Hey!" she said.

"Antoinette," Theo said. He started to cry. A line of cars formed behind the stopped cab. Antoinette leaned in to pay the driver and Theo took in a huge gulp of autumn air. A sense of peace settled over him. He'd found her.

The cars honked. He moved the bike to the sidewalk and she came to him.

"What are you doing here?" she asked.

Theo wiped his eyes. He couldn't answer. Sabrina had been right, and the Madame—Antoinette was alive. But then confusion rattled his brain. This wasn't Antoinette. Or rather, it was Antoinette, but younger, prettier even. It was Lindsey. Her daughter Lindsey.

"Oh, shit," Theo said. His whole body was shaking. "Shit, I thought you were Antoinette."

"You thought wrong," she said. "I'm Lindsey. You're Theo."

"Yes."

"Yes, well, I'd think you'd have better things to do with your time than wander the streets of Boston looking for a dead woman."

"Antoinette's not dead," Theo said.

"Oh, really? She's turned up?" Lindsey said. "News to me."

"She didn't turn up yet," Theo said. "But that doesn't mean she's dead."

Lindsey snickered. "You should see the look on your face. You are such a sorry sight." She hitched her backpack over her shoulder. "You were in way over your head, baby. Now if you'll excuse me, I have to meet someone."

"Wait," Theo said. He followed her. "Wait, I want to talk to you."

"I don't want to talk to you," Lindsey said. "You

and your mother are responsible for what happened, and I can't tell you how it burns me up. Your mother should be thrown in jail. She should be on death row. I'd like to see a white person get it just once for killing a black person."

"No," Theo said. "Because. Well, you don't know the whole story."

"I don't care anymore," she said. "I've been in therapy for almost three months over this, and I don't need you appearing like some ghost bringing all the bad shit back. Now quit following me, or I'll call a policeman."

"I loved your mother," Theo said. "She was pregnant with my baby."

"I know," Lindsey said. "And the thought of it makes me want to vomit. Now please!" She crossed the street against the light, running in front of two cars. Theo had to wait for a stream of traffic to pass; he watched Lindsey hurry down the next block. He should just let her go—she hated him, she probably would get a policeman after him, and he didn't need that kind of trouble. But, God, what were the chances? She wasn't Antoinette, but she was *close*, a whole hell of a lot closer than he'd gotten in months. So he mounted the bike and chased after her, weaving among other pedestrians, and an old man with a dog. When Theo was within feet of her, she whipped around and screamed at him.

"What do you want from me?"

"I want to talk."

Her brow creased and her eyebrows met sharply in the middle, two angry diagonal lines. An element of her face that did not belong to Antoinette. Weird.

"Antoinette used to talk about you. I could tell you what she said."

"Why should I care what she said?" Lindsey asked. Although Theo knew from the sound of her voice that she did care. Three months of therapy aside, she did care.

"Because she was your mother," Theo said. "Because she loved you."

She agreed to have coffee with him—his suggestion, because having coffee was an adult thing to do and Theo didn't want to call attention to the fact that he was too young to drink alcohol. Plus, he only had ten dollars left in his wallet, which wouldn't go far with anything except coffee. They went to Rebecca's Café and stood in line for coffee, which Theo loaded down with cream and sugar. Lindsey got jasmine tea, and Theo said, "Do you want a scone or anything? I can pay for it. What about a *cwasant oh jam-bone ay fro-maj*?" He used his corniest French accent, a relic from his days with Brett and Aaron and his other school buddies a hundred years ago. It worked: Lindsey smiled the tiniest smile, and Theo rushed ahead of her to pay for "One large coffee and one jasmine tea, please." They sat at a very small round table in two uncomfortable wrought-iron chairs. Theo sipped his coffee and burnt his tongue.

Lindsey stirred her tea bag with a thin plastic straw. "Why don't you just tell me what you have to tell me?" she said. She looked at her watch.

"Do you really have someone to meet?" Theo asked. "Your boyfriend?"

"You may have been screwing my mother," she said. "But you're a far cry from being my father. Got that?"

"No, I didn't mean . . ."

"How old are you anyway? Nineteen?"

Theo was pleased that she thought he looked nineteen. "Almost."

Lindsey huffed. "Disgusting. My mother and you, I mean."

"It wasn't disgusting," Theo said. "Don't think that."

"Whatever," Lindsey said.

"Your mother is a beautiful woman," Theo said. "And you look just like her."

Again, the tiniest smile. "Please."

"It's true," he said. "She told me the whole story about how she was pregnant with you and what happened . . . with her husband . . . your father. She said she loved you. She loved you, but she gave you away because she was in so much pain."

"My father cheated on her," Lindsey said. "Antoinette told me that already, when I spoke to her on the phone. He cheated on her because that's what men do. They cheat."

"Hey," Theo said. "That's not fair."

"Life isn't fair," Lindsey said. "Like, I finally get the courage up to contact my mother and the day before I get to her, she vanishes into thin air."

"Why did you contact her in the first place?" Theo said. "If you don't mind my asking."

Lindsey leaned forward and parted her lips so that

Theo could see a tiny chip on her front tooth. "Because I wanted her to love me."

"I wanted her to love me, too," Theo said. He tried his coffee again, but now he had a sore, dry spot on his tongue. "She never forgave herself for giving you up. So I can't understand why . . . why she wanted to abort our baby. You'd think she'd want to try again, you know? Do things the right way?"

"I have no idea," Lindsey said. "I never met the woman. Never even seen a picture of her face."

"I have a picture of her at my house," Theo said. "A picture of her when she's twenty-seven years old. You should come see it. You'd see how much she looks like you."

"I thought you lived on Nantucket," Lindsey said.

"I do. I did. I'm spending this year with my grandmother. I go to Boston Hill."

"Boston Hill? You're still in *high school*?"

"I got held back," Theo said. "I should be a freshman in college."

Lindsey looked out the plate glass window at the dark street. Theo tried to predict his grandmother's reaction if he brought Lindsey home. It was almost five-thirty. She liked him home by six to eat dinner.

"So what do you say? Do you want to come see the picture? Oh, and I have something else you might want."

"What?"

"Just something. Come with me. It's not far. Marlborough Street. You can meet my grandmother."

"I don't think so," Lindsey said. "But thanks, anyway."

"Please?" Theo said. "Don't you want to see the picture? I'll give it to you if you want it. It's, like, the only picture of Antoinette in existence. Come on." He took her empty cup and his full coffee cup and threw them both away. "Follow me."

It was very cold outside. Theo wore a flannel shirt with a fleece vest. He shoved his hands into the front pockets of his jeans.

"I have to meet someone," Lindsey said.

"This won't take long," Theo said. He unlocked Antoinette's bike, and even considered telling Lindsey that it was Antoinette's bike, but he didn't want her to claim it as her own or anything. "I'll give you the picture and you can go. I promise." He walked the bike with confidence, checking twice out of the corner of his eye to make sure she was following him.

"I'm not staying long," she said.

"It's okay," he said. "We eat at six, anyway."

"And don't introduce me to your grandmother as Antoinette's birth daughter or anything. Just tell her I'm a friend from school."

"You bet." He slowed down a little so she could walk alongside him. "Was it you who turned my mother in to the police?"

"I didn't *turn her in*," Lindsey said. "I just told them what I knew about you and Antoinette. About Antoinette being pregnant. Those seemed like relevant facts, and your mother certainly wasn't going to come forth with them. That guy, John? He told most of it, anyway. He had it in for his wife and your mom."

"My mom didn't do anything to Antoinette."

"Prove it."

"I can't prove it," he said. "But they haven't found a body, have they? I'm telling you, Antoinette is alive somewhere."

"You can hold on to that fantasy if you want," she said. "But I'm not going to."

"My mother didn't do anything wrong," Theo said. "If you need someone to blame, blame me."

"I do blame you," Lindsey said. "High school. God, I can't believe it."

They approached his grandmother's apartment. He had his own keys now. Lindsey regarded the building. "Nice place," she said. "I'd hate to imagine the rent."

"Two thou," Theo said, though he had no idea if this was true or not. He locked Antoinette's bike up at the bottom of the stairs. "Where do you live?"

"None of your business," Lindsey said. He turned to look at her as they climbed the stairs, and she glared at him. "I don't want you stalking me."

"You *are* like your mother," Theo said. He took a deep breath outside his grandmother's door; then he unlocked it. "Sabrina?" He smelled roasting chicken, and Sabrina emerged from the kitchen wearing a flowing orange dress and a gold lamé head scarf. She shimmered like a flame. Sabrina on fire. Theo watched Lindsey's eyes widen; she was expecting another kind of grandmother, maybe.

"Well, helllooo," Sabrina said. "Hello, hello. I'm

Sabrina Montero." She smiled and offered Lindsey her hand.

"Lindsey Allerton." Lindsey transformed immediately into the kind of woman that one would want to introduce to one's grandmother. Charm lifted off her like perfume. "It's lovely to meet you. I'm a friend of Theo's from school."

Sabrina blinked. She looked between Lindsey and Theo. "Really?" she said. "How divine. Theo hasn't brought any of his school friends up to meet me yet. Ashamed of me, probably. Will you stay for dinner? We're having Cornish game hens—and you won't believe this, but I put three of those little yummies in the oven. I had a feeling company was coming."

Lindsey hugged her backpack close to her body. "Thank you for asking, but I'm meeting someone in a short while, so I'll have to pass. Too bad—it smells delicious."

"I'm devastated," Sabrina said. "But another time."

"Another time," Lindsey repeated.

Theo cleared his throat. "I have some assignments and stuff to give Lindsey. Okay if we go into my room?"

"Of course," Sabrina said. She winked at him, and his face grew warm.

Sabrina went back into the kitchen humming, "Try to remember the kind of September . . ."

So she knew, Theo thought. Knew something was up.

He led Lindsey to his room and shut the door. She sat on his bed, dropped her backpack at her feet.

"I love how you ask your grandma if you can bring me in here," she said. "Like we're going to make out or something."

"Shut up," Theo said.

"Just show me the picture," Lindsey said. "Because really, I have to get a move on."

"Okay," Theo said. He stood at his dresser. He couldn't believe he was about to share two of his prized possessions with a virtual stranger. His artifacts of Antoinette. But what choice did he have now? He removed the snapshot and the wrinkled cocktail napkin from his underwear drawer. He handed the snapshot to Lindsey. "Here she is."

Lindsey took the picture. "Turn on a light," she said.

Theo hit the overhead light. Even through the closed door, he heard his grandmother humming that song. Lindsey stared at the picture. She stared and stared.

"The baby in the picture is me," Theo said.

Lindsey stared.

"She looks like you, doesn't she?"

Lindsey didn't answer. Theo felt awkward standing in the harsh light. He wished Lindsey would finish looking at the picture and leave so that he could have dinner with his grandmother. He was going to tell Sabrina the whole story as soon as Lindsey left.

"Well?" he said impatiently. "What do you think?"

Lindsey raised her head. She was crying. Or not crying so much as leaking tears. "I can't believe it," she said. "We're twins."

"Yeah."

She wiped her face. "Sorry," she said. "It's just that my whole life I've never had anything biological. You know? My parents are wonderful people, but they're not related to me. The whole reason I started searching for Antoinette in the first place was that I wanted that void filled. I wanted a biological connection." She held up the picture. "This woman is related to me."

"She's your mother."

More tears fell as Lindsey studied the picture. Theo hurried to the bathroom and brought back a three-foot strip of toilet paper. Lindsey blotted her eyes.

"So I can keep this?" she asked, waving the picture.

His heart flagged. His only picture of Antoinette. The only picture of Antoinette in existence, that he knew of.

"Sure."

"Thanks," she said. "And you said there was something else?"

"Oh." Theo paused. He removed the napkin from his vest pocket. "Here. This is a note I found on her refrigerator."

" 'L. Cape Air, noon Saturday,' " Lindsey read. "*L*? That's me."

"Yeah."

Lindsey put the picture and the napkin in her backpack. She was taking them. Theo touched the sore spot on his tongue to his teeth.

"You realize," Lindsey said, "that if she were

planning on picking me up at the airport, then she didn't disappear intentionally. She drowned, Theo."

Drowned.

He shrugged. "Whatever. I can think otherwise."

"I guess you can. But why would you torture yourself? You're so young. You need to accept that Antoinette is dead and move on. Maybe you should see a therapist."

"Maybe." His throat clogged with impending tears. She was right: He *was* young, his life did have possibilities beyond this. He could marry someone else, father other children. Move on. Heal. But Theo's future would be colored forever by his love for Antoinette. This was what he couldn't explain to Lindsey, or to Sabrina, or to his parents—the way his love for Antoinette and for his unborn child haunted him. He heard it in the top note of Pachelbel's Canon, he tasted it in Sabrina's paella, he saw it in the slender, graceful arms of the ballet dancers at school. His love and his pain would follow him wherever he went next in life. They were all he had left.

Lindsey stood up. "I have to go."

"Okay," Theo said. The polite thing was to walk her out, which he would do, he would hold himself together until Lindsey left, and then he would shout and scream and cry. Sabrina would feed him; she would listen without asking questions.

Before she put her hand on the doorknob, Lindsey leaned over and kissed Theo on the lips. The lightest kiss, like a kiss from a ghost, Theo thought. A kiss from Antoinette.

"Thank you," she said.

Theo smiled. For a second, he felt transformed. For a second, he was just a boy of eighteen, kissed by a pretty girl. "You're welcome," he said.

Kayla

The first thing Kayla did when she stepped into the San Juan airport was to seek out the bank of pay phones. She lifted the receiver and punched in her calling card number. At home, on Nantucket, the answering machine picked up. Of course: The kids were at school, Raoul at work. "I arrived safely," Kayla said. "I love you all." Seven words; that was all she allowed herself. She hung up.

Kayla proceeded down the corridor toward baggage claim. She was wearing a new dress, a turquoise sundress with splashy pink flowers. She'd bought it out of a catalog, as a way to get excited about this trip. Six weeks by herself in sunny Puerto Rico, a new dress, a wallet full of cash and traveler's checks—no price was too high for Raoul to get her off Nantucket. She was being banished. Raoul said no phone calls—except for one letting him know she'd arrived safely—no postcards even. Just her alone, with too much time to think. This was her penance.

It had been over two weeks, and there was still no sign of Antoinette's body. Kayla hadn't ventured out of the house; she hadn't answered phone calls, although the phone rang constantly. Some people wanted to express their condolences—*We're sorry you lost your friend*—some people wanted an explanation. Raoul's name appeared in the police blotter for assaulting a police officer, and that instigated yet more calls. And even visits, concerned neighbors tapping on the sliding glass door. Kayla actually went so far as to lock that door and the front door. She stayed out of the kitchen.

Kayla plucked her suitcase off the carousel, extended the handle, and rolled it over to the rental car desks. Ten minutes later, Kayla stood out in the humid tropical weather as a young Puerto Rican man drove up in her car, a bright red LeBaron convertible.

The young man threw her suitcase into the trunk and helped her decipher her map. She was close to the highway, he said. The drive to Guanica was easy.

Kayla clipped her hair back into a barrette, put on her sunglasses, and hit the gas. It was liberating, and if she hadn't been so sad, she might have enjoyed it.

Three days later, she had a routine. She was staying in a pleasant one-bedroom unit at a place called Mary Lee's by the Sea. Her unit was decorated with tropical fabrics, plants, rattan furniture, and it looked out over the ocean. Kayla started her day with exercise—she walked past a seafood restaurant and a parking lot where a pack of mangy dogs barked at her from the other side of the chain-link fence, past the opulent Copamarina Beach Resort where wealthy

Americans played early morning games of tennis, down to the public beach, and back. At her unit, she showered and made herself a papaya smoothie. Then before it grew too hot, she drove the LeBaron into downtown Guanica, a dingy port town. She shopped at the bodega, cashed traveler's checks at the bank, visited a souvenir shop, and pawed trinkets and held up T-shirts, thinking, despite her best efforts, of her children. In the afternoons, she lounged on her deck. At five o'clock, Kayla showered again, drank some wine, and either cooked for herself or walked to the seafood restaurant. And every night after dark, she sneaked down to the end of the dock in front of the hotel office, slipped off her sundress, and swam in the lagoon. This was the only time that she allowed herself to think.

The entire situation with Antoinette had opened her eyes to several new ideas. One new idea was that she wasn't a very good mother. Another new idea was that she wasn't a very good wife. And a third new idea was that she wasn't a very good friend. Only weeks earlier, these three words— *mother, wife, friend*—would have been the exact three words Kayla would have chosen to identify herself. But not anymore. If she wasn't a mother, wife, and friend, then who was she? She didn't know.

The lagoon frightened her—it was bordered by the thick, gnarled roots of mangroves. She was afraid to put her feet on the bottom because there might be crabs, or snakes. And yet, being afraid cleared her mind—she spent the dark hours replaying moments from her children's early lives, especially Theo's, replayed them like she was a coach watching a game tape—searching for things that might have been done differently. Theo was her first baby. She hadn't known what she was doing. Did she breast-feed him too long or wean him too soon? Did she tell him she loved him too often or too infrequently? What had she done to make him sleep with her best friend? Somehow, she suspected, it was her fault. And how had she not realized what was going on with Antoinette? Now that Kayla looked back, she saw clues: Theo out on mysterious errands all the time, the way his shirts smelled when Kayla collected them for the laundry, the time he was so curious about Antoinette's past. But Kayla had been too busy, too blind, too naïve to see the clues. Antoinette was in one part of her life, and Theo in another. Even now, Kayla had a hard time believing in the affair. She couldn't bring herself to imagine their intertwining bodies.

Thinking about Raoul was even more painful. In the nineteen years of their marriage, Kayla and Raoul had only spent a handful of nights apart—the nights Kayla had slept on the beach at Great Point for Night Swimmers. Saying good-bye was difficult: Raoul took her to the airport while the kids were at school, so it was just the two of them in the near-empty terminal. Kayla had never said good-bye to Raoul before, and she didn't know how to act. Raoul tried to make light of her leaving by humming "Leaving on a Jet Plane," and when Kayla grew angry at him for this—saying he couldn't carry a tune, so please save her ears—Raoul grew angry at her.

They'd ended up sitting side by side, arms crossed, staring at the woman who worked the Cape Air counter as she helped another customer with a fouled-up ticket. Then, when Kayla's plane was called, Raoul took her elbow and walked her to the gate and kissed her as sweetly as he had ever kissed her, and Kayla cried.

Kayla missed the sound of Raoul's voice, the feel of his scruffy face when he didn't shave for a day or two, the way he touched her in the middle of the night as if making sure she was still there. She missed hearing him talk to the kids, she missed his smell of fresh lumber and plaster and paint, she missed pulling crumpled pink receipts from Marine Home Center out of his pockets when she put his clothes into the hamper at night. But she hadn't been a good wife. She'd suspected him of adultery for years—she admitted this now—and so she harbored old anger about being deceived along with this new anger about being deceived. And then Jacob. God, Jacob. Every minute of this vacation was a struggle not to fall into a pit of self-loathing.

While there was a chance that her marriage would survive, Kayla understood that her friendships with Val and Antoinette were over. Val had turned Kayla in to the police, and Kayla slept with Jacob. Both actions were unthinkable. Or rather, what was unthinkable was that after twenty years a friendship as strong as theirs could be so violently destroyed. Torn apart in a matter of twenty-four hours. Kayla had packed up all of Val's things and sent Theo to drop them off at her house.

At the end of her evening swim, as Kayla climbed out of the water, dried off, and walked back to her unit, she asked the question that became her mantra, her *raison d'etre*: *What had happened to Antoinette?* Was she alive? Dead? Here, Kayla was flummoxed. She'd asked Raoul to leave a message at the office of Mary Lee's as soon as a body was found, but she'd heard nothing. And as far as she knew, the police were conducting what they called a limited missing-persons investigation, but again, she'd had no news. Everyone thought, or had grown to accept, that Antoinette drowned during Night Swimmers. She'd been drinking, true; the water was tricky, the riptide fierce and unpredictable. But something nagged at Kayla, and that something was Antoinette herself. She was too capable, too strong, too *clever* to let herself get swept away. It sounded stupid, but it wasn't Antoinette's *style*. She was a survivor. So where was she? Hanging out with the Jim Morrison groupies at Père Lachaise cemetery in Paris, or trekking on the back of an elephant in the teak forests of northern Thailand? Mostly, Kayla thought of Antoinette as vanished. Not alive, not dead, just gone. Meaning, she could turn up again somewhere. Resurface.

Kayla had been dreading this vacation from the beginning, and yet, when the six weeks were over, she panicked at the thought of returning to Nantucket. She thought back to the words she once heard Antoinette say: *"I'm lonely all the time, every day. But there are far worse things than being lonely. Like being betrayed."*

Kayla didn't want to relinquish her solitude, her simple routine, her ocean view or her solitary night swims. She thought brashly of writing a forbidden postcard, *Decided to stay here for the rest of my life. Love, Kayla.*

She returned on the sixth of November, and as her plane flew over the island, Kayla was filled with trepidation. The first landmark she spotted was Great Point lighthouse, which from the plane looked like nothing more than a white stake planted in the ground. A stake marking the site of her sadness. Then Kayla took in the cranberry color of the moors, the dark blue ponds, the amber and green plots of Bartlett's farm. Autumn had come while she was away.

She didn't know what to expect when she entered the airport. She almost walked past Raoul—he was sitting on a bench reading the newspaper—but he reached out and caught the skirt of her dress. He looked the same, the most beautiful man she had ever known, but his face had changed, too. He looked sad; he looked scared. Both her fault.

She didn't cry. She just stood and ate him up with her eyes, and when he said, "Do you need help with your bags?" she let him come to her rescue.

Kayla stifled all the questions that had been running through her mind for the previous six weeks: *Do you still love me, can we make this work, will you ever trust me again?* She reminded herself that Raoul was a builder; he believed in process. The relationship would have to be restored one brick at a time. There was no quick fix, and there were no easy answers.

Still, she felt she had to be the first to say something. As they stood at the baggage claim waiting for her suitcase, she spoke up. "I missed you."

"Oh, yeah?" he said.

She swallowed. "Yeah. Did you miss me?"

He turned and took her in his arms, and she pressed her face into the side of his neck and wondered how she'd made it through six weeks without him.

"Oh, yeah," he said.

By Thanksgiving, things appeared, on the outside, to be back to normal. Kayla ventured out of the house again, although she spoke to no one about what had happened Labor Day weekend. When people asked about Theo, she told them he was attending Boston Hill to improve his chances of getting into a good college.

Raoul went to court and was fined five hundred dollars and sentenced to fifty hours of community service. He offered to build a new jungle gym for the elementary school playground, and he let Luke help him design it. He and his crew started work on a house on Eel Point Road. The client bought the sixty-five-acre parcel of land for almost twenty million dollars and he told Raoul he wanted a house that would make the Tings' look like a scallop shanty.

The kids—Jennifer, Cassidy B., and Luke—still didn't know the whole story. They became absorbed with school and friends and pretended to forget all about it.

Raoul and Kayla called Sabrina to find out how Theo was doing. He was hurt, Sabrina said, but healing. Kayla wanted to talk to him, she wanted to see him, but he wasn't ready. He needed space, he needed time. Kayla, more than anyone else in the family, understood.

In the *Inquirer and Mirror* in the middle of November, Kayla saw that John and Val's house had sold for over a million dollars. A few weeks later, the Nantucket Bar Association placed an ad wishing Valerie Gluckstern "lots of luck in her new practice in Annapolis, Maryland." Kayla felt a sense of loss, but more than anything, she was relieved.

On the outside, everything appeared to be back to normal.

And then, December. The day that Kayla went Christmas shopping in town, the day when everything seemed so festive, so right. The day the phone call came that nearly stopped her heart.

"Kayla," the voice on the answering machine said. "This is Paul Henry. I have news. Please call me."

I have news. Kayla walked aimlessly through the house, trying to control her breathing. She entered Theo's room. It was pristine—dusted, vacuumed, bed made. The way Kayla always imagined it would look once Theo went to college, until she and Raoul bought a large piece of exercise equipment, or decided to redecorate and make it a guest room.

I have news.

What was she afraid of? The reality of Antoinette's death—perhaps even the physical reality of it, the remains of Antoinette's body. What would that look like now, after so many months? A skeleton? A blue, bloated corpse? Once Kayla saw the body, the body that contained her grandchild, it would haunt her forever. She would see it in her sleep, she would become afraid of the dark. The finality of it: a dead body. Not to mention the possible criminal charges, the word *murder* silently attached to Kayla's name. Or not so silently: If the detective drummed up enough evidence, there would be an indictment, a trial.

I can't do it, she thought, longing for her one-bedroom unit at Mary Lee's by the Sea. *I can't call him back.*

What was more terrifying was the thought that Antoinette might be alive.

She tried to forget about the message. After all, it was Christmastime. Kayla convinced Raoul to take the next day off of work and they flew to the Cape to do some Christmas shopping while the kids were in school. They bought Luke a North Face jacket and a Razor scooter, Cassidy B. a complete set of grown-up art supplies: oil paints, watercolors, pastels, charcoal pencils, sculpting clay. They bought Jennifer a leather skirt and Rollerblades. They bought Theo a computer and arranged to have it sent to Boston. Then, exhausted, they ate lunch in the noisy, crowded food court, where kids too young for school screamed and smashed French fries into their hair.

There, amid the din, Kayla heard Paul Henry's voice. *I have news.*

Kayla listened to the piped-in Christmas music, Karen Carpenter singing, "Have Yourself a Merry Little Christmas." She wanted to disappear into the glitter and tinsel and spun sugar of Christmas at the Cape Cod Mall. Forget about drownings and love affairs and detectives. But the specter of Paul Henry crunched into her Christmas spirit like the Grinch. Kayla tried to smile at Raoul across the dinky Formica table.

"Is something wrong?" he asked her. "You seem preoccupied."

"I have to make a phone call," she said. "Where are the pay phones?"

"Who do you have to call?" Raoul asked.

"Your mother," Kayla lied. "There was something else she said Theo wanted, something for school, but I can't remember what."

Raoul nodded and Kayla ran around the perimeter of the food court until she found the corridor with the rest rooms and the pay phones.

"Come in," Paul Henry said.

"I can't," Kayla said. "I'm in Hyannis. Christmas shopping. Just tell me what the news is, Paul. Did you find a body?"

"I'll tell you when you come in," he said. "This

isn't something I'm willing to tell you over the phone. Tomorrow morning?"

"Fine," Kayla said. She slammed down the phone.

"What did mom say?" Raoul asked when she returned. He was busy finishing her chicken teriyaki and didn't notice her agitation.

"Sabrina wasn't home," Kayla said.

"Probably out shopping for dinner," Raoul said.

The police station was decorated for Christmas—a row of garlands across the front desk, blinking white lights in the window. The officer behind the glass shield was wearing a Santa hat. He took one look at Kayla and picked up a phone. Paul Henry emerged from the hallway ten seconds later. He reached for Kayla's hand and, incredibly, kissed her on the cheek. Kayla hadn't slept at all the night before. She lay next to Raoul counting his breaths, imagining possible scenarios. Kayla realized she was grateful for one reason. She wanted an end; as gruesome or as scary as it might be, she wanted closure.

She followed Paul Henry down the dim hallway to his office. Paul Henry sat down behind a kidney-shaped desk. Kayla collapsed in a needlepoint chair while Paul Henry opened a manila file folder. He read. Kayla studied the photographs on his desk— his wife, Carla, their kids, a grandchild. Kayla studied his hands—he wore a gold wedding band. Raoul never wore his wedding ring because when he built houses it could catch on something. Instead, he kept it in a plain white box in his sock drawer. A lonely gold band with her name inscribed inside and their wedding date, June 1, 1981.

Kayla looked expectantly at Paul Henry.

"I have to tell you, Kayla, I called the woman's daughter yesterday. Told her who I was. She hung up on me, and I haven't had any luck reaching her again."

"Okay."

Paul Henry took a small notepad and copied something from the file. Like a doctor writing down the diagnosis of a terminal disease, Kayla thought. He slid the paper across the desk. Kayla was afraid to look at it. "Can't you just tell me?"

Paul Henry put down his pen. "Ms. Riley is living on Martha's Vineyard."

"She's *alive*?" Kayla's stomach dropped; she started to sweat. "For the love of God, Paul, she's *alive*? Living on the Vineyard? Are you sure?"

"Detective Simpson was conducting the missing persons, and he subpoenaed pertinent information from Valerie Gluckstern's office."

"What kind of information?"

"Information about Ms. Riley's assets. Back when this whole situation started, John Gluckstern told us that his wife had convinced Ms. Riley to take her assets out of Nantucket Bank and invest them with a broker in London."

"London," Kayla repeated.

"We finally tracked down the guy in London, and he refused to answer our questions, so we went to his supervisor and what we found out was that the bank has been sending Ms. Riley money to an address on the Vineyard the first of every month . . . since, well, since September."

"You're kidding." Kayla nearly swooned. She put a hand on Paul Henry's desk. "Did Val know? Did Val know this whole time that Antoinette was alive?"

"I called Valerie myself and asked her because I couldn't believe it. She said she merely put Antoinette in contact with the London broker and that she knew nothing of their arrangements." Paul Henry smoothed his crew cut. "If Valerie knew all along that Ms. Riley 'ran away,' as it were, we can slap some fraud charges on her. Detective Simpson has big hopes for this. I don't. This police station isn't set up to handle big cases. I'm just glad Ms. Riley is alive."

Kayla looked at the piece of paper. "This is Antoinette's address?"

"Supposedly."

"What should I do with it?"

Paul Henry shrugged. "Whatever you want. Go see her. Don't go see her. I guess Detective Simpson was hoping you could give him a positive ID so that he could close the case." Paul Henry reddened. "You certainly don't have to do anything for Simpson's sake. He was awfully rough with you, Kayla. I'm sorry."

"Val was rough with me. I really can't believe this. I can't believe Antoinette is alive. I thought . . . really, I don't know what I thought."

"Well, again, I'm sorry for what happened. I don't like to see good people, good Nantucketers, take it on the chin like you and Raoul did. And your son."

Kayla stuffed the paper into her purse. "Okay," she said. She knew Paul Henry was looking for some sign of forgiveness, but she couldn't give it to him. She had to get out of there. "Thanks."

On the way home, Kayla stopped at Hatch's and bought a six-pack of beer and a five-dollar scratch ticket. Antoinette was alive, on Martha's Vineyard. Kayla laughed in the check-out line.

Later, she sat at the breakfast bar and drank two beers with her lunch. A cream cheese and grape jelly sandwich and eight Lay's potato chips. *Val had known the whole time.* There wasn't a doubt in Kayla's mind. She scraped the silver film off her scratch ticket with her thumbnail. Nothing. She used to find old scratch tickets all over Theo's room. He'd bought them at the Islander Liquor Store, back when he used to hang out with his friends. Back when he was a normal kid. The word that filled Kayla's mind was *outrageous*, because at the center of that word was rage. *Antoinette is fucking alive. On the fucking Vineyard.* And Valerie knew. Now things started to make sense. Val pretended that Antoinette had drowned so no one would suspect otherwise. She threw Kayla to the police to keep the police from investigating any deeper, but she knew Kayla wouldn't get into any serious trouble because a body would never be found. Kayla had left Great Point for at least half an hour when she went to call the police. There was plenty of time for Antoinette to crawl out of the

water and escape. Maybe she'd left her bike somewhere along the way, maybe she rode to Val's house
and hid out there until morning when the ferry left
for Martha's Vineyard, which on Labor Day weekend would have been filled with tourists. Or Antoinette could have taken a motor boat; she knew how
to operate one—Kayla remembered the trip to Tuckernuck with Theo years before. It mattered very little
at this point how Antoinette got to the Vineyard.
Once there, she was safe. The Vineyard was the perfect place to hide. It was too close, too obvious, and
for these very reasons it was the last place anyone
would have looked.

But why, Antoinette? Why run away?

Kayla had to go see for herself.

With the kids at school and Raoul at work on his
huge new project, it was easy to slip away the next
day. There was one ferry to the Vineyard in the
morning, and one ferry home in the afternoon. Kayla
was one of three people on the boat. She hunkered
down in a window seat and inventoried the damage
that Antoinette had caused—Theo's heart, for starters; Kayla's good reputation; Kayla and Raoul's
marriage; Kayla and Val's friendship; Ting. If Kayla
did find Antoinette on the Vineyard, what could she
possibly say? Only this: *You ruined everything.* Outrageous.

Martha's Vineyard was much bigger than Nantucket;
it had seven towns to Nantucket's one. The town of

Vineyard Haven, though, had the same slow pace of Nantucket in winter. When Kayla arrived, there was a line of taxis, each with a Christmas wreath tied to the grille, and the drivers were clustered together, warming their hands around cups of coffee. Kayla stood by the passenger door of the first taxi in line until the driver, a man with long, deep lines in his face, tore himself away from the group. He wore jeans, a gray hooded sweatshirt.

"Where you headed?" he asked.

"I'm not sure," she said. The paper said: *52 Painted Rock Road, between Chilmark and Aquinnah.* When they climbed into the car, she handed it to the driver.

His face creased into more lines. "Well, I know where Chilmark and Aquinnah are, but I've never heard of Painted Rock Road. You sure that's the right name?"

"No," Kayla said. "This is just an address someone gave me. A . . . a friend of mine lives there."

"I've lived here twenty-six years," the driver said. "Been driving cab fourteen and I have never heard of any Painted Rock Road."

That sounds like Antoinette, Kayla thought. She was forever stumping the taxi drivers on Nantucket. Even with the address they couldn't find her house.

"Can you take me out that way?" Kayla asked. "You can drop me off, maybe, and I'll look for it?"

The driver shrugged. Kayla saw on his license that his name was Eddie.

"Okay," Eddie said. He shifted his car into gear.

"We'll give it a whirl."

They drove out of Vineyard Haven and hopped on the state road. "I'm headed up-island," Eddie said into his radio. "Don't know when I'll be back." Kayla looked out the window at the acres of open land, farm land, pine forest. It was turning out to be a nice day; the sun came out for brief periods before disappearing behind white puffy clouds.

After a while, they passed a hand-painted sign that said *CHILMARK CHOCOLATES*.

"So we're in Chilmark, then?" Kayla asked.

"Yep," Eddie said.

"We should start looking for signs," Kayla said.

"If there's a sign for this Painted Rock Road, I've never seen it before."

"Oh," Kayla said.

Eddie picked up his radio. "Hey, anybody out there ever heard of Painted Rock Road?"

Static.

"Hey, Norm, you out there? Carrie, doll?"

A woman's voice. "I'm here, Eddie. Can't help ya."

More static.

Kayla watched mailboxes sail by. Eddie was driving pretty fast. "Maybe we should slow down," she said. "So we can look?"

A man's voice broke the static. "Painted Rock's off the left hand side of State, Eddie. Two turns before the Kaiser place."

"You're kidding," Eddie said. "There's no houses down that turn, though, Norm. There's no sign."

"Nope, no sign. Just a rock there at the turn with blue paint. You've probably never seen it," Norm said. "And there is one house back there, Eddie. I know because I dropped off the woman who lives there a week or so ago."

The woman who lives there.

Eddie nuzzled his radio. "Thanks for the tip, Norm." He looked back at Kayla and shrugged. "Learn something new, et cetera, et cetera."

Kayla was suddenly too petrified to speak.

With this information from Norm, Eddie found the road almost instantly.

"No shit," he said. "A rock with blue paint. There it is."

Kayla fumbled through her purse for money. "You can just leave me off here," she said. "I'll walk to the house. Truth is, I'd like to smoke a cigarette before I get there."

Eddie pulled over to the side of the road just past the blue rock. "No problem," he said. "Fifteen bucks."

Kayla gave him a twenty and told him to keep the change. He smiled. "Have a nice visit with your friend," he said. "And Merry Christmas."

It was sunny but cold. Kayla wore jeans, a turtle-neck, and a black corduroy jacket. She put on her gloves and began to walk. Painted Rock Road was a dirt road surrounded on both sides by thick trees. It felt eerily familiar. Same setting, different island. Kayla saw other footprints in the dirt. Antoinette's footprints? Or the footprints of some other woman? Kayla followed the footprints to a clearing, a small yard, a house. The house was long and narrow, a bunch of rooms lined up like boxcars on a train. Cedar shingles, forest green shutters, empty window boxes. A stucco chimney gurgled smoke.

Someone was home, enjoying a fire.

Kayla crunched up the gravel driveway. Fairy tales played through her head: "Hansel and Gretel," "Goldilocks and the Three Bears." An evil-looking crow cawed from the roof. Kayla knocked on the front door three times. A friendly knock.

No answer.

Kayla knocked again, this time a little more aggressively. She wondered if someone was watching her from behind the curtains.

Still no answer.

Kayla rounded the side of the house with the chimney and stepped into the back yard. She was alarmed to discover the back of the house had huge windows and glass doors. Kayla could see right in— the beautiful cherry cabinets in the kitchen, the bar stools, one with a paperback copy of *The Bluest Eye* splayed on top. A small Christmas tree glittered with white lights on the kitchen counter. Behind the kitchen was a living room with a huge stone fireplace—and lying on the sofa in front of the fire, Kayla saw Antoinette, fast asleep.

Pregnant.

Kayla gasped. She should leave. Right now, leave. Give the detective his positive ID—*Yes, that was Antoinette. Case closed*. But Kayla couldn't help herself. She walked closer to the glass doors;

she pressed her face against the glass because she had to be sure.

Antoinette lay on her side, her hands resting on her swollen belly. She wore a pleated white blouse. Antoinette in white—it seemed odd. Her hair was loose, frizzed out on the sofa cushion, her eyes were closed, and her mouth hung open slightly. Kayla stared unabashedly. She remembered the incredible exhaustion of pregnancy, how it had weighed her down. And now here was Antoinette pregnant-tired with Kayla's grandchild. Kayla reached for the handle of the sliding glass door. It was open. Kayla walked right in and tiptoed over to Antoinette; she stood so close she could hear Antoinette's breathing. So close she could touch Antoinette's forehead, which was shiny and dotted with small pimples. After all this time, months of speculation, here she was. *You ran away from us*, Kayla thought. *And in so doing, you ruined everything*. But staring at the roundness of Antoinette's body, Kayla softened. Antoinette had kept the baby, after all.

And then, without warning, Antoinette's eyes opened, and she looked at Kayla.

Kayla smiled at her. "Hello, old friend."

A baffled expression crossed Antoinette's face; her brow wrinkled. "You found me?"

"Apparently so."

Antoinette blinked, confused. "Apparently so," she repeated. She put a hand on the sofa beneath her in an attempt to push herself upright.

"Don't get up," Kayla said. "I'm not staying."

"Do you have a gun?" Antoinette asked.

"A gun?"

"Don't you want to kill me?"

Kayla laughed. "Sort of, yeah. But I don't want to kill what's inside you."

Antoinette relaxed; she rubbed her stomach. "It's a girl, Kayla."

Tears sprang to Kayla's eyes, and she stared into the fire. "A girl, huh?" She began to cry, unsure of how to feel. On the outside, things seemed to have gone back to normal, but inside of Kayla, everything had changed. The things that money couldn't buy— a happy marriage, good kids, loyal friends—floated in the air around Kayla like snowflakes. At one time, she'd had them all, but now they were gone, and in their place was this news. A baby, after all. A baby girl. Kayla wiped her tears away with the back of her hand and took a deep breath, but when she turned back to Antoinette, she broke down again.

"Why the hell did you . . . and Val . . . she didn't tell me . . . she *accused* me . . ."

"I made Val promise," Antoinette said. "I swore her to secrecy."

"But the two of you are supposed to keep secrets with me, not from me."

"We wanted to protect you."

"Protect me?"

"Protect Theo," Antoinette said. "He can't know about this. It will only set him back, Kayla. He needs to move forward. You know I'm right about that. Please don't tell him."

"He's heartbroken," Kayla said.

"So am I," Antoinette said. "At least he has me

to blame. I have to blame myself. I do, you know—accept the blame for everything. I will feel guilty for the rest of my life."

"Good," Kayla said. If Jacob Anderson had taught her anything, it was that guilt was the worst that life had to deal out. And Antoinette deserved the worst. "You hurt a lot of people. You hurt me."

"I know, Kayla. I'm sorry."

Kayla stuffed her hands into the pockets of her jeans. She and Antoinette looked at each other for a long moment—Kayla really looked. Her friend dressed in white for the first time, the frizzy hair, the swollen belly—a woman she'd never understood, but had loved anyway. Kayla wondered what Antoinette saw: A wife? A mother? A friend?

"I have to tell Theo," Kayla said. "There's no way I can keep this from him."

"You can't tell him," Antoinette said. "He deserves a second chance—at love, at a family. Once he's older."

"Yes, but . . ."

"Kayla," Antoinette said. "Twenty years ago we made a promise to keep each other's secrets safe from the rest of the world. That includes Theo."

"He's going to find out sooner or later," Kayla said.

"Then let it be later. Promise me he won't hear it from you."

Kayla nodded and warm tears spilled down her cheeks. "Will you raise her well?" Kayla said. "This little girl of ours?"

"I will," Antoinette said. "This is my second

chance. I waited a long time for this, Kayla."

"I didn't know you wanted a second chance," Kayla said.

"That was my confession," Antoinette said. "I want a second chance. Please."

Kayla didn't know how to respond, and she sensed she never would.

"Merry Christmas," Kayla said. She walked back to the door and stepped out into the cold, bright day. When she turned around, Antoinette's eyes had fallen closed once again and Kayla watched her deep breathing resume, her chest rising and falling in a rhythm as perfect and steady as the waves of the ocean.

Kayla walked all the way back to Vineyard Haven; several cars stopped to offer her a ride, but she declined. She was in a trance of sorts. She replayed the conversation over and over and had to quell the desire to return and bombard Antoinette with what remained: her anger, her questions, her remorse. But those things were rapidly losing importance, and in their place, Kayla felt a growing sense of freedom. It was over. Complete. Ending not with a death at all, but with a life. Her granddaughter's life would be the last Night Swimmers secret, the secret that would bind her to Val and Antoinette even if she never saw them again. The hardest secret to keep.

Forgive me, Theo, Kayla thought. *Because I am a mother, too, I understand.*

• • •

As Kayla waited for the ferry to Nantucket, she thought about the little girl who would be entering the world soon, a little girl connected to Kayla's life, and to her husband, and to her son, and to her dear friend. This little girl changed things, transformed them. Kayla hoped Antoinette would raise the baby to be strong and wise and yes, sensitive, like her grandmother. Maybe someday Antoinette would tell her the story about Night Swimmers, about three women who shared secrets that they couldn't share with anyone else. Maybe when this baby grew up, she would have female friends of her own. To be friends with another woman was difficult, Kayla thought, and painful and complicated. But when a friendship between women was good, it had a sacred, shining power. Kayla gathered up memories of this power—and there were many—as she stepped onto the ferry and headed for home.

Acknowledgments

My deep and unending gratitude to:

My agent, Michael Carlisle, who is a safe place for me in the chaotic world of New York publishing, and Jennifer Weis, my editor at St. Martin's Press, who knows commercial fiction like nobody else.

Jeff Allen, of the Nantucket Fire Department, for his detailed descriptions of open water rescue.

The women in my life who have taught me about friendship. (You know who you are.)

Clarissa Porter, for reminding me that I had a literary mind even when I was up to my elbows in baby food, and Mimi Beman, of Mitchell's Book Corner, for her enthusiastic support of my work.

Heather Osteen Thorpe, always my first reader.

My mother, Sally Hilderbrand, for my roots and my wings.

Most of all, thank you to the men in my life, or should I say, the men who are my life: my husband, Chip Cunningham, and our shining star, Maxwell.

Read on for an excerpt from
Elin Hilderbrand's next book

Summer People

Now available in paperback from St. Martin's Press!

Chapter 1

Driving off the ferry, they looked like any other family coming to spend the summer on Nantucket—or almost. The car was a 1998 Range Rover in flat forest green, its rear section packed to within inches of the roof with Pierre Deux weekend duffels, boxes of kitchen equipment, four shopping bags from Zabar's, and a plastic trash bag of linens. (The summer house, Horizon, had its own linens, of course, but Beth remembered those sheets and towels from her childhood—the towels, for example, were chocolate brown and patterned with leaves. Threadbare. Beth wanted plush towels; she took comfort now wherever she could find it.)

Three out of the four passengers in the car were related, as any one of the people milling around Steamship Wharf could tell. Beth, the mother, was forty-four years old and at the end of pretty with blond hair pulled back in a clip, a light tan already (from running in Central Park in the mornings), and green eyes flecked with yellow, which made one think of a meadow. White linen blouse, wrinkled now. A diamond ring, too big to be overlooked. One of Beth's seventeen-year-old twins, her daughter, Winnie, slumped in the front seat, and the other twin, her son, Garrett, sat in back. That there was no father in the car was hardly unusual—lots of women Beth knew took their kids away for the summer while their husbands toiled on Wall Street or in law firms. So it wasn't Arch's absence that set their family apart from the others on this clear, hot day. Rather it was the dark-skinned boy, also seventeen, who shared the backseat with Garrett: Marcus Tyler, living proof of their larger, sadder story.

Beth lifted her ass off the driver's seat. She'd driven the whole way, even though the twins had their learner's permits and might have helped. She'd been awake since five o'clock that morning, and after four hours on the highway and two on the ferry, her mind stalled in inconvenient places, like a car dying in a busy intersection. In her side-view mirror, Beth checked on the two mountain bikes hanging off the back of the car. (It had always been Arch's job to secure them, and this year she did it herself. Miraculously, they were both intact.) When she brought her attention forward again—she couldn't *wait* to get off this boat!—her gaze stuck on her diamond ring, perched as it was on top of the steering wheel. This wasn't the ring that Arch had given her twenty years ago when he proposed, but a really extravagant ring that he presented to her last summer. He called it the "We Made It" ring, because they *had* made it, financially, at least. They had enough money that a not-insignificant amount could be wasted on this diamond ring. "Wasted" was Beth's word; she was the frugal one, always worrying that they had two kids headed for college, and what if the car got stolen, what if there were a fire? What if there were some kind of accident?

You worry too much, Arch said.

A rotund man wearing a Day-Glo vest, long pants, and a long-sleeved shirt in industrial blue, even on this sweltering day in June, motioned for Beth to drive off the ramp, following, though not too closely, the car in front of her. Seconds later Beth was not on the ferry anymore—not on the ferry, not on I-95, not in a parking garage on East Eighty-second Street. She was on Nantucket Island. The rotund steamship man waved at her—(she could see him mouthing, "Come on, lady, come on," as if she were just another elegant housewife from Chappaqua,) but he didn't know what had happened to her. He didn't know that, along with the Pierre Deux bags and the expensive mountain bikes, they'd brought along the urn that held her husband's ashes.

Beth's forehead grew hot, her nose tingled. Here, again, were the tears. It was the new way she evaluated her day: On a good day she cried only twice, in the morning shower and before her Valium kicked in at night. On a bad day, a *stressful* day, it was like this—without warning, in front of the kids, while she was *driving*, in *traffic*. Tears assaulting her like a migraine.

"Mom," Winnie said. She'd slept for most of the drive and the ferry ride, and now she gazed out the window as they cruised past the bike shops, the ice cream parlor, the Sunken Ship on the corner. The whaling museum. The Dreamland Theater. People were everywhere—on the sidewalks, in the stores, riding bikes, eating ice cream cones. As if nothing bad could happen. As if nothing could hurt them. Meanwhile, Beth negotiated the traffic surprisingly well at full sob.

"Mom," Winnie said again, touching her mother's leg. But what else could she say? Winnie pulled the neck of her sweatshirt up over her nose and inhaled. It was her father's old, raggedy Princeton sweatshirt, which he'd worn often, sometimes to the gym in their building, and it smelled like him. Of all their father's clothes, the sweatshirt had smelled the most like him and so that was what Winnie took. She'd worn it every day since he died, ninety-three days ago. Winnie tried to convince herself that it still smelled like him, but his smell was fading, much the way her father's vivid, everyday presence in her mind was fading. She couldn't remember the whole of him, only bits and pieces: the way he loosened his tie when he walked into the apartment at the end of the day, the way he ate a piece of pizza folded in half, the way he'd fidgeted with a twig when he told her and Garrett the facts of life one warm and very embarrassing autumn afternoon in Strawberry Fields. (Why hadn't her mother done "the talk"? Winnie had asked her mother that question a few weeks after the memorial service—now that Daddy was dead, certain topics could be broached—and Beth said simply, "Your father wanted to do it. He considered it one of the joys of parenting.") A whole life lived and all Winnie would be left with were snippets, a box of snapshots. She breathed in, listening to the atonality of her mother's sobs as if it were bad music. The sweatshirt no longer smelled like her father. Now it smelled like Winnie.

The Rover bounced up Main Street, which was paved with cobblestones. Garrett shifted uneasily in his seat and checked for the hundredth time on the urn, which was a solid, silent presence between him and Marcus. It was embarrassing to have his mom losing it with a stranger in the car. Beth kept Garrett awake at night with her crying and he had a weird sense of role reversal, like she was the kid and he was the parent. The Man of the House, now. And Winnie—well, Winnie was even worse than his mother, wearing that sweatshirt every day since March sixteenth—every day: to school over her uniform, to sleep, even. And Winnie refused to eat. She looked like a Holocaust victim, a person with anorexia. And yet these two loonies were far preferable company to the individual sitting next to him. Garrett couldn't believe their bad luck. The last thing Arch had done, practically, before his plane went down, was to invite Marcus Tyler to Nantucket—not for a week, not for a month—but for the entire summer. And since a dead man's words were as good as law, they were stuck with Marcus.

Your father invited him to come along, Beth said. *We can't exactly back out.*

Yeah, Winnie said. *Daddy invited him.*

Garrett tried to talk to his mother about it, using

the most powerful words he had at his disposal, the words of their therapist, Dr. Schau, whom they all saw together and separately.

We need to heal this summer, Garrett said. *As a family.*

Your father invited him for a reason, Beth said, though Garrett could tell even she wasn't sure what the reason was, and Garrett called her on it.

We need to help those less fortunate, his mother responded lamely.

Why is Marcus less fortunate? Garrett said. *He has a father.*

You know why, his mother said.

Because Marcus was the son of a murderer. Even as the Range Rover jostled up Main Street, Marcus's mother, Constance Bennett Tyler, was locked up in Bedford Hills Correctional Facility because she had killed two people. Arch had been Constance's defense attorney, and he'd gotten to know Marcus and like him. That was why Garrett shared the backseat with this huge black kid, this refugee from one of the most talked-about court cases in New York City in years. And because Marcus was the same age as Winnie and Garrett they had to be friends. Because of the tragedies in life that had converged on the four people sitting in this car, they had to join together. Empathize. It was the most twisted, unfair situation Garrett could imagine, and yet it was happening to him this summer.

Garrett glanced sideways at Marcus. Marcus was wearing an expensive-looking white dress shirt with his initials—"MGT"—embroidered on the pocket. It was the kind of shirt one wore to brunch or a college interview, though it was inappropriate for seven hours of car travel. Marcus had been sweating the whole ride and now the shirt looked like it'd been plucked from the bottom of a laundry hamper. Marcus had shown up at their apartment that morning wearing a squeaky new pair of dock shoes, which looked so unlikely on Marcus's feet that Garrett wondered if he'd worn the shoes to mock them somehow, to mock this trip to Nantucket. He'd taken the shoes off before they even hit Connecticut and his enormous bare feet gave off an odor that nearly caused Garrett to gag. Before Garrett could dwell on the other aspects of Marcus's appearance that bothered him—his closely-shaved head, his heavy-lidded eyes that made it seem like he was always half asleep—Garrett realized that Marcus had his elbow on the urn. He was using the urn as an *armrest*. Garrett held no fantasies about the contents of the urn—it was only ashes, another form of matter. There had been a few weak attempts at levity since the urn arrived from the crematorium—one night, Garrett set the urn at their father's place at the dining room table—but Garrett didn't believe the urn in any way contained his father. Only the remains of the body that once belonged to his father. Still, using the urn as an armrest was *not* okay. Garrett glared at Marcus, but refrained from saying anything. They'd made it all the way from New York City without incident and Garrett didn't want to start trouble now, when they were almost at the house. An instant later, as if reading Garrett's mind, Marcus lifted his oxford-clad elbow and Garrett moved the urn into his lap, where it would be safe from further indignities.

Marcus was the only one who thought to offer Beth a tissue. She seemed genuinely grateful, turning her head so that he could see her try to smile. "Thanks, Marcus," she said. She stopped crying long enough to blot her eyes and wipe the runny stuff from her nose. "Here it is your first time on Nantucket and I'm blubbering so hard I can't point things out. I'm sorry."

"S'okay," he said. He'd gotten the gist of the place already: the gray shingled houses, the cobblestone streets, the shops with expensive clothes and brass lanterns and antique rocking horses in the windows. White people everywhere all excited about summer.

Beth stopped crying and put on her sunglasses. Marcus wasn't sure what to make of the woman. He couldn't tell if she was being nice to him because she wanted to, or because she felt she had to—if pressed, he would lean toward the latter. She spoke to him like he was in nursery school. (At McDonald's that morning for breakfast, with a pinched smile, "And, Marcus, what would *you* like? How about some pancakes?" As if he was too simple to navigate his way around the menu.)

Marcus had met the twins twice before. The first time was when Arch brought them along to visit Marcus and his family in Queens. The twins had stood in the apartment looking around like they were on a field trip about poverty; he could almost hear them thinking, "So this is where it happened." The second time Marcus met them was at Trinity Episcopal Church on East Eighty-eighth Street, at the memorial service for Arch. The twins' father, Arch Newton, had been the gold standard of human beings (Marcus intended to use this phrase in the book he was writing), the only white person in all of America who was willing to help save his mother's life. And for free—an expensive Manhattan lawyer who offered to defend Constance Bennett Tyler against the death penalty, even though everyone knew she was guilty as sin.

I'm going to help your mom, Arch told Marcus. *I'm going to see that she gets the best possible defense.*

Arch was there through the worst of it: the hot hours in the courtroom, the cold visits to Rikers, the reporters, the TV cameras, the disturbing photographs in the *New York Times,* especially the one of Candy's body being carried from the building, all of her covered by a sheet except for her patent leather shoes, the shoes that, ironically, Constance had bought for her. They reprinted this photo a lot; it became the icon for the case. Every time Arch saw the photo, he tore it in half. *They love it because it screams, "Baby killer!"* he said. If it weren't for Arch's powerful, steadying presence—his defense less a legal term and more like a physical shield that he held over Marcus and his family—Marcus never would have made it. But then, on the evening of

March fifteenth, flying back from Albany, where Arch had traveled to meet with an attorney he knew who was close to the governor and might be able to speak out on Constance's behalf, Arch's plane crashed into Long Island Sound. Ice on the wings. It was a week before the trial was to start, and bizarrely, Arch's death added an element of humanity that had been missing from the defense's case; the media softened, hailing Arch as a hero for the common man, specifically, for a woman facing death row with no resources to fight it. Another attorney from Arch's firm took the case to trial, which lasted only three days. The jury convicted Constance of one count of first-degree murder, and one count of second degree murder, but the judge spared her the death penalty, and nobody protested. It was as if Arch had taken the punishment for her.

Offering Beth a tissue was the least Marcus could do. Because what all four people in the car knew but nobody acknowledged out loud was that if Arch hadn't been defending Constance, he wouldn't have died. And so, Marcus *would* be a slave to these people if that was what they wanted. He'd haul out the garbage cans, he'd sweep sand off the porch, he'd rub oil onto their backs so they didn't burn in the sun. Yes, he would. Before Marcus left New York, his father, Bo, said, *These people didn't have to invite you, son. So be a big help, and make me proud.*

As they drove out of town, the houses grew farther apart. Then Beth signaled left and they turned onto a dirt road. Bumpy. Dirt and sand filled the air, gravel crunched under the tires.

Marcus would offer to wash the car.

He saw the ocean—it was in front of them suddenly, glinting in the sun like a big silver platter. Beth shut off the air-conditioning and put down all four windows.

"We're here," she said. She pulled into a white shell driveway that led to a house—a big, old, gray-shingled house—which sat on a ledge overlooking the water.

"Whoa," Marcus said.

Beth shut off the engine and climbed out of the car, raising her hands to the sky. "It takes my breath away every time. I feel better. Kids, I feel better already."

Marcus stuffed his feet into his very uncomfortable white-person shoes, wondering if he should help unload the car, but before he could make a move, Winnie took his hand and pulled him to the edge of the bluff. "Look, Marcus. What do you think?"

Marcus thought he might be experiencing some kind of reverse claustrophobia. Because he felt queasy, unsettled, unable to place himself. He was used to the Elmhurst section of Queens, and Main Street, Flushing. He was used to dirty streets and bodegas that smelled like too many cats and the long line outside the yellow brick public health building on Junction Boulevard. He was used to Shea Stadium and LaGuardia Airport—obnoxious Mets fans in their blue-and-orange hats crowding the subway cars, jumbo jets overhead at any given moment. He was used to sitting in the back row of the classrooms at Benjamin N. Cardozo High School so nobody could stare him down. He was used to a dark, low-ceilinged apartment that he shared with his father, his sister LaTisha, and the belongings of his mother—her head scarves, her record albums, her knock-off Prada bag—things that now simply took up space because she would never be back to reclaim them. He was *not* used to this—a Range Rover with leather seats, a white shell driveway, a golden beach, the Atlantic fucking Ocean, not to mention people who were civil to him even though they knew his mother was a murderer.

"It's cool," he said.

Winnie steered him toward the front door. "Come inside," she said.

Beth pulled the key out from under the welcome mat.

"Has that been there all winter?" Marcus asked.

"It has," she said. "And this is the last time we'll use the key until we leave in September."

"You're kidding," Marcus said. "What if somebody steals your stuff?"

Beth laughed. "That's the beauty of this place. Nobody's going to steal our stuff."

When Marcus got inside, he realized there wasn't much worth stealing. He followed Beth through the rooms, nervously thinking of Garrett behind him carrying bags. He should be helping Garrett. But Winnie had taken his hand and now he was sandwiched between Beth and Winnie both asking him, *Didn't he just love it? Didn't he think it was magnificent?*

The house was big. Marcus could say that with confidence. There was a hallway where you walked in with a living room on the right. A flight of stairs on the left. Past the stairs were a kitchen and dining room that had a row of windows and glass doors looking out over the water, and a deck beyond the kitchen with a green plastic table and chairs. The house was big but not fancy. The furniture was white wicker, except for one nasty-looking recliner the color of a dead mouse. The pictures on the walls were faded watercolors of the beach; the curtains were a creepy filmy material. The floorboards creaked and the house had a smell. An old, grandmother smell. Marcus wasn't sure what he'd expected—he guessed he'd pictured something like a fashion magazine, something more like the Newtons' apartment on Park Avenue which he'd seen for the first time that morning—with real antiques and Oriental carpets and brass candlesticks and sculpture. This house didn't feel like poverty, just like a house owned by white people who'd stopped caring. How had Arch described it? *A funky old summer cottage*—and Marcus had pretended to understand what that meant. Now he knew, it meant this. This was how white people lived when they relaxed at the beach.

Marcus checked out the view from the deck and then wandered back through the first floor. Garrett brought in a second load of stuff and dropped it at Marcus's feet in the living room. Marcus was looking for the TV; he didn't see one anywhere.

"Is there TV?" Marcus asked.

"No," Garrett said. "Sorry, man, you're going to have to do without *Bernie Mac* for the summer."

"Hey," Marcus said, straightening his shoulders in his new white shirt that was so fine it felt like money on his back. *Fuck you* was on the tip of his tongue. What the fuck was that supposed to mean? Was that a racial comment already? Well, why not? Why not put him in his slave's place right away? Before Marcus could prepare a response, Garrett was headed out the door again, aiming for load number three. Marcus followed him out.

"I don't appreciate your tone," Marcus said. He sounded, ridiculously, like a homeroom teacher. Garrett didn't even turn around. "I'm sorry I'm bumming you out. I don't want to ruin your summer with your family." Marcus couldn't believe he was talking like this. What he'd learned in the past nine months was that the easiest response to other people's shit was silence. Let his eyes drop to half mast, pretend like he hadn't heard. Pretend like nothing they said could bother him. Marcus would get his revenge on everyone later, once his book was published.

"Why did you come, then?" Garrett said. "I know my mother offered. But you could have said no. You could have spent the summer at home. Closer to . . . your own family. Why did you come with us?"

Marcus felt guilt rising in his throat along with his long-ago-eaten breakfast. He *should* be at home. His father was going through a very stressful time trying to live without Mama. But things at home had gotten so horrible that Marcus needed to escape. At home, the phone was always ringing, the press calling, or people who had somehow gotten their number who wanted to share their feelings about what a monster Constance was. Marcus had lost all his friends, he suffered cold-eyed glares from his neighbors and teachers and people he didn't even know. He couldn't get an aspirin from the medicine chest without seeing all of Constance's half-used makeup, the tubes of lipstick, the skin stuff she loved that made her smell like apricots. He couldn't walk in or out of the apartment without thinking of Angela's and Candy's bodies bleeding onto the floorboards. The worst had passed—the weeks after the murders when they were forced to stay in that fleabag motel, the humiliating afternoon in the swim team locker room—but Marcus's life in Queens, his new identity as the *murderer's son,* suffocated him. His mother was gone forever, but at the same time she was everywhere, tainting every moment. He wanted out. On the whiter, brighter side, there was Marcus's book deal, Mr. Zachary Celtic, true crime editor at Dome Books, the thirty-thousand-dollar advance that no one knew a thing about except for Marcus and his English teacher. At home, Marcus would have had to get a job. Here, he had the luxury of a summer without work—long days of quiet hours to write the truth about his mother, whatever that was.

But he couldn't say any of that to Garrett. He reached past Garrett into the car for his own bag—a black leather duffel that had cost him nearly two hundred dollars. He'd bought it to impress these people, but in the Nantucket sun, Marcus saw it was all wrong. It looked like a drug dealer's bag with garish brass buckles and a strong smell of leather.

"I don't know," Marcus said. "But here I am. A nigger boy on your turf."

Garrett glared at him. "That's a low blow. You're calling me a racist, and that's not what this is about."

"What's it about, then?" Marcus said. He felt himself sweating and worried about the expense of dry-cleaning his new shirt. It was at least ninety degrees out.

"It's about us losing our father," Garrett said. "That's what this summer is about. That's what every day has been about since his plane crashed. That's the only thing anything's going to be about ever again, okay?" Garrett got tears in his eyes, but because his hands were full, he wiped his face on his shoulder.

"Okay," Marcus said. He was proud of himself because he understood not only what Garrett was saying, but what he hadn't said. *Our father is dead because of your mama. If he hadn't been defending her, he wouldn't have gone to Albany. If he hadn't gone to Albany, his plane wouldn't have crashed.* Arch was another victim of the day Connie Tyler lost her mind. Marcus wanted to apologize on his mother's behalf, but apologizing wouldn't help. If Garrett hated him, Marcus would have to live with it. It wouldn't be worse than the other stuff Marcus was living with.

Suddenly Winnie appeared, tugging on Marcus's arm in an eager, excited way, like a little kid. All three of them were seventeen, but Winnie seemed younger. Maybe because she was a girl. Or because she was so skinny. She had no body to speak of, certainly not the way some of the girls at Cardozo had bodies—with huge tits like balloons under their sweaters and curvy asses. Winnie was a stick person—right now she was wearing jean shorts that showed two Popsicle-stick legs, and her torso was swimming in her sweatshirt. She had blond hair like her mother and she was cute in a way that elves are cute. But not womanly. Even Marcus's twelve-year-old sister LaTisha had more action going on than Winnie.

"Come on," she said. "I'll show you your bedroom."

"In a minute," Marcus said. He wanted to finish with Garrett, although he could see that the moment had passed. Garrett walked by them with his load of luggage and Marcus slung his bag over his shoulder and reached for another box. He needed to catch up.

"Come on," Winnie said. "Please?"

Marcus managed to stave her off until he and Garrett had unloaded most of the car. In silence, except for the squeaky complaints of Marcus's shoes.

"Come on, Marcus," Winnie said.

Marcus picked up his leather duffel, which looked nothing but ugly compared to the Newtons' luggage, and followed Winnie up the stairs.